coq

coq

ALI BRYAN

Freehand Books acknowledges the financial support for its publishing program provided by the Canada Council for the Arts and the Alberta Media Fund, and by the Government of Canada through the Canada Book Fund.

Freehand Books
515 – 815 1st Street SW   Calgary, Alberta   T2P 1N3
www.freehand-books.com

Book orders: UTP Distribution
5201 Dufferin Street   Toronto, Ontario   M3H 5T8
Telephone: 1-800-565-9523   Fax: 1-800-221-9985
utpbooks@utpress.utoronto.ca   utpdistribution.com

Library and Archives Canada Cataloguing in Publication
Title: Coq / Ali Bryan.
Names: Bryan, Ali, 1978– author.
Identifiers: Canadiana (print) 20230152694 | Canadiana (ebook) 20230152740 | ISBN 9781990601255 (softcover) | ISBN 9781990601279 (PDF) | ISBN 9781990601262 (EPUB)
Classification: LCC PS8603.R885 C67 2023 | DDC C813/.6—DC23

Edited by Kelsey Attard
Book design by Natalie Olsen
Cover photo © Dream Lover/Stocksy.com
Author photo by @PHOTOPHILCRO
Printed on FSC® recycled paper and bound in Canada by Friesens

for Big Frat

one

"JOAN, YOU ARE *NOT* WEARING THAT," I say, staring at her baby pink bandeau top. "It's not appropriate for a wedding."

"Joan-*é*," she snaps. She swipes gloss that probably contains moondust and truffle oil and placenta across her lips, and then smiles with her mouth closed to conceal her braces. She has Glen's lips, pouty and bee-stung. She looks eighteen, not thirteen. She takes a selfie and sends it to God knows who. I ignore what looks like the remnants of a hickey on her neck.

I study my own lips and wonder if they're shrinking. I resemble a hamburger bun.

"Gimme that." I snatch the lip gloss and apply it in broad strokes. It's too shiny. I try to rub it off with a Kleenex, but the tissue breaks down.

"It doesn't just come *off*," Joan says. "You have to use this."

She hands me a special lip-gloss remover that smells like turpentine. I'm not convinced it won't dissolve my teeth or remove my lips entirely, which might not be a bad thing. I could get mouth replacement surgery. I'm sure I can find a spare mouth in a bin of Mr. Potato Heads in the basement.

Wes half-knocks on the door. He wears a grey suit with suspenders and sneakers, and a pink tie. He is six foot five with a baby face and bayou hair, wild and unwieldy.

"Wes, hon. Why are you still here? You should be at the church. You have to walk Mona down the aisle."

"I don't want to walk Mona down the aisle. I barely know her."

"You know her enough."

"How come *he's* allowed to wear pink?" Joan adjusts her bandeau.

"It's not the colour I have a problem with, Joan, it's the size. That's not even a shirt. It's not even half a shirt. It looks like you tied one of my running headbands around your chest."

"You don't run," Wes says.

"Are you slut-shaming me?" Joan replies.

"I'm not slut-shaming you, Joan —"

"Joané."

"Fine, Joané! But half-shirts aren't acceptable attire for church weddings. What would Grandpa think?"

"Grandpa bought it for me."

"Well, he obviously didn't know what he was buying. He probably thought it was a napkin."

I glance at my phone. It's twenty to eleven. "We're going to be late." I shoo them from the bathroom and tell Joan to get a sweater from my closet. If I tell her to change, we'll get into a fight. She'll call me a bad feminist, accuse me of trying to silence her and take away her power. Tomorrow I will hide the bandeau. Or wear it as a mask.

"Can I drive?" Wes asks.

"Not today," I say. "We're in a rush. Maybe you can drive home."

Wes sighs, but doesn't complain. He hands me the keys. I slip on a pair of ridiculous heels. I've managed to coax Joan into a reasonable pair of childlike sandals. She doesn't put up a fight but I'm certain it has more to do with the blister on her heal from her new soccer cleats than a desire to comply.

We settle into the car. I avoid checking myself in the rearview mirror and head toward the church. We're in the middle of a heatwave. Neighbours water their lawns, dogs pant. It's been a summer of scorchers, sunburns and drought. For my dad, a summer of love.

I pull into the church parking lot next to my brother Dan's ancient blue Dodge Caravan. There's no sign of Allison-Jean's tidy Jetta with the heated seats and low mileage. It's been almost six months since they separated. He still thinks there's a chance they'll get back together despite the fact Allison-Jean now hosts a podcast called *In Your Next Life, Lesbian*.

"Where's Uncle Dan?" Wes asks. "He was supposed to meet me in the parking lot."

"I don't know, text him."

There are strangers fanning themselves, crowding the church's sloping front yard. They must be on Mona's side because they are all short and homely. One cowers under a golf umbrella to escape the heat.

"Shouldn't we be in there already?" Joan asks.

"Soon," I reply, smoothing down my blue dress. I still taste the lip remover. "We'll go in last."

I think about my dad pacing in a vestibule. The colour scheme was his idea. Grey made his hair look whiter. He's proud of his hair. It's a snow white, not smoker yellow or wizard charcoal like his friends. I'd combed his curls out this morning, adjusted his suspenders, pinned a clump of bulky pink carnations to his lapel. Mona wasn't fussy, he'd said about the flowers, and about the industrial park buffet where'd they'd booked their reception. He didn't seem to mind that they'd probably be taking pictures outside of an MMA gym or equipment yard.

A tap on the shoulder. I spin around, startled. Dan stands there, sweating, with twisted suspenders and a prepubescent moustache.

"You look like shit," I say.

He rubs his face, blinks. "Barely slept. Hann — Harrison — was up all night."

Hannah, who loved horses and French braids, is now Harrison, lover of anime and biceps. Of mine and Dan's collective offspring, he was the last one anyone expected to be gender nonconforming. Bets had been on Joan, who went through a suit phase, which I let everyone think was a case of gender dysmorphia when I knew it was actually because I'd let my six-year-old binge-watch the *Godfather* series. If not Joan, votes went to Emma, Dan and Allison-Jean's youngest, who at the tender age of four was into muscle shirts, ham radios and top hats.

"Do you have anything?" Dan asked.

"What, like speed? No, sorry, I don't. Aren't you supposed to be in there ushering?"

"I got Harrison to do it."

I nod. Harrison would like that. "Why don't you go with Wes? He's supposed to walk Mona down the aisle. Give him some tips or something." Before he leaves, I shove a breath mint in his mouth.

Joan, who's been hovering with her shoulders in a perpetual teenage slump, says, "*Now* can we go in?"

"Put your sweater on." I speak through clenched teeth. She mimics me, saunters toward the car. Dan and Wes round the back of the church. I glance at the cemetery, where my mom's headstone rests, and a pang of grief, so acute it leaves me breathless, rips through my body. What would she think of this? Dad remarrying a retired party-planner with a herniated disc and five children, all of them short and in the military?

It's been almost ten years.

Joan drapes my mother's green sweater over her shoulders. Of all the sweaters.

"What?" she says. "It was the only one I could find."

I take her arm and pull her in the direction of the church. We are greeted by two men in Air Force uniforms. The younger one looks at Joan. At all of her. "Don't worry," she whispers, before he whisks her down the aisle, "I'm more into Army boys."

The other pilot, who looks about my age, and is hot in a dad way with salt and pepper hair and a square jaw, reaches for my arm, but just as I'm about to hook on, Harrison swoops in.

"Auntie Claudia," he says in a voice matching Wes's. "You look beautiful." Harrison, one year a boy and already a gentleman. I smile and compliment his bowtie. In his left ear, one of my mom's diamond earrings sparkles, catching the light bending through the church's stained-glass windows. He seats me next to Joan in the same pew we sat in for Mom's funeral.

Harrison winks and returns to his duties. The organ player is twelve and I'm pretty sure is playing an elevator rendition of "Enter Sandman," which seems appropriate, given that my father looks old and nearly mythical.

"I don't see why he's allowed to change his name, and I'm not," Joan whispers.

"We've been through this a thousand times. Harrison identifies as male. His new name affirms that."

"Well, I identify as French."

I give her a nudge as my father enters from a door beside the choir benches, accompanied by his friend Harold Pugh and my brother who looks . . . high? OMG, Wes. I search for him at the back of the church, where Mona's five kids are in formation, looking like they're planning an attack.

The minister arrives. A woman with big teeth. The one who presided over Mom's funeral died of Covid last year. The organ player clears his throat and begins to play something military, French. Joané approves, sits up tall. I catch my father's eye. He's noticed his late wife's sweater draped over his granddaughter's back. My mom's favourite sweater. His mouth falls open, just enough to see the heartache in the back of his throat, and then he slowly presses his lips together to welcome his new bride.

I shift in my pew to watch the procession and there, in the last row, is Glen looking dapper and tanned. Alone.

two

WES IS STONED. I can tell by his overzealous broadcaster expression. I'm gonna kill him. He towers over my dad and brother. His stance suggests his shoes are too tight but there's something endearing about his folded hands and drooping corsage. The softness in his shoulders. He's still my baby. Meanwhile, Dan resembles the Philadelphia Flyers mascot, Gritty. I stare, willing him to look less like a child's nightmare but he misinterprets my intent and smiles. With his teeth.

Joan whispers, "What's wrong with Uncle Dan?"

The minister prays and riffs about second chances, mature love, Gerald and Mona. Dad cups Mona's hands, strokes her knuckles with his thumb with airy precision. Did he do that when he took my mother's hand in marriage? What had the minister said about love back then when my mom and dad were mere twenty-somethings, optimistic and bright-eyed, with a first-floor apartment and a hand-me-down van? 'Til death did them part.

"He's hot." Joan nods at one of Mona's adult children. The one in the Navy with the eyebrow scar and tight pants.

I whisper, "He's probably my age."

"Hot like in a Clint Eastwood way."

My daughter thinks I'm an octogenarian. I shush her and focus on the ceremony. The minister doesn't ask if anyone objects to Dad and Mona's union and I can't help wonder, if she had, whether my mom might go full on poltergeist. Toss a hymnbook, play a few keys on the organ. Set the alter on fire. I think not. Ghost Janice would more likely be sitting proper in the front row, hoping my dad remembered to take his diabetes medication. That he didn't forget to wear a belt.

I steal a glance at Glen. It's been a month since he returned from a year-long trip, in which he cycled from Singapore to Rotterdam with two hundred euros and the burden of his life choices. When Dad invited him to the wedding he had initially declined because he was "still processing his journey."

I'm still processing the carrot cake I ate for breakfast. My stomach gurgles in fits and spurts and Joan slides away from me as if I've farted. I pinch the back of her arm and she stifles a yelp.

Mona's maid of honour, her eldest granddaughter, hands Mona the vows she's written. The paper has been wound into a tight scroll and it takes Mona several tries to unravel the page and pull it taut enough to read.

"Gerald," she squeaks, through orange frosted lips. "The first time we did deep water aquafit —"

Wes starts to laugh.

"I knew you were special."

"Grandpa does aquafit?" Joan asks.

"The way you moved with such commitment and vigour and spunk and sang along to the music. How you let all the ladies pass when we ran in a circle. You helped me into the hot tub when I tore my meniscus."

Joan leans in. "I thought he did lane swimming."

I picture my dad egg-beating to the Neutron Dance.

"The way you leant me your goggles after my cataract surgery."

"This is getting awfully anatomical," Harrison whispers from the pew behind us.

A woman coughs and a boy shifts in his seat. Mona's voice cracks and the church falls into contemplative silence. The beads on Mona's youthful gown sparkle from the light of a decorative candle and the air feels simultaneously light and warm.

"You made me want to live again," she continues. "You made me want to feel an inch worm crawl on the back of my hand. You made me want to splash in a puddle, kick a ball, lick the syrup from my plate, wave my hand out the window of a moving car."

At least he doesn't make you want to start a hoard, I think.

"You bring me the kind of joy I haven't felt since I was a child growing up in Petawawa."

I didn't know children found joy on army bases.

"Every day that I'm with you, I'm reminded that happiness doesn't come from the big stuff. It's not the luxury trips or big screen TVs or season tickets to the Mooseheads. It's the little things. Sharing a scone, watching the stars. It's waking up next to you. It's —"

Mona's TED Talk is interrupted by Dan's sobbing. Instead of patting his uncle on the back or taking his arm, Wes shouts in a loud voice, "What do I do?"

Dad intervenes. He hands Dan a handkerchief — probably used — from his pocket and explains to the guests, "His wife just left him for a woman."

I scan the church for Allison-Jean. She had planned to attend, but her partner was having minor foot surgery and there was a chance she wouldn't make it. I don't see her.

The minister urges Mona to continue.

Mona clears her throat, stands tall. "What I'm saying, Gerald, is that you bring me joy and I promise to return it every day, as long as we both shall live."

I wonder what joy looks like. A parrot? An icicle? A foil

balloon? I imagine these items being passed back and forth between Dad and Mona. Joy hot potato.

Dan blows his nose and Mona takes the soiled handkerchief and gives it to my dad, who stuffs into his pocket. He's forgotten his belt. From the other pocket he retrieves a folded piece of blue paper acquired from my office notepad: *Claudia Sinclair, VP Sales & Marketing.*

"Mona," he starts. "When I first saw you at aquafit —"

Wes starts laughing again.

"I was taken by your incredible energy. Your smile, your enthusiasm. The way you responded with the loudest *woo-hoo* every time the instructor asked *how are we doing, team?*"

Dan shouts, "Woo-hoo."

Joan snaps a selfie making either a peace sign or a gang symbol and then asks if Uncle Dan is "having a nervous breakdown."

I glare at her.

Dad continues. "When you first asked me to see the live remake of *Pinocchio*, I was so nervous. I didn't know what to wear or what to order at the concession stand or whether it was okay to put my arm around you. But after I picked you up and you wore those little dangly popcorn earrings and you'd stuffed your purse with bottled water and black licorice and a first-aid kit, I knew we were meant to be together."

"Why would they need a first-aid kit? Do old people get injured going to the movies?" Joan asks.

It's getting increasingly hot. I wave the wedding program in front of my face. The ceremony continues. Dad and Mona finish their vows and they kiss like high-schoolers. A military march plays while they sign the registry. The minister presents my dad and Mona to the crowd. With all the juvenile talk about licorice and inch worms, I half-expect them to exit via matching

Shriners' cars. Instead, they link arms and lumber, first down the stairs, and then the aisle, Mona's train the length of a first marriage dragging behind her.

Wes whoops, Dan whistles, and in the back, I recognize Glen's sharp methodical clapping. Extended family I don't know wipe tears from cheeks. The wedding party exits the altar. Dan has forgotten how to walk. His steps are tiny, as if he's wearing a kimono. I mouth, "What are you doing?" but Wes pushes him forward.

Joan nudges me from behind. "Go, Mom," she says as the pew across from us begins to empty. But I can't move. I'm rooted to the church's sloping floor. "Mom," she says impatiently. "Go."

I motion for Joan to go around me. As she passes, her sweater snags on my corsage. Petals sail to the ground. The sweater slides from her shoulders and I catch it mid-air. Unencumbered and now uncovered, she catwalks the church aisle like a Parisian model, a little *fuck you* mixed with a healthy *je ne sais quoi*. Plus a little . . . tattoo?

For frig's sake. There's a lily climbing up between her shoulder blades. Her middle name. Mom's favorite flower. The church continues to empty until I'm alone and the flame from the only candle goes out.

three

WES AND JOAN HEAD TO the reception buffet in a "cousins' car" driven by Harrison. I congratulate Dad and Mona before slipping into the cemetery with its lumpy plots and sprawling oak trees. Clumps of faded plastic flowers are nestled against grave markers and a crew of pigeons wanders the grounds.

Mom's headstone is simple, granite, bevelled. Fresh lilies matching Joan's tattoo fan from the base of her headstone. I run my finger along their coarse stems, trace my mother's name. I haven't been here for months and yet I feel like I'm always here, liaising with the dead to understand the living.

I fish a pair of glasses from the thick grass near the base of the stone. They are black and masculine.

"You found them."

I turn to find Glen behind me, presumably blind, in his wedding suit and cycling shoes. A yellow helmet dangles from his wrist.

"You left the lilies?" I ask.

He nods, accepts the glasses and polishes the lenses with his shirt cuffs.

"They're pretty," I say, admiring their delicate filaments.

"I used to grow them," he says. "After she died. Joan loved them. She used to shove her face into the flowers. *Grandma lilies*, she called them. That's why the tip of her nose was always orange."

"Joané," I correct.

"Oh God," he replies. "What's up with that?"

We share a laugh. "Did you know she had a tattoo?"

"Not until yesterday. Aren't there rules about tattooing minors?"

"Apparently not in Nova Scotia."

"Claudia —" he starts.

I wait for him to continue but he pauses, mouth open, as if the words are caught in the back of his throat. Odd, given that Glen has always had something to say. About the way I cut the tomatoes, or organized the cupboards, or parked the car. How I paid more attention to the kids, or laughed too loud at parties. The way I was. The way I wasn't.

"What?" I reply.

His eyes flicker. "I think I made a mistake."

I glance down at his fluorescent cycling shoes.

"We all do. That's what they neglect to tell you when you're born. That you'll make all the mistakes. You'll fall in love with the wrong people, pursue the wrong career, live in the wrong place, abuse your body, shatter your heart, ignore your inner voice, and then you get hit by a banana boat." I throw an arm toward my mom's headstone.

"Uh," Glen fumbles. "I meant that I'd made a mistake biking to the church. I didn't realize how far the reception was."

"Didn't you just bike from Asia to Europe?"

"Not in a single afternoon."

"Where's your bike?"

He gestures toward the church parking lot.

"Fine." I crouch in front of the headstone and whisper to my mom, "I miss you." I will never stop missing her. I pluck a lily from its stem and twirl it between my fingers. Glen extends a hand. I accept his help because I rage-ran fifteen K yesterday and my quads feel like cannonballs.

He takes the flower and says, "Here," tenderly tucking it behind my ear.

I simultaneously think *fuck off* and *do it again*. In the car, I set the flower on the dash while Glen maneuvers his stupid bike into the trunk.

"Are we dropping it off at your place or taking it to the reception?"

"As long as you don't mind driving me home, I'd prefer to drop it off. That way I can change my shoes."

I nod. He sits with his helmet on his lap and I notice his hands look middle-aged and mottled. Like mine. I can barely remember his younger hands. Just that they were there cradling Wes in the infant bathtub, fixing the front steps, playing with my hair and then they were gone and that's how the last decade has felt. Down a set of hands. Handless.

I pull up to his tidy wood-and-slate townhouse with the astro-turf lawn and blast the air conditioning.

"You can come in," he says, through the open trunk where he's trying to remove his bike.

How long does it take to change a pair of shoes?

"What for?"

"I dunno." He shrugs. "We can have a drink? Before the reception? I don't think Barry's All-U-Can-Eat has the best selection in wines."

I turn off the engine and grab my purse. It would be nice to freshen up in a real bathroom and I would like a glass of wine. It's my job at the reception to welcome Mona into the family and I haven't prepared a thing.

I haven't been in Glen's house since before his road-trip and even then, mostly stuck to the driveway or foyer, usually to drop off Joan's forgotten backpack or cleats or Wes's Cineplex uniform. The house is spotless.

I hoist myself up onto a futuristic stool at the kitchen island and check my phone.

A text from Wes: *Do we have to be there for pictures? Harrison said there's pictures.*

I remind him they aren't doing formal family pictures as Glen slides a glass of white wine in my direction.

"Pinot Grigio. That okay?"

I take a sip and study his fridge.

"Whose baby?" I ask, pointing to the jointless bald blob.

"Kara's."

"She sent you a picture of her baby?"

I think of his ex. The woman he'd moved on with so quickly after our split, eliminating any chance for us to reconcile. I remember her long legs and white teeth. The way she perfectly braided Joan's hair or tied Wes's skates. The goddamned notes I'd find in the kids' lunch bags. *You got this! Be kind! Know your strength.* God, she was awful. God, she was good. I'm glad she has a baby.

"Who's the father?"

"A guy she met on a plane to New Zealand."

People still meet people on planes? Gross. I take a drink. "Did you and she ever think about having kids?" I know it's none of my business, but Glen and I are an ancient thing. A landline.

"We tried."

He doesn't elaborate. He pours himself a glass of whiskey and I imagine a scenario where my kids have half-siblings. I'm relieved they don't. Glen opens a bag of chips. I take a handful and eat them one at a time. We talk about the coming school year. Indoor shoes, bus fees, soccer evaluations. He tops off my glass and then leans on the island.

"Back at the cemetery," he starts. "When you said we fall in love with all the wrong people. Did you mean that?" He fiddles with his glass. The ice cubes clink.

I shrug. "My track record would suggest, yes." I wink. "Yours too."

"I don't know that *wrong* is the right word. Relationships aren't binary."

I think of Harrison. "No, they're not."

"I think we just fall in love. We're human, we're flawed. Relationships are just messy." He pushes off the island. "Right and wrong don't exist."

I wonder if this is how he justifies moving in with Kara so soon after our split. When our first kiss and the nights we made our children were still remembered by their calendar dates and not a single Christmas tree ornament had broken. Our relationship had been that precious, that new. That right.

That wrong.

"We should go," I say, downing the last of my wine.

He clears the glasses and I go to the bathroom to fix my makeup. I look okay. I notice an empty box of Just for Men hair dye in the trash, and in the bath tub, pomegranate body wash. After all these years, he's still using it. I blush at a sudden memory of going down on him in the shower. Of getting pressed up against the tile, which was cool, despite the steam and want.

"I'll meet you in the car," I shout, but Glen's at the door, ready to go in his regular shoes.

"You look great, by the way," he says as we get into my car.

I shift into reverse. "I know."

four

I MAKE A BAD TRAFFIC DECISION and consequently have to crawl through a construction zone. We're late for the reception. Dad and Mona are already seated at the head table with the mishmash wedding party. Glen disappears to a corner table. Dan stands to pull out my seat. Somehow, I've ended up with a wheelie chair. I look to my brother for an explanation, but he is coming down and useless, shoes off and eyes fixed on his empty plate.

The crank is missing from the office chair I've been assigned so when I wheel myself in, the table comes above my chest.

"Wes, fix my chair," I whisper. He's watching TikTok videos on his phone under the table.

I ask one of Mona's sons wearing a beret for help, but he doesn't hear. This must be the one who had half his face blown off in Afghanistan. The side I can't see. He rearranges his flatware, adjusts his water glass with a melted hand.

Another of Mona's sons approaches the podium. He welcomes everyone to the reception, points out the washrooms and escape routes, outlines the rules for the buffet. Before inviting the head table to get started, he bows and says grace.

Mona's Saturday Night Fever shoes prevent her from getting her own meal, so Dad does it for her. He's selected things that can't be eaten with a fork as if it was a Jeopardy category: chicken wings, wontons, roasted corn on the cob, buns. She accepts with childlike fervor, clapping her hands.

I cut in front of Joan and take a bun. I filled up on chips at Glen's. I shuffle from chafing dish to chafing dish in search of something light. Joan dips out of line and joins Wes at the dessert station. They fill bowls of soft-serve to overflowing. Their cousins join them, adding sprinkles and sauces and chopped allergies. Allison-Jean would never let this happen. She'd have given each kid a vegetable quota.

Joan puts a maraschino cherry on her tongue and takes a selfie.

"Delete that," I whisper as I pass, stopping the bun from rolling off my plate.

The head table looks like the Last Supper before a lockdown. Someone in Mona's family dissects a crab leg with the intensity of a medical examiner while my dad playfully feeds Mona a spoonful of peas. Peas.

Peas.

I watch Mona chew. She must have borrowed Joan's military-grade lip gloss because her mouth remains perfectly orange and frosted, except for the bits of green. When a pea falls down her dress, I have the sudden urge to be single for the rest of my life. I set my dinner-for-one on the table and cross my heart.

By the time I've finished my bun, my shoulders already ache from trying to reach my cutlery. Beside me, Dan has a plate consisting of nothing but eggrolls. Another thing Allison-Jean would never have allowed. He tears open a packet of plum sauce with his teeth and pipes his eggrolls in zigzags. "Oh my God, Dan, just friggin' dip them like a normal human being."

"She'll be here in twenty minutes," he says, tearing open another packet.

I'm assuming he means Allison-Jean.

"You'll be fine," I encourage, uncertain he will. "Just remember we're here for Dad. Keep it about him."

He licks a blot of plum sauce from this pinkie. People return to the buffet for seconds and this is my cue to welcome Mona into the family. I snake my way to the podium, bend the mic toward my face.

"A few months ago . . ." I wait for the clatter to settle. "I picked my dad up from the curling club and there was something different about him. He told me he that he had met someone at the pool earlier that day and when I asked him to tell me about her, he simply said, 'She's Mona.' That's all he said. 'She's Mona.'"

A light chuckle travels the room.

"I thought about that for days. How that's all he needed to say. That a name could be enough. That everything I needed to know about Mona could be inferred from that simple phrase: *She's Mona*. And then I met Mona."

"Uh oh," someone hollers from the back. Mona's sons snort, my dad hoots, Dan drops an eggroll on the floor. Old people jokes zip around like rumours there's a sale on Voltaren. Mona loves the attention. She laughs an outrageous laugh and slaps the table. She stands and my dad salutes her. A Russian salute? I try to reign the audience back in, but someone starts clinking his glass with a knife. Dan's crying again. Wes dips onion rings in his ice cream.

The glass clinking grows in volume until Dad plants an R. Kelly kiss on Mona's lips. I clear my throat in a joking manner to make them stop even though I very much want them to stop, because, fuck. I'm sure I saw a pea roll onto the floor.

"As I was saying, and as you just saw —" I gesture toward the couple. "Mona doesn't need any further introduction. She's the life of the party, a warm and generous grandma and a loving partner to my dad." My voice catches. Emotion gathers in the back of my throat like a choir behind a curtain, threatening to belt out a tune at the exact wrong moment. Threatening to weep. "On behalf of my brother and myself," I croak, "would you join me in raising your glass to officially welcome Mona to the family."

I swallow, lift my trembling hand, and gaze at the guests. She's gone ten years and all I can think of is how I want to call my mom and tell her about the wedding. About Mona's cleavage, the handwritten vows, and the fact that the soya sauce tastes off. The terrible crepe paper decorations. My hunch that Harold Pugh has had a stroke. And this. This moment of seeing strangers, distant friends, and family members raising a glass to her replacement.

"To Mona," I squeak.

I shoot my wine, bury the glass inside the podium atop someone else's speech, and make a beeline for the bathroom. There's no one inside. I lock the door and slump down on the toilet seat. What am I doing? I rub my temples and search my purse for Wes's confiscated vape. I'd smoke anything right now.

"Mom?"

"Joan?"

"Can I come in?"

I slide open the deadbolt and wave Joan in. She's wrapped in Mom's sweater.

"Your mascara's running." She tucks her hand in her sleeve and dabs my cheek. "I thought you were happy for Grandpa?" she says.

"I'm very happy," I say. "Sometimes I just think about my mom." The toilet automatically flushes.

Joan nods. "Maybe we can do something special, you know, to like . . . honour her. That's what Libby's family does every year on the anniversary of her dad's death."

I remember Libby's dad. His emaciated body. His ashen skin and wooden cane.

"They take a trip to one of his favorite places."

We intended to do that. Some type of family tradition to mark Mom's passing, but it never worked out. Someone always had a soccer game, a conference call, a tee time. We carried on because of and in spite of our grief. We remembered her privately. Me at the bird sanctuary, Dan at the cemetery, Dad parked and idling across the street from their old house.

I pat Joan's hand. Her nails are ten inches long and shaped like claws. "I'll think about it," I say, mustering a smile. "Thanks."

She slips out of the stall and I take a moment to wipe my nose.

"Can I have a glass of champagne?" she asks.

"Absolutely not."

The lineup for the dessert station bends around the restaurant and I return to my seat at the head table with minimal fanfare or notice. Somehow my seat seems to have deflated another six inches so the table comes up to my neck. A bowl of partially melted ice cream is set at my place with a vanilla wafer sticking out of it like a cocktail pin. Glen.

I look up and he watches me from the corner table, an unfamiliar baby on his lap. Is this a thing? Is he courting me at my dad's wedding? I eat the wafer as one of Mona's bereted sons welcomes my dad into their family. As he finishes his speech, a bagpiper appears suddenly and plays a reel. People sing along. Mona is the loudest. I tap my foot to the music. Someone's refilled my wine and I down it brazenly.

Restaurant staff clear tables with rubber bins and a trolley. Chairs are dragged to the side where the DJ — a friend of Wes's — has set up a table. Multicoloured spotlights line the perimeter of the "dancefloor" to give the place a "club feel" per Mona's request. Next, we'll hit the Neverland Ranch for the afterparty.

The DJ plays "Sexual Healing." I search for Wes, who curated the playlist, but he's fled to the parking lot with the rest of the teenagers to watch desperate CrossFitters flip tires in the alley. I can see them through the back door.

Allison-Jean congratulates my dad and Mona who are still seated at the head table. She looks happy with her short hair, crystals and burlap dress. A ripple of sadness passes through my chest when I remember Dan's frantic call. *She doesn't want me anymore.* How gutting and small to be unwanted. How barbaric. How human.

"Do you want to dance?"

I spin around to object, but a beautiful man in a pin-striped suit stands there with a presumptuous outstretched hand. He's caught me off guard and knows it. He smirk-smiles and I take his hand with the boldness of a Mona or Joané. Nothing says romance like dancing to "Sexual Healing" at your elderly father's wedding while your kids spy at you from the back door.

"Bjorn," the man says, moving his pelvis in hypnotic circles.

I try to create space, but Bjorn wants to make precious furniture together. He presses his allen key into my hip. I dance away, but he tugs me back in with a touch of violence, his goatee grazing my cheek. He smells like a rum-soaked forest, and I am here for it. Heat courses through my body. Too much heat. I spin away to recover at the edge of a circle where someone is twerking. My dad. Joan probably taught him. People cheer him on.

Outside the human boma, Bjorn stalks. He wants to build a bedroom set. In a different lifetime, I'd have brought the screws. Before Bjorn can make his next move, Dan materializes out of nowhere like a Scooby Doo villain and pushes me into the circle, where Dad and Mona are performing a geriatric version of the Humpty dance.

I keep right on going, and fall into the burnt and capable arms of Mona's disfigured son. He invites me into a synchronized step-touch. He dances with conviction. He dances like nobody's watching. Or perhaps like everyone's watching, footloose and totally present. I make it to the next chorus and plan my exit. There's a hole in the circle between Harrison and Mona's granddaughter. When the route is clear, I shimmy through and out the front door.

The humidity's burned off and a breeze cools my skin. I lean against the hood of my car, take off my shoes. I can still hear the bass from the speakers. Through the restaurant's tinted glass, I watch wedding guests move on and off the dancefloor like shapeshifters, in pairs, in groups, in broken Conga lines. I feel my aloneness. The wind on my bare shoulders. The space.

five

I WAKE UP the next morning hungover. I skip the post-wedding brunch and take an Uber to the restaurant to pick up my car. Shreds of crepe paper litter the parking lot along with a pair of forgotten stilettoes.

Glen texts and offers to take Joan to soccer. Her game's in the valley an hour away. Wes slept at a friend's house. I grab coffees and pastries from a bakery and nudge Dan awake. With Dad married off, Dan's taken over my guest room.

"Your breath is terrible," I say, dumping a chocolate croissant on a plate.

He rubs his eyes, adds cream to his coffee, checks the time. "I have to be at the community centre at noon."

His monthly Fathers of Trans, Non-Binary and Gender Expansive Youth support group. Harrison has technically aged out of the corresponding teen program, but it's been a safe space for Dan, even more so since Allison-Jean left him. I offer him a ride, but he says he'll walk.

We pick at our croissants while Joan's alarm goes off. She was up late and will be in a foul mood. I've already filled her water bottle and set her cleats by the door, things I shouldn't be organizing for her at her age but do on occasion, to avoid the wrath.

"Allison-Jean wants Cindy to move in."

"That's ridiculous," I reply. "It's only been a few months."

"She says it's temporary. Just until Cindy gets the cast off. She's been looking after her."

"How much looking after does she need? She's got a boot. It's not like she's immobile."

Dan shrugs. "I never thought I'd be alone," he says, voice a whisper. "It was supposed to be forever."

He sounds so pathetic and yet I know it's what he thought. He wanted what Mom and Dad had. The silver anniversary gift. The pearl, the ruby, the gold. The dusty photo albums, full medicine cabinet, the his-and-her track suits.

"I know," I say, peeling a stick of chocolate from his croissant. "You'll find someone else."

He raises his brow.

"What?" I say defensively. "I never really tried. I was too busy with work and single parenting. I did fine by myself." Of course, there were others since Glen. Executives, playboys, single dads.

"At least you had Dad here."

My jaw tenses. "God, for the first five years it felt like having a third child around. He could barely do anything after Mom died. It was like those people that come back from war and need to learn how to walk and talk again."

"Speaking of war," Dan says, slurping his coffee. "Did you see that guy at the wedding with half his face blown off?"

"Rodney," I reply, having learned his name. "He was actually hot in a rugged, I-almost-died kind of way." I blow on my coffee. "Terrible dancer though."

"Aren't you lonely?" Dan asks.

Joan appears in the hallway, partially dressed in her uniform, last night's makeup still on her face. She stretches and asks for food. I point to the bag of pastries on the counter. She takes a Danish and disappears back down the hall.

"I don't know if I'm *lonely*."

"Of course you are," Dan insists. "Saw it last night."

"You probably saw a lot of things last night. You were friggin' stoned."

"Doesn't matter. I could tell." He takes a second croissant, peels off the end, talks with his mouth full. "Remember the summer we moved to Clayton Park and I had friends from Scouts and baseball and you didn't know anyone and you just kind of floated around the neighbourhood looking for someone to play with?"

The loneliest summer.

"You had that same look on your face last night as you did then."

"I drank a bottle of wine."

"Before that."

"At the church?"

"Claudia," he says, exasperated. 'Just admit it! You're lonely. You haven't been in a serious relationship since Glen. Your kids are pretty much grown, you're a VP . . . why aren't you out there trying to meet someone? It's not right to be alone."

"I'm scared," I blurt.

Am I? Is that what I am? I take a sip of coffee. It burns my throat.

We hear someone coming up the front walk and both watch the door in anticipation. Dad barrels through.

"Well, if it's not the Hotstepper," I say, noting his dishevelled hair and knock-off Birkenstocks. "How was brunch?"

"I can't find the ring," Dad replies, his face draining of colour.

Dan and I stare at his tree-branch fingers.

"You're wearing it," Dan says.

"Not this one," he says, irritably stroking the thick band Mona managed to jam on there yesterday. "Your mom's."

"What do you mean?" I sit up straight, prompting a headache.

"It's in the floral pouch with her earrings and the little pewter prayer hands she used to carry around."

Dan looks at my father. "You have the prayer hands?"

Dad paces the kitchen.

"Why is your knee blue?" I stare at his bloated joint.

"I took the ring out of the pouch," he says. "I wanted to have it at the wedding." My dad opens cupboards. I pour him a glass of water and motion for him to sit. He stumbles.

"I wanted your mom to know I hadn't forgotten about her."

"You checked your pockets?"

He gulps his water and it goes down the wrong way. He sputters and coughs, spraying the table. Dan and I lean away.

"When's the last time you saw it?" Dan asks, stuffing the last of his croissant in his mouth.

"I think at the church."

"It'll turn up," I say. "We'll call them today. And the restaurant."

Joan pads into the kitchen and pours herself a giant glass of juice. We've been over this a thousand times. She's supposed to use the small glasses in the cupboard near the sink. She drinks half, refills and then digs in the hall closet for her shin pads.

Dad rubs his watery eyes and the atmosphere in the kitchen feels weary and grey. My neck tenses.

"It was a nice wedding," Dan offers.

"I feel guilty," Dad says.

"It's just a ring," I say. "We'll find it."

"Lying in bed next to Mona. I feel guilty. Like I'm doing something wrong."

"It's a bit wrong."

"Dan!" I shove his arm. "There's nothing wrong with Dad moving on and remarrying. It's been a decade. You just finished saying we're not meant to be alone."

"I know, I know." Dan shifts in his seat. "Sometimes it feels like she's just gone away. Or that she never really left. Or that she's going to come back." He throws an arm toward the front hall. "Like any minute now, she might walk through that front door and make everything okay."

Glen slips through the front door, gently stomps his feet on the mat. "I tried to text," he says.

My phone is on the counter. "Joané, your dad's here," I holler.

Joan's fixed her hair into an extreme ponytail. The 1 on the back of her jersey is peeling. "I don't want to be called that anymore," she huffs.

I don't ask why because this is thirteen. Tomorrow she'll probably tell me she's a cat. "Have a good game," I call, as she rams her feet into a pair of slides. "Love you."

She leaves behind a scent trail of teen deodorant and half a glass of orange juice. I collect the juice from the hall console and pour it back into the container.

"Sick," Dan says.

Dad nods approvingly.

"Are you sure you didn't put the ring back in the pouch after the ceremony?" I ask. This is a man who once put on his goggles to search the pool for his missing goggles.

Dad unzips the floral pouch from his pocket, and dumps the contents on the table. Mom's ruby earrings tumble out, followed by the prayer hands. No ring.

The prayer hands are narrow and grooved, misshapen. Dan snatches them up and holds them to his chest. The earrings are tiny. Striking. They seemed so big in Mom's ears. I still remember sitting on her lap and twirling them. Have they shrunk? A flutter of panic: I can't remember her scent. Chanel? Leaves? Lavender?

"We should do something," I blurt. "To commemorate the tenth anniversary of Mom's death."

Dad looks up, the ruby studs now resting in his palm, nestled in his lifelines. "A service?" he asks.

"A dinner," Dan suggests. He holds the prayer hands to his cheek.

"A trip," I reply.

"Where?" Dan says.

"I don't think I can go back to Cuba." Dad clears his throat. "I can barely go to a beach without thinking about the accident. Pineapple triggers me. And Spanish greetings. Whenever I hear 'Hola!' it sounds so friendly but all I see is your mother covered with bandages." He waves his hand across his forehead.

"Sable Island!" Dan shouts.

"There's nothing to do there," I say.

"There's wild horses."

"And?"

Dan sits back, deflated. He exhales, then holds the prayer hands up to the chandelier. "She always wanted to go to Paris," he whispers.

"Paris?" Dad spouts.

I think of Joan formerly identifying as French and of travelling to Paris with my brother and Dad. The city of lights and love and catacombs and protests. I can't think of a worse idea.

My dad gingerly returns the studs to the floral pouch.

Dan tucks the prayer hands into his breast pocket. "I need them more than you," he says to me, though I had no plans to object.

"Do you know *why* your mom always wanted to go to Paris?"

My brother and I sit up expectantly. Truth is, I'd never given it much thought. Everyone, at some point, wants to go to Paris. Like New York or London or Disney World. It's a rite of passage.

To see the Eiffel Tower, sip the wine, stroll the Seine. Step in the dogshit.

"She fell madly in love with a French exchange student in high school."

"Huh?"

"What?"

"His name was Émile."

"How did I never know this?" I brush croissant flakes onto my plate.

"Because it was in high school," Dan reasons.

"They wrote letters well into their twenties," Dad says. "He desperately wanted to marry your mother." He goes to the fridge and drinks the orange juice straight from the container. I flinch, but Dad smiles, a bravado smile, a coq one, an I-won one. My mother, the prize.

I glance up at one of the mugshot roosters caught mid-strut on my kitchen border and I say his name in my head: *Émile*. I harshly can't imagine my mom attracting the affections of a Frenchman with her practical sneakers, drab hair and elasticized pants. But I also can't imagine my mom in her twenties. I can't imagine her not-a-mom or not-a-teacher. I can't imagine her as a young woman, with desires and dreams. Lovers, secrets.

"Might be weird to go to Paris," Dan concludes.

"He's still alive," Dad says, backwashing the juice. He screws the lid on the container and slides it back into the fridge.

"You looked him up?"

Dad nods. "He didn't age well."

"Dad!"

"Maybe we should just go to New Brunswick or something," Dan offers.

But I can't stop thinking about France. About my mother's strange lover and the Moulin Rouge and the small angry cars and beautiful small men. I'll visit French grocery stores and write off part of the trip. We could toast my mother in the rain from the top of the Arc de Triomphe. God, she loved the rain. A memory of my mom standing in the backyard in a Nova Scotia storm, arms outstretched like Christ the Redeemer, flows to the surface. I see her face, squinting up at the sky. I see her gaping rubber boots and sopping hair. I see her.

I choke down the dredges of my coffee. "Paris is always a good idea."

six

WES MAKES A BRIEF APPEARANCE to shower and change into his work uniform. In the car, I lecture him about getting himself and his uncle high at his grandpa's wedding. He claims it was an accident. He pops open the glove compartment and digs out a nondescript package of watermelon-flavoured cannabis gummies.

"Whose are those?"

"I assumed they were yours," he says.

"I don't take gummies and neither should you." We slow to let a dump truck peel off toward a construction site.

"Well, they're not mine," Wes says.

Whose are they? Glen wasn't in the car until after the ceremony, and they can't be Dan's, judging by the way he behaved at the wedding. Maybe they're Dad's. To put his joint pain, his hoarding tendencies, his guilt, at ease.

"Regardless," I scold. "You shouldn't have taken them. They'll mess up your brain. And you know your uncle's vulnerable right now."

"Sorry."

"Have you eaten anything?"

He shakes his head and I give him a twenty. "Get something healthy," I say as he straps his Cineplex visor to his head. His nametag says MARY-BETH. I point to it. "Wes, come on. It's unprofessional. Where's your actual nametag?"

He winks and gets out of the car, meets up with a blond in a matching uniform and they saunter toward the theatre entrance. In a few weeks, he'll be in grade eleven. I don't think ahead to grade twelve or graduation, or the fact that this time next year we'll be navigating early admission, recruitment fairs, finals, firsts.

I stop at the mall, pleased that I have a few hours to myself before Dan returns from Group and Joan from soccer. I need new running sneakers and a bra. Instead of hitting up Sport Chek, I find myself at a trendy boutique with a minimalist aesthetic and a security guard patrolling the front entrance. Everyone inside looks like Joan: polished, coiffed, computer-animated. One of them asks if I need help and I say that no, I'm just browsing. "For yourself?" she says, tilting her head.

Yes? No? Am I too old to shop here? There are a few halter tops, but most of the clothes are black and reasonably sized. I pass a mirror. Maybe it's my eyebrows. Or my hamburger-mouth. Or my hooded eyelids. I see why everyone in my office gets Botox. Even the babies. Until now, my high cheekbones have done an exceptional job holding things in place, but even these seemed to have given up, packed it in, taken a midlife cycling trip oversees.

"How would you describe your style?" another associate asks. She's shorter than the other girls, with frizzy hair, but more confident.

My style? Somewhere between Homo erectus out for a Sunday stroll and a WalCrotch shopper on Black Friday.

"I'm not here for style," I say, grabbing a pair of socks from a rack.

The sales girl says, "Socks are life," and makes a heart with her hands.

She's not wrong. I could paint a series. *Still Life with Socks*. Wool, soccer, tube, diabetic, hard.

What I really want is an outfit for Paris. Something chic and age appropriate. I try on a black dress with a fitted bodice and sheer overlay. The neck is high and scalloped, the sleeves wide, wrists cinched. I pull the dress over my head. I can't tell if it's too short. My legs, for the most part, are strong and toned from years of running away from myself, but my skin has the appearance of partially-shucked corn.

"How are we doing in there?"

We? I stare into the mirror. Is this an existential question? As in how am *I* doing, but also how am *I* — who *I* think you think *I* am — doing.

"I'm doing okay," I reply, attempting to shimmy the dress over my head. But *we*, we are stuck. On so many levels.

I can't manipulate the garment over my back. It's trapped on my rib cage. A faint *rip*. Real or imagined? The temperature in the change room rises. Sweat forms on my forehead. I exhale and try again, praising Jesus as I tug. Progress, until a thread snaps. The price tag dangles from an elegant navy cord pinned somewhere near my head. Two hundred twenty-nine dollars. Also, a UK 6, which means a US 4, neither of which accounts for my Canadian double-double back.

"Do we need another size?" a voice on the other side asks.

No, Ava Rose or Kylie or Kayla or Shayla or whatever your name is, I need a pair of scissors.

"I want to see how it looks with the socks." For fuck's sake, why'd I say that?

My phone trills from my purse. Why can't Dan just text like everyone else?

"Hello?" I whisper into the speaker.

"Oh, Claudia," Dan whimpers. "Today's Group was so hard."

"I'm sorry that happened to you," I say. "Really, I am, but I need you to come to the mall."

"Aspen had top surgery and they are experiencing some type of horrible regret or withdrawal."

"Yeah, well, I'm about to need top surgery myself and I'm also suffering from horrible regret. Can you just come to the mall? I'm in a store called Bougie and I'm stuck in a dress."

"Bougie? Harrison used to shop there. That's like a teen Balenciaga. Why are you there?"

"I dunno, Dan. Maybe we hate ourselves."

"Who's we?"

"Hurry up."

I wave the heat from my face and crack open the door. "I think this would go better with a pair of leggings."

The sales associate tries to spy on my legs. "Medium?" she asks.

"Extra-large."

She prances off.

Group is not far from the mall. Providing Dan has only just left, he should be here within ten minutes. I will try on the whole store to stall. After three pairs of leggings, I hear Dan's voice. I fling open the change room door before he tells them I'm trapped, and usher him inside.

"Um," the sales girl starts, "only one person is allowed in the dressing room at a time."

"It's okay, I'm her brother," Dan says.

I hit him in the arm. "That sounds creepy."

"Sorry," I explain. "I'm shopping for a dress for our mother's memorial service. I want to make sure I choose the right one."

"Uh," she hesitates, "okay."

"Terrible choice," Dan says, shaking his head. "Looks like those weird baby doll dresses girls wore in the nineties."

"You've got a pedophile moustache."

He runs his thumb across his upper lip. "You've got dad's nose."

"Okay, that's just mean."

"Meaner than being called a pedophile?"

"How's it going in there?" Annabelle Olivia Rose asks.

"Great," I shout and then whisper to Dan, *"Help me get it off."*

"Are you wearing a bra?" he asks.

"Never say that again," I reply, knocking over my purse. "Just pull it over my head."

He gives a hearty tug. "It's stuck on your boobs."

"Pull them."

What happens next will never be spoken of again. When we emerge from the dressing room, I don't take the time to confirm whether I've ripped the dress. I buy it, and leave.

Dan stops at every hand sanitizing station we pass on the way to the car. We don't speak or make eye contact the whole ride home. Only when I pull into the driveway does he say, "I need a new Group to . . . uh . . . deal with what just happened." As if he has PTSD.

There's drizzle on the windshield. I flip on the wipers. "We need a Group too."

seven

MONDAY MORNING, I text Dan from the boardroom and ask him to follow up with the church and restaurant for Mom's ring. He says to *remind me later* because he's driving Emma to a wilderness camp outside the city.

An office temp sets a fruit tray on the table while an IT intern fiddles with the projector screen. The CFO eventually appears in his oval home office. We're discussing the acquisition of an organic supermarket chain that started in British Columbia and that has expanded across the prairies. Modelled after Okanagan fruit stands and the sidewalk markets in Europe and Queens, Fresh Life's market share is rapidly growing alongside its patented vertical hydroponic greenhouses.

No one agrees with the company's valuation. Our Chief Operating Officer calls the acquisition price outrageous. The CFO vehemently disagrees. He's tasted the company's arugula, and claims the arugula alone is worth the six-million-dollar purchase price.

"Six million? Their setup reminds me of something you'd find at a NASCAR race or a protest camp. For that price we could just buy a few shipping containers and a bunch of tents from Canadian Tire."

"Low carbon footprint," I offer, stabbing a piece of cantaloupe with a toothpick.

"And their greenhouses are covered in graffiti."

"The company's founder would call that art." The cantaloupe has a touch of slime. "They commission locals to paint murals reflecting each community's relationship with food."

The CFO pushes a muffin off camera.

"Has anyone seen the *Beyond Van Gogh* exhibit?"

No one answers.

A colleague turns his laptop screen toward me and shows me a live stream of his dogs fighting over a toy at daycare. He beams.

I didn't even check to see if Wes and Joan were alive this morning.

I skim over Fresh Life's financials.

"You know this hydroponic-market thing started in France. A little start-up called Petit Vert."

I glance up at our business development manager.

"In a Paris suburb," he says.

"I'll go," I say.

"To Paris?" the CFO asks. His wife appears in the background of his screen, setting a bag of McDonald's on his credenza. He doesn't turn around.

"Look at the numbers." I point to a column on the spreadsheet. "When's the last time you saw growth like that?"

The CEO makes a face like he's never seen growth like that.

"I have to go anyway," I say. "To Paris. We're doing this family trip."

"When?"

"Soon." Soon?

The executive team shrugs and we move on to Health and Safety. By the time I get out of the boardroom I have a thousand unread texts.

Wes: *can i eat the last cheese bun?*

Dan: *ring not at the church*

Joan: *where's my flat iron?*
Dad: *send this to ten friends . . .*
Glen: *there's a flat iron in my trunk*
Dan: *ring not at the restaurant*
Wes: *can we order Skip?*
Mallory: *have u seen this?*

Mallory Pepper, whose luggage I stole and whose maternity pants are still hanging in the back of my closet. I remember teaching her how to breastfeed from a Calgary hotel room. And I must've done a good job because her son, Arthur, is now ten and a dozen cheeseburgers taller than his classmates. He's on my fridge in the form of a hockey card.

Mallory's my travel agent. I click on the link, hoping she's sent me a flash seat sale to Paris or a hot deal on an all-inclusive, but the link takes me to a blog: *A Journey to Self.* The hell is this? I scroll through broken landscapes and National Geographic–style street scenes, including one image of a fruit stand that seems to stretch an entire city block. Does Mallory know about Fresh Life?

When I click on the ABOUT tab, a picture of Glen pops up. He looks thin and gay. Probably taken in France. Did he even travel through France? How does one get from Rotterdam to Singapore via bicycle? And since when does Glen have a website?

Last year, I took a sabbatical from my medical sales job in Canada and cycled 16,000 km from Singapore to Rotterdam. What started as a freewheeling adventure to inject more impulse and immediacy into my life evolved into a spiritual awakening. One of awareness and healing. Reconciliation and peace. I went to see the world, but what I saw was myself.

What the actual fuck. Impulse? What is impulse if not leaving your partner and two small kids to then go play house with another woman? What is immediacy if it's not waking up to a kid barfing in her bed, or getting a text from your dad that he's having a panic attack at Canadian Tire, or an email from your son's teacher that your kid probably has lice. It's a stroke on a plane.

"Claudia?" Marcus from Business Development raps on my door.

I wave him in.

"Check it out." He shows me an image of a Petit Vert in a Northern Paris suburb. In addition to greens, it includes a community fridge, a cheese cooler and a small-batch baguette oven. Mismatched chandeliers dangle from a painted ceiling. The staff wear green-striped aviation-style coveralls. "Cool, right?"

I nod. If Petit Vert's uniforms reflect current fashion trends, I can skip shopping and wear Dad's pajamas to Paris.

"See this?" Marcus points to a row of five vintage yellow seats, inside the entry of Petit Vert's. A sign in front of them invites Parisians to *sit and reflect about a time they had to wait.*

So much for immediacy. Marcus flips his laptop shut, and stands. "I'll send you some stats," he says taking an apple from my fruit bowl. "The graphics will blow your mind." He mimes an explosion with his hand.

I go back to Glen's website and study the pictures. He has an eye. His subjects seem to have enjoyed being photographed by him. The people smile, the trees perform, the pigeons are proud. Even the inanimate seems alive. Waving Jeeps, frowning concrete, buildings that hum.

A one word reply to Mallory: *weird.*

This is a Glen I don't recognize. A Glen who supersedes co-parenting arrangements, complicated surnames, and shared Christmases. And yet the images also show a side of him I remember from before we had kids. A Glen who explored abandoned buildings, invited strangers for dinner, and jumped from planes.

I used to explore abandoned buildings, invite strangers for dinner, and jump from planes.

Mallory texts: *go to the events tab.*

Glen has a arranged a speaking gig at the library, this Friday. The talk's title is ripped from his bio: *I went to see the world, but what I saw was myself — an evening with Glen Hopper.*

Mallory: *Read the last line.*

I skim through the lengthy blurb . . . capuchin . . . flat tire . . . yak butter . . . lost wallet . . . temple . . . Claudia. I stop at my name and read the line aloud: Leaving Claudia was a mistake.

My chest heaves and dips.

This is what I'd think about at the Petit Vert in north Paris. How I've waited a decade, pinned to a seat, for Glen to admit any type of regret. I feel a mix of vindication and shame. A touch of rage. Vindication for being regretted, shame that it matters. Rage that it doesn't.

I remember Wes coming home from school in grade one, and asking if it was true that he came from a broken home, and all I could do to keep my legs from buckling was to agree because luckily, the fridge wasn't working at the time. I'd spent the night trying to fix it. This was before YouTube had really taken off, and I could only find one video and it was three and a half hours long, and I cried through every twist of the screwdriver. When Wes got up the next morning, I showed him my handiwork. I made him stick his hand inside the crisper so he could feel how cold it was. I assured him his home was no longer broken, even if I was cracked in half.

I hoist myself up from my chair and gaze at a picture of Cathy and me taken at a Spartan race a few years after Mom died. We're both covered in mud, both laughing; me keeled over, heaving, her upright and bent skyward, clutching her chest. God, it was a terrible race. She was so elated to finish. I don't remember what was so funny but it's my favourite picture of her. It was on our way home from the race in a Dairy Queen drive-thru she told me she had cancer. I still have the red plastic spoon on my desk.

I touch her face, imagine she's laughing at Glen's bio, which is — admittedly — a bit Pinterest for my tastes. She would balk at the thought of me getting back together with him and understandably so. It was her who stepped in to replace him during those middle years when the kids always seemed to have overlapping schedules. She'd pick up Wes from swimming lessons, drive Joan to soccer, come with me to hockey games and movie nights and school concerts. Deliver a forgotten lunch kit to the school. Once she even attended Wes's Cub Scouts BBQ. On Father's Day. And for a woman who was frequently misgendered and anxious about her tremendous height, it was the ultimate act of friendship. The ultimate act of love. She died too soon.

eight

MONA AND DAD are playing Boggle at my kitchen table when I get home from work. This is not what I imagined when I told Dad to keep his key and drop in anytime. Mona's using one of my office notepads to keep score. Wes and Joan are plugged in front of the TV, watching a murder show and slurping takeout Pho.

"Check it out," Dad says. "I spelled SURPRISE. That's worth eleven. Most points I ever got."

Surprises should be worth zero points, I think, sizing up the garbage bag in the kitchen. Why is the oven on?

"What's in the bag?"

"The old comforter," Dad says, flipping the sand timer.

Not *my*, not *our*. *The* old comforter. Such an impersonal article for such a personal article. As though that comforter didn't shroud my parents, their marriage, in warmth.

"We thought you might want it. I know there wasn't much left after . . ." Mona's voice trails and Dad immediately disassociates, because this is what he does. He's physically still here staring at the Boggle tiles but his mind is elsewhere. The seventh hole, the seventh planet, drowning in the seventh sea.

I finish the sentence. Not much left after the hoarding. Mona's right. Not much survived my father's stint of grief-induced garbage collecting. But I'm not sure I want the comforter. It's too intimate, never mind too floral. And yet I understand how it would be weird for Mona to lie in bed with the ghost of my mother on top of her.

Wes and Joan have both pushed their takeout containers aside.

"Did you guys not get me anything?"

"Dad paid for it because there was no food."

I open the fridge. "There's tons of food. I went grocery shop-ping yesterday."

"Joan was craving pho," Wes says. "And you didn't answer your text."

"Dad always lets me use his account," Joan adds.

"What do you mean by *always?*" There's half a pound of luncheon meat in the drawer, yogurt, cheese. A whole god-damned Petit Vert on the bottom shelf.

"She orders Starbucks all the time," Wes says.

"Coffee?" I ask.

Joan spins a chopstick between her fingers. "Non-fat soy Frappuccino, double whip, caramel drizzle."

"It'd be weird if we got you something on Dad's account."

"I wasn't expecting you to pay for it from his account. Joan, don't drink coffee. You're too young to get addicted to caffeine." I turn back to my dad and Mona. "Did you guys eat?"

"We went to Denny's," Mona replies, furiously scratching words on the notepad.

Dan charges through the door, wipes his feet on the mat. It must be raining because his hair's sopping and his pants are spotted.

"Is that Edo?"

"Starving," Dan replies. "That wilderness camp is nearly an hour's drive."

"So, everyone's eaten?"

"I can make you something?" Mona offers, flipping the sand

timer on its side to pause the game. She lumbers to the fridge, takes a quick scan, touches a few things. "Not much in here," she says, frowning.

Dan sets his Edo on the table beside Dad. "Claudia, pass me a fork."

"Can you get your own fork?"

"I had a hard day." He shakes a tiny container of sesame seeds over his bowl of noodles. "When are we doing this trip to Paris? Because I gotta talk to Allison-Jean."

"Paris?" Joan squeals. She jumps from the couch and races to the kitchen. All I see are legs. "We're going to Paris?"

Dad's face turns red. He hasn't told Mona. Dan dumps hot sauce on his noodles.

"Paris?" Mona shrieks, pushing away from the table. "Gerald, was this the surprise?"

Dad looks at me, mouth open.

"Do I have to go?" Wes asks.

Mona is still waiting for Dad to reply. Her fingers are braced against the table's edge, and turning white. Oblivious Dan shovels noodles into his mouth with game show desperation. Dad leans away. "Daniel, slow down. You're eating like a starved horse."

Mona cannot come to Paris. It's a memorial trip, not a honeymoon.

"France sucks," Wes says. "Can't we go somewhere cool? Like the Maldives?"

"Do you know expensive the Maldives are?" I know because Glen once sent me a postcard from there. A university friend's wedding. Mallory said he would have paid a thousand bucks a night for the resort he stayed in.

"Gerald?" Mona says, her voice cracked and quiet.

"No," he finally replies. "The surprise was that I got us tickets to see the Van Gogh exhibit."

Disappointment ripples through her jangly cheeks until she can close her mouth and clench her jaw.

"I heard it's lovely." I stare at Dan, imploring him to say something.

"Romantic," he adds, wiping his chin with his sleeve.

"Van Gogh killed himself," Joan says.

"Yeah, shot himself in the chest. I saw it in a meme." Wes turns off the TV. "His last words were 'The sadness will last forever.'"

Mona swallows. "And this was what you had planned for our honeymoon?"

Dad shakes the Boggle case. "Not our honeymoon per se, just a post-wedding date night."

"So, Paris is still a thing?"

"Look, Mona," I say. "Dad probably didn't tell you because we only discussed it yesterday but we were thinking of going to Paris — as a family — to commemorate the tenth anniversary of my mom's death."

Silence. No one says anything because everyone is trying to discern what I mean by family. We hadn't even discussed bringing the kids. Allison-Jean would probably say no. Glen would probably say yes and then have a conflict in his schedule that would prevent him from "babysitting" his children. And Mona and Dad have only known each other a few months. A few months gets you Van Gogh. Not Paris.

"I've always wanted to go to Paris," Mona says.

"So did my mom," I quietly reply.

Mona pries the lid from the Boggle case, plucks the letters off one-by-one and drops them into the sack. I think of the floral pouch, Mom's missing ring. Wes throws his takeout container in the trash and leaves for a friend's house. Joan hands Mona an Edo napkin. Dad reaches for Mona's hand. Her ring is sapphire, cut like a second helping.

"Sorry, Mona. It was something we should've done ages ago. Life just kind of kept happening. Kept getting in the way. We figured this would be a way to get some closure. To say good-bye."

"I understand," Mona replies. She tears the scoresheet from my legal pad and throws it in the garbage. "Gerald," she says, "I'd like to go."

"To Paris?" he replies, standing.

"Home."

Home. Family.

Dad gathers game parts to put away. He's frazzled and can't fit everything inside the box. He does the best he can, but the timer rolls onto the floor and he throws everything into Dan's empty plastic takeout bag.

Mona slips into her sneakers. She struggles to pull the heels up over the backs of her ankles. I hand her a shoehorn. Without wedding makeup, her skin looks like time and worry. My mom's face didn't reach this hallmark and I'm both sad and relieved by this. Mona sits down on the padded hall bench, passes the shoehorn to Dad. It takes him three and a half minutes to put on one shoe, untied. Mona gets down on her knees, on the hardwood no less, to tie his laces. I imagine her tying the laces of each of her five boys. Boys who would grow up and get dispatched to Bosnia and Eritrea, blown up in Afghanistan. No wonder her wrinkles are trenches. No wonder she wants to go to Paris.

I hug them both, thank Mona for the comforter.

"Drive safe," Dan says. "It's raining."

I flip on the outside light and they slowly descend the front steps towards Mona's giant pick-up. Dan watches over my shoulder.

"Are we mean to exclude her?" I ask. "From Paris?"

My brother shrugs. "I think she'd feel out of place. Besides, they're going to Van Gogh." He towel-dries his hair on one of my hoodies.

"That's not much of a honeymoon." I call the restaurant down the street and order pasta for one. "Maybe we can send them away for a few days. Somewhere special. Beyond Van Gogh."

"There's that new bed and breakfast close to Oak Island. They love the show."

It's a great idea. Mona's obsessed with the Lagina brothers.

"But I don't have any money," Dan adds.

"Whatever, I'll pay for it. You organize it."

Joan is already planning the trip to Paris. She comes out of her room with a list of five-star hotels near the Champs.

"Look for a Holiday Inn," I say. I'm not wasting five stars on my family.

My pasta arrives and I carry it to the couch. Dan is texting Allison-Jean about driving Liam to the dentist. Liam is older than Wes but hasn't bothered to get his license. Or a job.

Dan says, "It's cold in here. Can you turn the heat up?"

"It's August, no."

My brother rips open the garbage bag in the kitchen and tugs out the comforter. He brings it back to the couch, and spreads it over both sets of our legs. I jab a meatball with my fork. The comforter is so worn, our kneecaps protrude. I can smell Dad.

"Can I have a bite?" Dan waits with his mouth open wide. He looks old and small. The stress of his marriage has left him with dark circles under his eyes, thinning hair and loose clothing. He's down at least ten pounds.

"You need some new clothes." I pass him a meatball and we stare at our reflection in the blank TV.

nine

ON TUESDAY, I work from home because there's a power outage by the office. This is a mistake, because Dan's also working from home. From my home. His stuff's spread over the kitchen table. I'm set up in the living room, my laptop perched on a stack of textbooks that Wes failed to return at the end of last school year.

I'm in the middle of a Zoom meeting, where our ad agency is presenting creative for a new series of web ads, when Glen texts: *can we talk?*

About what? I text back.

Dan starts his own Zoom call. He's yelling. I motion for him to go in the other room, but he explains through hand gestures that his laptop's plugged in. I turn my camera off and go down the hall. By the time the agency is finished its presentation, Glen still hasn't replied to my last text and it leaves me irritated and curious. I spent years processing our failed relationship. I met some good men. Why then do I care so much that he has something to say? Why have I let him lock his bike to the only sliver of my heart still capable of receiving love? I hate myself.

I set my phone facedown, turn on my computer mic, say the usual post-meeting pleasantries and disconnect.

Dan is shouting projections from the kitchen. Wes's school emails to say timetables have been posted online. One week till the kids go back. I'll have to take them shopping for school clothes. Or give them money to go on their own.

Between meetings, Dan and I book Dad and Mona's getaway. I arrange to have a bottle of champagne in the room. Dan's managed to book a private Oak Island tour through one of his clients. Mona is ecstatic and we both feel better about leaving her behind. Next, we tackle Paris.

"Should we bring the kids?"

"That's a lot of kids," Dan replies, microwaving a Pizza Pop.

"Harrison isn't exactly a kid."

"He isn't coming." Dan lingers beside the microwave. "He can't miss school. Too many labs and depending on when we go, midterms."

"I kinda don't want to bring the kids."

Dan's phone rings. He answers, while transferring his Pizza Pop to the table.

I heat up leftovers. Mom's funeral bulletin is still on the fridge, faded and curled at the corners. *She was their grandma*, I think, studying her picture, but I don't know that Joan remembers and Wes doesn't even want to go. After reviewing my calendar, I text Dad about the last week in September. It's soon. Flights will be outrageous. God knows about hotel bookings and whatever else it is we're planning on doing. What *are* we planning on doing?

When Dan gets off the phone, we examine our calendars.

"I don't know if Allison-Jean will let them miss school." He plucks a dry meatball from my plate.

"Liam doesn't even go to school."

"Online he does," Dan argues.

For grade twelve? Or terrorism? All Liam does is play first-person shooter games. And yet Dan and Allison-Jean are more concerned about whether he eats his broccoli, drinks his whole milk, and takes his vitamins: C, D. AK-47.

"I can't leave the kids behind," I say.

"I thought you wanted to go without them."

"I won't be able to relax."

"You never relax." He says it, rinsing his plate in the sink.

"That's not true."

"Oh, Claudia." He rolls his eyes. "Everyone knows you can never just relax and go with the flow."

"Okay, Yoda. You cancelled Christmas last year because you couldn't find Turtles."

"That was Mom's fault," he says, shaking his mouse to jump-start his computer screen.

"There was a global shortage of pecans."

"And what did Mom always say? You can't have Christmas without Turtles."

Dan starts typing, and everything about him looks hard. Concrete shoulders, lead fingers, metal veins. The one on his forehead doesn't even pulse. I turn away and stare at the fridge. There's a picture of Dan and me at his wedding. His arm's around me and I'm sort of hunched, mid-laugh, a glass of champagne dangling dangerously from my hand. Dan's boutonniere is upside down. In the background, Glen. I have no idea who took the picture or why it's on my fridge. It's not even a nice photo. It's slightly out of focus, grey-tinged and date stamped with ugly alarm clock digits. My right side is cut off.

I consider us both now: middle-aged, alone, a litter of kids and a ribbon of sadness between us. Maybe France will fix us. Maybe we'll find our old selves or reinvent new ones or simply see the world in a new light. It seems to have worked for Glen.

Dan is hyper-focused on whatever he's typing. I move the picture to the centre of the fridge so nothing else touches it. His phone chimes. "Allison-Jean says I have to take Liam and Emma to Paris. She can't single-parent and study."

Alison-Jean is going to mortuary school.

"I thought Cindy was moving in."

"Cindy doesn't know how to parent. She doesn't have any children."

"So, I guess we're bringing the kids."

"Have you talked to Glen?"

We haven't spoken since he texted asking if we could talk. I phone him. He answers from the car. A siren wails and then fades into the background. I explain the plan.

"You're taking a family memorial trip to Paris a month after your dad remarries? A bit weird, no?"

"That's kinda why. The whole wedding thing was almost a sign that it was time to do something so we could all just move on."

"What's remarrying, if it's not moving on?"

"Forward. He's moving forward," I say. "You don't move *on*. Moving on implies finality. You make it sound like we're replacing the dishwasher with a new model."

"But you just said you were going to Paris so you could move on."

I want to tell him to die in a hole, but he's right. I said that. "I meant forward."

There's a long pause. I hear a truck pass, the pleasing click-click of a turn signal. "You never really move forward."

Preach, Plato.

"Time is a construct and we're nothing but energy moving directionless in and out of the light."

"I'd like to move forward with this conversation. Do you mind if I bring the kids?"

"Will Joan miss evaluations?"

"They'll be finished by then. The most she'll miss is a few practices."

Another long pause. I imagine Glen moving directionless in and out of the traffic lights, lost. If I hold the phone close to my ear, I can tell he's playing flute music again.

"Are you listening to Zamfir?"

"I could always come to Paris."

I recoil, as if he's suggested we make love on a Paris rooftop in matching striped shirts. "Why would you come?"

"I could help with the kids. Take Joan to a PSG game. Entertain Wes. If he's still into war stuff I can take him to Normandy."

"Football doesn't start until October."

"A training session? I think they're cheap."

"And Wes hasn't picked up a history book since he learned he could play War on his Xbox."

Cold, street, civil, guerilla.

"I'm trying to be helpful, Claud. You said I was never helpful."

"I needed help taking the kids to preschool, getting their eyes checked, building the stupid cars they had to design in grade four. Did you ever see what they ended up taking to school? Wes's car looked like a hot dog on wheels and Joan's was two-dimensional. For a unit on 'vehicles that move forward' she raced a piece of cardboard."

"Claudia," Dan interrupts. "You're yelling. I have to make a call."

I want to suggest Dan go to his own house, and fix his marriage. Now, before he's still unpacking it ten years later, a box of junk in the basement overflowing with miscues, missteps. Mistakes. A sarcophagus of emotion.

"Mona's not even coming," I say.

"If you change your mind . . ."

"I won't."

"When the time comes, I'll talk to Joan's coach. In case she does have to miss a game."

"That would be helpful."

"But if you did let me come, I would take you to every god-damned romantic corner of the city. Every lover's bridge, every candlelit alley, archway, balcony, platform. Every rooftop."

What. The actual. Fuck. When Glen said *I went to see the world, but what I saw was myself*, did he see himself as Jerry Maguire or Jack Dawson? Or that lovelorn creeper from *Love Actually* who confessed his feelings to Keira Knightley with a stack of giant recipe cards and a ghetto blaster?

And yet the idea of standing on a Paris rooftop with Glen actually makes me feel like I'm standing on the edge of a roof right now: curious and awakened. Alive.

Enough, now.

ten

GEORGIA IS JOGGING on the spot by the time I reach the trail-head. "I'm already at ten thousand steps," she says, checking her watch. She wears running gear as orange as a pylon and cut for a college athlete, of which she is not. She doesn't care about creases and folds or high-waisted panels. She cares about steps.

She gives me no time to warm up. As soon as my foot touches the pathway, she's off, as if looking for a new husband. She's been married three times — proudly — and loves like she runs: reckless and hard. A hundred metres in and twice she's nearly run me off the trail.

"Why were you late?"

"I was talking to Glen."

"He cool with the whole Paris thing?"

"He wants to come to the Paris thing."

Georgia slows and whacks my arm. "The hell for?"

"To help," I say, making air quotes.

She picks up her pace. We round a bend and take a foot-bridge in single file. Ahead of us, a single tree has gone rogue, its leaves sharp and yellow in defiance of summer.

"I suppose that wouldn't be the end of the world if you have to visit a few grocery stores while you're there."

I'd forgotten all about Petit Vert. In fact, I'd forgotten about the memorial. The whole reason we're going. I'm turning Paris into a goddamned fantasy.

"Right" is all I say, dodging a fallen branch.

"Maybe he can watch the kids some night and you can go out dancing."

"By myself?" How tragic.

"I would," she counters.

I agree. "You would."

We run the next leg of the trail in silence. Too many hills. Georgia's most recent divorce was finalized last winter. She celebrated by hiking Machu Picchu alone and then spent a week immersed with a group of local farmers growing quinoa. At home, she harvests men.

I blurt, "I think Glen wants to get back together."

"Splendid," she replies. "I mean, most men hit midlife and they want to leave their wives. That's very avant-garde of Glen, never mind romantic." She kicks a rock out of the way. "What more can you want in a man?"

One who never left in the first place.

I change the subject and we spend the next five K discussing everything from bitcoin to Botox. We're holdouts on both. Liam has supposedly made a few bucks on digital currency but I still don't fully understand how it works. I never anticipated seeking investment advice from the generation that ate Tide Pods.

We pass an older couple out for a stroll. Birders, on account of the binoculars. Georgia and I nod, before we blow past them.

"That could be you and Glen," she says.

It could be my dad and mom, if she was still alive. This is exactly how they would have done their seventies: nature walks, sun hats, sandhill cranes. With Mona, it's a different future. One I'm still trying to figure out, but I suspect will include trips to Las Vegas, shot glass collections and inappropriate T-shirts. Dad always liked gag gifts: passive-aggressive notepads, fanny packs made to look like beer bellies, bathroom putting greens.

An impossible thought strikes me and I stumble as we near the final bend of the trail. Which of those men is my real dad? Canoe man or cruise ship karaoke participant? Man nursing a scotch or man doing the macarena while polishing back a margarita? Pavarotti or Elvis impersonator? Janice or Mona. If mom had a sophisticated French lover, then maybe Dad has a secret penchant for American gameshows and grannies with fake eyelashes. Of course, I'm assuming Émile was sophisticated. A financier or maître d'. But maybe he just repaired shoes.

"Whatcha thinking about?" Georgia asks. She's accelerating toward the parking lot and I can barely keep up.

I can't speak by the time we sprint through the gate. A few wobbly steps to orient myself and I hunch over, elbows on my knees. My head spins and it takes me a few minutes to catch my breath.

Georgia's parked near the trailhead. She pops the trunk of her Lexus, then fishes through layers of real estate signs before uncovering an ancient case of water. "Here," she says, tossing a bottle in the air. I mouth "Thanks," unscrew the cap with a trembling hand and take a long sip. From the front seat, she grabs her own bottle, stainless steel, and mixes in a tiny packet of flavour.

"You think it's possible we can spend an entire marriage, a whole life being someone else?"

"No," she replies, furiously shaking her head. "Why do you think I've been married three times?"

Because you're shitty at relationships? Work too much? Talk through movies? Have the worst taste in Christmas decorations?

"Because marriage is a construct."

For fuck's sake. First time, and now marriage. A distant jackhammer splits the air into pieces.

"This notion that we can only love one person, that we

have to pick one and say together until end times doesn't work for me. I want to be with as many people as I fall in love with and die."

"Then why even bother getting married? Why not just date whoever?" I feel my heart rate starting to drop and at the same time I notice a dull and persistent ache in my chest.

"Because I do love a wedding," she replies wistfully.

It's true. Georgia's had some spectacular ones.

"And I'm sorry I missed your dad's," she adds. "Open house."

An elderly woman in a beige Corolla pulls into the lot. She inches her way into a parking spot and Georgia and I watch, waiting for her to bump the crumbled concrete marking the edge of the pavement. She comes within inches, but never hits it. The woman slowly unbuckles, swings her legs out of the vehicle like they might be made of plastic or straw, and stands.

"What if you end up alone?"

Another car pulls in.

"Alone implies you're only qualifying romantic relation-ships. Whether I have a man or not, I'll always have you, my nieces, colleagues, friends. Barney."

I'm not sure she'll always have Barney. He's blind and has been on specialized cat food imported from Germany for nearly a decade. His mews are laments.

Another elderly lady joins Straw Legs. This one is wiry and fit with a big mouth and tinted hair. They are happy to see each other. It seems like it might have been a while. After a few min-utes of catch-up they select the smaller trail loop and disappear into the woods.

"What is all this?" Georgia waves her hand from my face down to my torso, like a disappointed fairy godmother. "You're all out of sorts. Is it the wedding? Your dad getting remarried? Your brother? Glen?"

That's a lot of things. I shrug, as if it's none of these things. Fuck, and I'm tearing up.

The old couple we passed earlier emerges from the trail, like a pair of great explorers. The man is recording something in a notebook with a voting pencil. I imagine his letters, shaky and slanted. His wife stoops to tie her shoe. A flutter of wings. We all look up and a great blue heron lopes across the sky. It looks out of place. Too heavy. Like it might plummet to the earth at any second. But then it climbs, higher and higher, before coming to a graceful stop atop a power pole.

I smile, shielding my eyes from the sun. When I lower my hand, Georgia is right there, a foot from me. She stares at me, deep and thoughtful. This is why she's single. She can see past masks and personas, profile pictures and tweets. She can see your shame, your secrets, your naked beating heart. She's terrifying.

I say nothing, willing myself not to cry.

She takes another step so our noses are practically touching and then her eyes grow wide, her mouth drops open and she says, "After all these years . . . you're still in love with Glen."

eleven

IT'S SUNDAY AND ME AND THE KIDS are on our way to Dad and Mona's for an Oak Island marathon. The invitation arrived in in my mailbox on Wednesday. No envelope. It was shaped like a treasure chest with a fastener screwed through the top so the chest could be opened. I hadn't seen anything like it since Wes and Joan were tiny and for a minute, I contemplated the joy and horror of children's birthday parties. The loot bags, themes, decorations. The kids. So many.

"I'm going to kill myself," Wes says from the back seat.

"Not appropriate," I scold, glaring at him in the rear-view mirror. "This is important to Mona. And Grandpa."

I'd assumed the card had been delivered in error. A young family had just moved in next door and the bungalow beside them housed a family of six, but when I opened the treasure chest, I learned it wasn't a mistake. The marathon was a pre-honeymoon celebration and our attendance was expected.

Wes says, "I'm only staying for one episode."

"Me too," Joan chimes. "Libby's doing my nails."

"What do you mean she's doing your nails? Like, painting them?"

"Gel."

"You just had your nails done for the wedding."

"Yeah, well, she's giving me Paris-themed ones. See?"

She shoves her phone in my face and I nearly drive off the

road. I bat her away and ponder what Paris-themed nails might look like. Guillotines, snails, love, rage.

"Make sure she cleans the tools or whatever. I don't want you getting an infection."

"When can I tell Hudson to pick me up?" Wes asks.

I pull up to the curb, put the car in park and turn to address my kids. "Neither of you are leaving until I say it's okay. We skipped the wedding brunch, so we have to do this. Be nice."

"I'm not participating in anything," Wes says.

"Who says you'd have to?" I collect the bean salad from the front seat floor.

Wes pulls at his hair. "The invitation said there's going to be a money cake and Oak Island–inspired games and food. I'm not playing any games."

Joan stares at the elderly bodies crowded behind Dad and Mona's picture window. "I'm going to kill myself."

"*Stop* saying that," I holler. "If I hear either of you say that again, today, or any other day, I'm taking your phones away for a week. Final warning."

Wes and Joan slink out of the car. "I'm still only staying for one episode," Wes says.

We knock and Mona answers the door wearing a gold dress and enough Mardi Gras beads to choke a stripper.

"Welcome!" she says, presenting us each with a string. I get purple. "Come see what your dad made." Mona pulls me toward a table draped with a disposable paper table cloth and crowded with serving dishes and trays. She holds up a bowl of Hersey's Kisses, chocolate gold coins, Ring-Pops and candy necklaces.

"What is it?" I ask, knowing there's an answer beyond the obvious.

"Top pocket finds." She giggles, unwraps a Kiss and pops it

in her mouth before sashaying her way back toward the front door to greet another guest.

Dad is in the kitchen washing dishes. His bent frame resembles papier-mâché. The rubber gloves go up to his elbows. I offer to dry and he gestures to the linen drawer with his foot. Mona's kitchen is small but functional. Loads of cupboards, an island of drawers, an entire shelf of Company's Coming cookbooks. Dad points to where things go, some of which I'm certain he's wrong about. The Tupperware, for example, that he's told me to put in the bottom drawer with the handheld beaters and electric meat cutter. It took him months to figure out my kitchen when he first moved in. I eventually cleaned out a drawer and made it his: bowl, plate, favourite spoon, insurance mug, and a cloth napkin that survived the great hoard because my mom had previously sent it home wrapped around an ice pack after Wes hit his head on the coffee table.

A stranger pops her head in the kitchen to indicate that the first show of the marathon is about to begin. Mona has curated a playlist of her favorite episodes. The ones where the searchers actually find something other than earthworms and rocks.

Dad hangs the dish towel on the oven door. The beads weigh him down and leave him hunched. His shirt is damp.

"You coming, Claud?" he asks. "The first one's my favourite. I like when they dig at Smith's Cove."

"I'll be right there," I say encouragingly. "Just getting some water."

When he's gone, I grab the Tupperware from the bottom drawer and search for its rightful place. Where there is one Tupperware, there are thousands. I search junk drawers and pot drawers, cereal cupboards, open shelves of teacups. I try the pantry. On the top shelf is the *Wizard of Oz* teapot I gave my mom on her sixtieth birthday. An audible gasp escapes my lips and I glance around to make sure I'm still alone. Dad told me he couldn't find it.

Someone comes into the kitchen. Mona's friend. I recognize her from the wedding. I tuck into the pantry while she goes into the fridge, removes a tray, samples one of whatever is on it and then ferries it back to the living room.

I take down the teapot, remove the lid and look inside, for what, I don't know. A tea leaf, a stain, some sign of her. The spout is chipped. I run my finger along the break, rough as a cat's tongue. I want the teapot back.

More noise from the kitchen and a burst of activity from the living room. Rick, Marty and the rest of the Oak Island team must have found something in Smith's Cove. A loonie, a zipper pull, a Happy Meal toy from 1995. The cast will spend the next twenty minutes debating the origins of each. Is it a Templar loonie? The zipper from a Rosicrucian's backpack? Jesus's Happy Meal?

I return the teapot to the shelf, spout turned in, and notice a row of neatly labeled bins on the bottom rack of the pantry: BIG, SMALL, LIDS. Perfect. I remove the lid from the unit my dad washed, place it in the corresponding bin, and then open the container marked SMALL. There must be a hundred pieces of plastic: round, square, coloured, opaque. At the bottom, someone's put an orange container back with its lid on. High grade, original Tupperware brand. I pry off the top to put it in the correct bin. My mother's ring is inside.

I fish it out, examine the stone and the two diamond clusters in the dull glow of the pantry light. Definitely hers. Why is my mom's ring in Mona's pantry?

"Mom?"

Wes. I slip the ring in my pocket, put the lid back on the container and nudge all the bins back in line.

"I'm here," I call, exiting the pantry, closing the door behind me.

"They're making us play a game."

"Who's they, and what kind of game?" My face is flushed, my ears hot as heat lamps.

"The old people," he says. "They're making us guess the number of chocolate gold coins in a glass jar."

"So? Guess. That's harmless. You made it seem like they'd asked you to swallow fire." I feel like I've swallowed fire.

"We're the only people here under eighty," he complains. "Mona's grandkids didn't have to come."

"Most of them live in Ontario. Just get through this episode."

Wes makes a noise akin to a grunt and goes back to the living room. I follow behind, sit in a cane chair next to the food table. Dad and Mona are squeezed together on a recliner. It seems Dad has earned some new beads since rejoining the party. Joan is in the corner snapping selfies. A cheap crown is fixed to her head. Could it be the crown of Duc d'Anville?

The cane chair is uncomfortable. Without getting up, I ladle myself a serving of punch. On the TV, one of the Lagina brothers is getting emotional. You'd think it would be because he's spent the last decade defacing an island in search of a treasure that most of us accept has long since been dug up, its bits distributed, its riches spent on wenches, fine liquor, whole towns. If in fact there ever was a treasure to begin with. Maybe the whole thing was a ruse. The real treasure's probably barely buried on the next island over in someone's Tupperware bin.

I want to text Dan and tell him about the ring. He only got out of this to take Liam to a community college open house. But I don't. It's the first time Liam's taken any interest in anything outside of his bedroom. Dan needs to be fully present.

Mona's son Rodney arrives with a bottle of Goldschläger. I take a shot when he comes around with a platter of mismatched glasses. He's hotter than I remember from the wedding. There's something about his weariness, the "awayness" in his face that I find intriguing, sexy. An island to dig.

By episode two, I've given away all my beads and finished the punch. Mona pauses the TV before episode three and makes us play a memory game. She sets a tray of treasure-themed items on the coffee table. Dollar-store rings, pirate patches, a fleet of tiny model ships. We are given ten minutes to memorize everything on the tray. I take note of Wes. His eyebrows furl, giving away his enthusiasm. I will remind him later that he enjoyed this game, a game my mom used to play with him when she took him for sleepovers.

When the ten minutes expires, Mona covers the tray and carries it to the kitchen. She comes back with a timer. "You have three minutes to write down everything you can remember that was on the tray."

The timer starts and I draw a blank. I stare at the Lagina brother frozen on the paused screen, the same one who was getting emotional on the previous episode. He shares that same "awayness" in his eyes as Rodney. It's a look somewhere between hope and despair.

Wes furiously scratches items on his notepad. I catch Joan, phoneless, standing at the back window staring into the backyard. I wonder what she sees, what she thinks.

The timer continues to tick. In my head I imagine it's getting louder as it counts down. Many of the adults have given up on the memory challenge. Pens and pencils are cast aside, lists are flipped over and concealed, the food table is perused. Mona's friend hurries down the hall toward the washroom.

My paper remains blank. All I can feel is my mother's ring

denting my back pocket. I don't remember the things on the tray. I stare at the sad Lagina. There is no treasure. I think, deep down, he knows this. *Despair.* But he searches anyway because he needs to. *Hope.*

The timer goes off and Mona stands on a corner stool. Someone has returned the tray and she begins to call out the items.

"Give yourself one point for each item you remembered." She clears her throat. "Fleet of ships. Toonie. Gold watch. Green clip-on-earrings. Silver button —"

Janice's ring.

I excuse myself and go to the washroom. Mona's friend has just left. The sink is full of suds and the whole place smells like lilacs. I flip the toilet lid down, sit, and pull out my phone.

Glen texts a single black heart. How can an emoji wield so much power?

The bathroom walls feel like they're closing in. I delete his message, rinse my hands and return to the living room. Wes has won the memory game. His prize is the kind of generic medal Joan used to get in Timbits soccer.

The show is unpaused and the cast of *The Curse of Oak Island* are gathered around a bunker table pretending they've found something of interest. The waxy-looking scrap of paper at the centre of the table resembles the jokes that used to come wrapped around Bazooka Joe bubble-gum. It's either that, or a piece of one of Shakespeare's original manuscripts. A tragedy.

Not ten minutes into the next show and Mona calls for another game. This time, treasure-themed charades. I want to kill myself.

twelve

WE'RE SITTING AT the gate waiting for our flight to board. None of us talks because each of us left packing until the last minute and we are all exhausted and disgruntled. That's the problem with taking the Red Eye. You feel like you have all day and the next thing you know, the Uber's arrived, you can't find the passports and you second-guess everything you packed and everything you didn't. I play a bubble-popping game on my phone, unconvinced it's not giving me brain damage.

Dad was too nervous to eat dinner, and picks away instead at a Tim Horton's bagel he bought after going through security. He's wearing an Oak Island golf shirt purchased during his weekend getaway with Mona and the same track pants he wore when I met him in a Yarmouth motel, the day after Mom's stroke. The room had been dark, black-out drapes pulled, half-full bottles of water scattered over every surface, the faint scent of suntan lotion and his sock tan the only evidence that the nightmare we were facing had started as a romantic island getaway.

I slip Mom's ring from my finger and zip it in my pocket, before patting his knee.

Across from me, the kids lounge and take up space. Liam and Wes man-spread. Everything about them is big: headphones, sneakers, backpacks that spill into the aisle. I nudge Wes's bag with my foot. Emma, dressed in a panda onesie, is tucked into the end seat like a cannonball, gaze fixed on the screen of her iPad. Joan is stretched out across three seats with a Greta Thunberg book, her hair in a loose bun, no makeup. She was reading travel beauty tips at breakfast and learned a fresh face was the best face for a transatlantic flight. Certainly no eye makeup. Smart. I think of the eighteen coats of mascara I applied only an hour ago. I will look like the hood of Emma's panda onesie by the time we touch down in France.

The gate agent announces that our flight is full and asks for volunteers to check bags. No one moves. I watch Dan from a distance, stocking up on flight supplies at a kiosk. He pays and meanders back towards us.

"Check this out," he says, pulling items from the bag and placing them on the seat beside me. He's bought a neck pillow, a magic spy book with an invisible ink pen for Emma, cashews, scotch mints, gum, water, the latest issue of the *Economist*, and an eye-mask stenciled with tiny stars.

I hook the mask's elastic band with my pinkie. "Can I have this?"

"Why don't you buy your own?"

I check the time. Still twenty minutes before we board.

"You got it there?" I point to the kiosk he's just come from.

"Further up," he nods. "That one only had kid sizes."

Dad is trying to open a packet of jam. A flimsy plastic knife is balanced on his lap. His hands tremble.

"Can I help?" I ask, reaching for the packet.

"Please," he says. I spread jam on his bagel, and set it on my vacant seat so he can use it as a table.

I announce to anyone listening that I'll be right back. A man in the next row of seats over is the only one to acknowledge. At the adjacent gate, toddlers roll on the carpet. Further up, a volleyball team with matching backpacks boards a flight to Frankfurt. Grandparents in airline wheelchairs wait, expressionless, for attendants to deposit them onto their connecting flights.

I pass a few kiosks before I notice the sleep masks arranged on a mobile display outside a terminal convenience store. I choose an "Ooh La La" mask for Joan, a plaid one for Wes, and a polka dot one for myself. I'm in line to pay, when something catches my eye. Some*one*. A woman, short and rotund with an elderly gait, drags a silver wheelie suitcase through a crowd of passengers just arriving from gate thirty-six. The suitcase bounces, catches on the wheels of another. Mona? I can't see her face through the crowd, only the back of her red cape-style shirt, flowing behind her like a silk tailfeather. She stops abruptly at the gate with the volleyball team headed to Frankfurt.

This is a pre-boarding announcement for passengers travelling to Paris on Air Canada Flight 872.

Frig.

"Can I help who's next?"

I slide up to the wicket and place the masks on the counter. The pre-boarding announcement continues. I glance back at the Frankfurt gate. No sign of the Mona lookalike, though I do see a man who resembles the friendly A&W spokesperson. I pay for the masks and return to the gate where everyone is still spread out and unmoving.

"Dad, we can probably board now. Passengers who may need a little more assistance. That's us." I motion for him to get up.

He shakes his head violently. "We'll board last."

"The flight's full. There won't be any overhead bins if we board last."

"I have to pee," Wes says, downing the dregs of his Starbucks.

"We're boarding."

Wes glances at the line. "I think we got time."

I order Joan to take Emma to the bathroom, and arrange my boarding pass and ID. The kids insisted on taking their own passports and boarding passes. I've honoured their request and wait anxiously for them to get organized and get in line.

Executive class is called, followed by the back of the plane. Dad has managed to sit on the jam packet.

"Did you bring a change of pants?"

"No, I didn't," he spits back. "Did you?"

His eyes bulge and his teeth clench. It's the angry face from my childhood. The one he'd make if Dan and I fought in public or kicked his seat or didn't clear the table. It's less threatening now, framed by his jolly hair and wiseman skin.

"Sorry," I whisper.

Still, he seems embarrassed, checking over his shoulder to see who might have heard, shielding the spot on his pants with a speckled hand. The boarding continues, the line dwindling. There won't be any overhead bins.

When the kids return, I motion for them to stand behind Grandpa while I dig a disinfectant wipe from my purse. Dan tosses the jam packet, and helps Emma with her passport. Dad makes slow work of the stain. It takes every bit of strength for me not to yell at him to hurry, or grab the wipe and do it myself.

This is a final boarding announcement for Air Canada Flight 872 to Paris. All passengers should be now on board.

Dan sprints to the gate. We marvel, for a moment, at his competitive spirit and then mobilize behind him. By the time we assemble at the gate, he's already disappeared down the chute.

"What the hell, Dad?" Emma mumbles.

There are no overhead bins available anywhere near our assigned seats. The boys and Joan sit in a row together. Behind them are Dan and Emma, while Dad and I are in a centre row with a stranger. I help Dad into his middle seat, arrange his airline blanket and pillow, and shove his carry-on under the seat in front of him. My face is hot from bending over.

A flight attendant materializes to help. She hates the bumbling assholes holding up take-off: us. She rearranges the bins to find room for most of our luggage. All except for mine. She takes my case.

"I'll find a place to store it for the duration of the flight." She disappears down the aisle, expertly dragging my suitcase behind her. I'm convinced she's going to open the rear door and toss it outside. I have a moment of panic, remembering what it was like to watch my suitcase accidentally be removed from my flight and sent away with a labouring Mallory. I want to ensure that my bag makes into an overhead bin, but another flight attendant arrives and wants me to sit down.

I slide in beside my father, fasten my seatbelt, and close my eyes. A feeling of joy and trepidation zips through my body. We are on our way.

thirteen

MINUTES AFTER TAKE-OFF, things are not right with Dad. He's yanked down his mask, which remains twisted on his chin, and he's gripping the armrests. He is ghostly, sweating, diminutive. I touch his hand.

"Dad?"

He turns toward me, his breath shallow, eyes frightened. I think heart attack, but he doesn't claw at his chest, double over or try to speak. I consider the facts. He just ate so he can't be hungry or low on calories. I made sure he had enough to drink and that he'd taken all his meds. He doesn't seem confused. I rack my brain for an explanation and then everything comes into alarming focus. It's the first time he's been on a plane since Mom died.

"It's okay," I tell him. "You're going to be okay. Focus on breathing."

I squeeze his hand and we breathe together, deep, fragmented breaths. Dad tries to unbuckle. The seatbelt sign is still on. I place a firm hand on his leg.

"I have to get up." His voice is shaky, thin.

"Not yet." I gesture to the seatbelt sign. There's no point in trying to engage Dan or anyone else. We need to get through the next few minutes. Once we hit cruising altitude, I can get him moving. I need to distract him.

"What was that song Mom used to sing when we were little?"

Dad shakes his head and I wonder if it was a mistake to bring her up, if it will only make things worse.

"The one she sang whenever we were stuck in line. Remember? Remember the long lines to get on the PEI ferry? Or the winding queues to feed the goats at the Christmas market?"

The memories come swift and desperate until I find myself transported back in time, standing in the funeral home receiving line, distraught that no one had mentioned how much my mom loved gingerbread or that she had a hidden talent for mental math. How unjust to have these details of her life dishonoured and forgotten.

Instead of calming my father down, my own heart gathers speed, dangerously, a bike travelling too fast downhill. I lean in and unclip Dad's seatbelt, hoping to give him the illusion of space, of safety, but the opposite happens and he springs up like a man half his age, making a beeline for the aisle, clambering over and crushing me in his wake.

The commotion alerts the flight attendant, who's still strapped in her take-off seat. She frowns and shouts something inaudible. I grab what I can of my father and try to wrestle him back into the row.

Dan unbuckles, dives into the aisle and takes my father's elbow.

"Does he need a doctor?"

I don't know who asks this. I'm hot with adrenaline and can't see much through my father's bent torso and flailing limbs. In the chaos I hear the telltale ding of the overhead light indicating the seatbelt sign has been turned off.

Dad is partially on my lap, and partway in the aisle, flanked awkwardly by Dan and the flight attendant. Another attendant asks over the PA system if there's a doctor on board. No one steps forward.

Dan manages to get my father to stand. Someone suggests that my dad place his hands behind his head. That this position will somehow help him. Dad obeys, but he still breathes in disturbing clips. I climb out of my seat and rest my hand on the small of his back.

"Panic attack," I whisper to the flight attendant, who nods sympathetically. He's middle-aged and square with hairy arms and faded tattoos. Un-flight attendant-like, but he's brought my dad water and a cool cloth, and he administers care like an army medic, direct and urgent. I brace myself despairingly between two seat backs, furious for forgetting that it's Dad's first time on an airplane since the accident. There've been a few road trips over the years, and a harbour cruise for Dan's fortieth, but the closest Dad's come to flying was chaperoning Joan's grade two field trip to an aviation museum.

My dad remains unsettled, unsteady.

"Gerald?"

We all turn around. Dad, Dan, the un-flight attendant.

Mona is standing in the aisle, her red blouse a super hero's cape. Before I can signal my body to let her through, Dad is pushing me out of the way. I move into the kids' row and watch him fall into her arms, weeping. My knees buckle.

Mona doesn't stumble. She holds their combined weight and his grief with unflinching strength. I watch, fascinated. Dan does too. After a minute, my dad resettles in his seat.

"Can you get off me, now?"

I look down at Wes, who I'm squishing. "Sorry," I mumble, collecting myself, finding my balance. Mona and I make eye contact. It's brief and loaded. I move into the aisle. Mona makes space and I lean in to kiss my dad's forehead. His skin is warm and he exudes an almost supernatural peace. I gather my pillow and blanket, and my purse from under the seat, and look to the back of the plane. The un-flight attendant agrees to fetch Mona's carry-on so she can stay with my dad.

We hit a patch of turbulence and the seatbelt sign turns on. After a few words with Dan and the kids, I'm forced to stumble down the aisle towards my new seat. It's easy to find because it's at the very back of the plane, the last row on the left by the washroom. The perfect place to hide when you've hijacked someone else's memorial trip. When you're travelling to Pairs, uninvited and unwelcomed.

The bearded man in the aisle seat stands to let me in.

The perfect place to process the hijacking and to consider that you might be wrong. You should've just invited her in the first place.

The plane is not full as the airline claimed. I'm relieved when the man in the aisle seat says there's no one in the middle. *Lucky*, he says. We're *lucky*.

I don't feel lucky. I feel tricked and grateful, nauseous and ashamed. What were we thinking, going to Paris? Planning excursions. Excluding Mona. Why didn't we choose something simple like a Sable Island picnic? A candlelight service by the old armoury. A long walk in the rain.

I don't like that the middle seat is empty. I want it to be full as a clown car. Packed with empathy and bulk and limbs. Give me a soft arm to brush up against, a thick shoulder to lean on, a knee to touch. In the quiet loneliness of row forty-two, give me Glen.

fourteen

"CAN I GET YOU ANYTHING FROM THE CART?" A bug-eyed flight attendant leans into the row.

I search for the seat menu, but it's gone. Mona probably stole it. My seatmate notices, hands me his. I thank him, scan the menu options, order a glass of white wine. I stare out the window into nothingness, a black sky, and somewhere thousands of metres below, the black ocean, frigid and swollen, dotted, I suspect, with container ships bludgeoning their way to New York under the light of the moon.

"You see anything?"

My seatmate is scrambling for a view. I attempt to put my chair back but forget we're in the last row. The seat positions are as fixed as toilets. I won't be able to sleep. None of this would have happened if I'd just invited Mona in the first place. If I'd been kind.

I take a sip of my wine. "I see dead people."

"Right, well, if you see my granny, tell her to bugger off, will you? I missed her funeral and she won't let it go."

A Brit. He raises his brows and takes a long swig of his drink, a Pilsner, and smiles. I make eye contact for the first time since landing in the back row. He's older than I thought, unmarried, his skin weathered, hair long and unruly and as gold as his beer.

"I'll do nothing of the kind," I reply, surprised and slightly ashamed by the ease, the elderliness of my banter. "What possible excuse could you have had to warrant missing Granny's funeral?"

"I was trapped in the ice on a cargo vessel off the coast of Greenland."

"Granny says that's a lie."

"You can see her now?"

I stare out the window. Still black. "I can. She's riding a horse. Chestnut. Blond mane."

He's quiet for a second. Dabs at a spill on his tray table with an airline napkin. "That's how she died," he finally says. "Fell off a horse. Hit her head."

I stare, trying to decipher whether he's being serious. He swallows.

"I'm sorry," I whisper. "I didn't mean . . ."

"I'm pulling your leg." His laugh is hearty, his smile mischievous.

I return his smile, sink back into my unmoving chair, take another sip of wine. The tension in my shoulders begins to wane and for a moment I forget about Dad's panic attack, Mona's sudden and timely appearance, the disaster trip I've initiated and have only just begun.

In the silence, my seatmate is pensive. He runs his finger around the rim of his glass. A science magazine flaps from the seat pocket in front of him. A scar bisects his right hand like a serpent mound. There's a small hole in the elbow of his shirt sleeve and I wonder if he knows. If there's not someone close enough to him who might've pointed it out when he got dressed this morning.

"She actually died of a stroke," he says, quietly. "My granny."

"That's how my mom went." Though I've said the words a thousand times, tonight they get caught in my throat, as if they've been altered by the plane's grim circulating air, or stiffened by the cabin's coarse lighting. "On a plane," I add.

"On a plane?" he says. "A curious place to go."

Curious is the correct word. I've both loathed and delighted over the details of Mom's death. The peculiarity, the odds of it happening on a plane, the publicness of it, the whimsy and horror. Her proximity to heaven. A place I still believe in if only to get through the day.

"She was only sixty."

"One always dies too soon or too late," he says.

Yes, I think, remembering not only my mother's funeral but of Cathy's and the cruel experience of seeing her parents draped on either end of her coffin, their grief so physical it took a team of attendees to help them back to their feet, to help them exit the church, to help them breathe.

"You know Sable Island?" I ask.

His eyes brighten. "Of course, I do. It's where my Granny learned to ride horses. Wild ones." He winks and then adjusts in his seat to face me, as if he's about to tell me a schoolyard secret. "I've been several times. You?"

I shake my head. I don't share with him the island's significance. That the location of my mother's plane was tracked precisely to Sable Island at the time of her stroke. That fact has always made her death somehow more tolerable, more poetic.

"It's a magic place," he says. "Sable Island is what brought me to Canada. I read about it in an old *National Geographic* I found at a doctor's surgery when I was eleven. It's why I became an oceanographer."

I remember the issue — Dad collected them — though there were US Air Force Planes on the cover, not scientists or seals or rogue horses. I'd found the soiled magazine while cleaning out my father's horde. It had been wedged beneath the faulty leg of a dining room chair. How absurd, I'd thought, that Dad had taken the time to make sure the chair was stable, comfortable, safe, despite the fact that it was nestled against a table piled high with food waste, winter coats, waybills, plants, and unopened mail. A platoon of mice.

Wes is standing in the aisle and my cheeks flush as though he's caught me doing something inappropriate. He makes it worse by shifting his gaze back and forth between me and my seatmate.

"What's up, Bud?"

"You got any headphones?"

I glance at the Beats folded around his neck. Wes notices, tugs them off.

"They're dead," he says. "Dad borrowed them and forgot to charge them."

At the mention of "Dad" my seatmate glances up from the magazine now spread on his tray table. Wes looks at him, then at me. He's obviously not brought the charger. I slither from my seat to fish a pair of earbuds from my carry-on and hand them to him. He thanks me. His eyes linger on my seatmate before he heads back to his seat.

I'm restless. Before stuffing my carry-on back under the seat, I yank my laptop from its sleeve and bring up a report I'd gotten halfway through reading before leaving for the airport. The report, conducted by a team of Finnish researchers, is from an architectural publication and examines sustainable design and best practices in the food sector from the building to the food itself. AI. HVAC. 3D Food Printing. Modular storage. Nano-fertilizers.

My seatmate orders another beer, and I get a second glass of wine. A vent is blasting hot air and I tear off my sweater, flap my shirt.

"Felix," my seatmate says.

"Claudia."

This is how it starts. All over. An exchange of names and somehow, saying it in the low light of the plane's overheated tail section while the rest of the passengers drift off feels bold and rebellious. Strangers no longer talk on planes. But Felix and I whisper: life histories, facts, confessions.

I learn that he's both childless and parentless. No siblings. Parents died in a bus accident in Italy. He's on his way to a climate conference. He studies currents, spent time in an ashram in his twenties. Former rugby player, divorcee, scared of the dark. A Japanese exchange student taught him origami and he folds me a little horse from a page of his ocean magazine. A galloping one with lean muscle, sharp hooves, a wavy mane.

He asks me about Glen, and the brazenness of his questions scares and thrills me. When did you fall in love? How did he show he loved you? Do you still love him? How private and inappropriate. How refreshing. He stops to retrieve a trio of pills from a sleek black pill organizer, swishes them down with bottled water.

In a few hours we'll part ways and I'll regret my honesty, my outrageous vulnerability. And his. In a few days I'll stand under the Arc de Triomphe with a satchel of my mom's belongings, recite a poem, speak of her gingerbread, her ability to solve for "x" and polish a doorknob, and I will know the quiet virtue of these things.

Lavender light fills the cabin. The sun is rising and Felix and I fall asleep, our bodies collapsing inward, over the vacant middle seat. I dream of my mother. It's so vivid I can smell her favourite nail polish, hear the musicality of her voice when she treated a split lip, a fractured heart. It's so real that when the flight attendant plunks down a tray of pale, jittery scrambled eggs somewhere off the English coast, I nearly reach for her hand.

After breakfast, Felix and I hold hands. Our grip is tight and primal as if we are trying to commit the experience to memory or biology. Fingerprint to fingerprint. Lifeline to lifeline. I check the map to see how far we are from Paris. Just under five hundred miles.

"Not much time left," Felix says, though his eyes are closed.

When Joan lines up to use the washroom at the back of the plane and sees me clutching a stranger's hand, I don't let go. If she finds it awkward, she doesn't let on. She only smiles, her un-makeupped face fresh and alive.

By the time she's out of the washroom, I panic, follow her halfway up the aisle, and tell her not to say anything to Grandpa or Wes. She nods. I'm embarrassed that she feels sorry for me, for my shame and desperation. Before I have to ask, she assures me my dad is okay.

When I get back to my seat, the breakfast tray is gone and the origami horse stands proudly in its place, gaze fixed on the window as if it knows we'll be landing soon and it will be free to roam the streets of Paris like an equine Joan of Arc.

I steal a glance at Felix's beautiful scarred hand and feel a dizzying loneliness I've never acknowledged before. I miss the brawn of a man's hand on my hip, clutching the back of my head, grazing the small of my back. I miss the chivalry, the dominance, the energy, the masculinity. Maybe it's the fatigue, or the emotional fallout of the trip, the pending jet lag, the anniversary of mom's death, or the strenuous act of being woman, but on some level, part of me wants a man just so I can stop having to be one. Let him chop the wood, scrape the windshield, change the oil, ship off to war. And let me, even if for a day, be she.

The plane touches down and taxis. We pack our belongings. I tuck the horse inside my purse. When the plane comes to a complete stop at the gate, it feels jarring and disappointing. Like the lights coming on at a bar. Closing time. I power on my cell phone and remember such a moment with Glen. Slow dancing on a rum-soaked floor on a snowy Saturday night. The lights coming on to reveal that we were the only ones there. What was the song? I push the memory away.

There's movement in the aisle. The doors are open and people are beginning to deplane. I hope my father remains seated and gives me a chance to catch up, to help him off. I find my suitcase, confiscated by the flight attendant when we first boarded.

Sensing the end, Felix says, "Thank you." It's a loaded state-ment. So lovely and true I imagine the horse whinnying in agreement from my purse. Felix has already told me he has no checked bags. From passport control he will bypass baggage claim and head straight through customs, where he'll meet an Uber to take him to the conference hotel and out of my life.

Men leaving. I feel an ache — regret? Separation anxiety? Recognition? — and I almost go after him. Shouldn't we ex-change emails? Itineraries? We held hands. I always wonder if I should've gone after Glen. Glen who left on a Tuesday night. After dinner no less. Tacos. How familial and cruel. He'd eaten everything on his plate, dumped the excess lettuce into the compost, loaded the dishwasher. Then, carrying a compact carry-on, not unlike Felix's, Glen walked out the front door and all I could do was lock it behind him.

I catch up with my family, spread in stunned disarray over multiple seat rows. Remnants of sour cream and onion chips speckle the carpet in the teens' row. Emma is sullen, Dan crusty, Dad and Mona chipper. Joan smiles kindly at me as though she can see my sad pink heart galloping in circles behind my rib cage.

Felix turns at the end of the aisle and smiles before disappearing into the catwalk.

"I remembered the song," Dad says. "The one your mother used to sing when we were stuck in line."

"What was it?"

"Now I can't remember."

It's Mona who rallies us off the plane and through Passport Control. It's Mona who finds the correct baggage carousel and directs us toward Customs. As I'm standing in line, my legs stiff as carboard, and mouth dry, I notice the phone number Sharpied into the inside of my left arm. The numbers are fancy. Ornate as a rich man's cane. I don't know whether to feel violated or pleased.

It's Mona who hollers for me to "Go!" when I've not noticed the line moving or the customs agent waving. It's Mona who gestures toward the Taxi sign when we reach the airport's arrival hall.

It's Glen who's standing in the sun-filled terminal in a beautiful grey suit and carrying a bouquet with more greenery than a Versailles grove.

fifteen

"**EW,**" **JOAN SAYS.** "Why's Dad here dressed up like The Bachelor?"

Wes makes a face echoing Joan's sentiment. I gape.

"Can we go now?" Emma whines.

"Glen!" I half-shout, delirious, shocked, pleased. It's outrageous how much the flowers work. I'm a greedy toddler. I want all the French flowers. I want fat blossoms and boozy fragrances. I want stems so thick you have to trim them with bolt cutters. I want hedgerows and rose bushes. I want a goddamn forest. In a fit of romance or rabid femininity, I snatch the bouquet and hug it to my chest.

Everyone stares. I catch my reflection in a plastic covered Metro map and it's no wonder they're staring. I look vaguely hysterical. My eye makeup is so smudged I could lick it from my cheek. My shirt's rumpled, arm Sharpied, I'm holding so many flowers it looks as though they've grown right out of my rib cage.

Glen seems surprised, as if the answer all along was flowers and he might've saved a couple grand on airfare and whatever fancy hotel he's booked.

"I love them," I say, burying my face in the petals. We both know I've said it with too much conviction for the moment to be just about flowers. It's a whole lifetime of love and pain. It's every balloon-heart high and every dehumanizing low. It's all of Glen. It's a little bit Felix.

I get closer to the Metro map and study the lines. Red, blue, orange, pink, purple. "There are so many green and yellow lines!" I holler. It's astonishing. "How do French people not get lost?"

"Probably because they're literate," Wes says.

"And not colourblind?" Joan adds.

"Your mom's tired," Glen whispers.

"Poissonnière," I read aloud. "Rue Saint-Maur. Trocadéro. Église de Pantin."

"Stop her," Wes says to Joan.

Dan comes up beside me. He's gotten himself, and no one else, a coffee.

"I want one."

"I don't have any more cash," Dan replies. "I didn't have time to get to the Exchange."

"I'm starving," Wes complains.

"Are we having breakfast here?" Dad asks. "I have to watch my blood sugar."

I look around the empty Arrivals Hall. It seems we are the only people left from our flight. No one else has come to Paris to hang out in the airport.

Liam is texting and Dan tells him to turn off his data.

"Why don't we grab a quick bite," Mona suggests. Like me, most of her makeup has worn off and she looks a bit like a circus performer after a hard night of clowning and cocaine.

We agree and shuffle like a simpleton tour group toward Brioche Dorée. The barista sees us coming and looks like he wants to kill himself. We crowd around two rickety café tables designed for elegant and agile Europeans, not for a riff-raff of overtired and poorly dressed Canadians. I hate Glen for being the exception in his slim-fit grey suit and daring sneakers.

The food soothes, the caffeine satisfies. I add another packet of sugar to my coffee, watching Glen as he does the same. What's he doing here? He must've arrived a few days ago. It'd have taken him at least a day to find the flowers. I can't process it. I don't remember the last time I texted him or that he said anything about travel. I still haven't fully accepted Mona's being here, except that I'm not sure Dad would have it made it past Greenland without her.

Greenland. I imagine Felix there trapped in the ice. Felix, about who I know so little but whom I can still feel in my fingertips and smell on my neck, trapped on a cold red ship measuring currents and counting narwhals. I remember his number inked into my arm and quickly check my sleeve to make sure it's hidden from view, like a cheap tattoo.

"What are we going to do?" Dad says, brushing crumbs from the table. "We can't check in for hours."

"You can come to my hotel," Glen offers.

"There's eight of us," I say.

"Harrison got an A on his Literature and Society paper." Dan says. His smile is charged and he doesn't look up from his phone. Liam rolls his eyes and I'm struck with a pang of understanding that I'm ashamed I hadn't seen earlier. Liam is not the underachieving middle child, the directionless gamer, the great disappointment he's been framed to be. He's the neglected brother in a household dominated by the high needs and stakes of a sibling in crisis. The product of two parents obsessing over the wellbeing of one child at the expense of another. I don't blame Dan and Allison-Jean. Harrison's transition was onerous, demanding, and fragile. Emma was still young and easy, appeased by playthings and playdates. By stuff. But Liam was in that delicate space between childhood and early adolescence where everything in life becomes more amplified: emotions, feelings, limbs. And he was ignored.

I hand Liam my second untouched pain au chocolat, hoping it will assuage my guilt for being a shitty aunt. He raises his brows, accepting.

Glen tidies the table. "I have a suite," he says. "Lucked out in one of those last-minute deals. There's a separate bedroom if anyone needs a rest."

Dad raises his hand.

I'm so tired, I'd sleep on a sidewalk if I had to.

"Can I take a shower?" Joan asks.

"Of course." Glen motions to the exit.

The flowers seem ridiculous now as I stand by the curb managing their leaves and my luggage. But part of me doesn't care. It's Paris and if they can still fuck around with mimes and can-cans and cigarettes, I'll fuck around with my handheld garden. Maybe I'll buy a fur coat while I'm here. Or a scarf so fine it will transform into a moth if touched.

Glen's hotel is in the 8th arrondissement. It's balconied and chic. The late September breeze is comforting, industrial, and a touch sweet, as I step out of the dark sedan and stumble toward the hotel's grand entrance.

"Why didn't we stay here?" Dad asks, touching the gold piping of a lobby chair and eyeing the portrait of a naughty-looking girl in ruffles.

Because it's probably a thousand bucks a night. Mom would be horrified.

Glen ushers us toward the elevators. The front desk staff pauses to watch us amble: Glen, a handsome Clark Griswold, and us, his gnarly inbred cousins fresh off the RV.

The room is contemporary. Palatial carpet, embossed wall-paper, pink furniture, green velvet curtains, a silver bucket with a bottle of champagne. Dad and Mona dump their baggage and hit the spare room. In minutes, Dad is snoring loud as a leaf blower.

I check on the kids. Joan's taken over the bathroom. The boys have figured out that the pink sofa is a pull-out, and with Dan's and Glen's help, they make it into a bed. Emma is curled fox-like on a stately chair with walnut armrests. I kiss her forehead. She misses her mom. Unbeknownst to Dan, I promised Allison-Jean I'd keep an eye on her. She didn't need to specify what that meant. Mothers know how to fill the gap.

I look for a place to collapse. Glen offers me the room's obscene king-sized bed with its taut marzipan covers and elongated pillows. I nod in appreciation, but first I step onto the balcony, touching the black rails and observing the street below. Compact cars zig-zag effortlessly into parking spots, and pedestrians move at a pace that is neither frenetic nor relaxed. Parisians move with intention. Everyone seems to know where they're going, and why.

Velvety smoke curls from a balcony two storeys below, and I crave a cigarette for the first time in years.

"Marlboros," Glen says, sniffing the air. He moves in beside me, leans over the rail. On the sidewalk below, a trio of pigeons exchanges places as they investigate a dropped sandwich.

"Why?" I ask him. "Why are you here?"

"Are you mad?"

"I'm tired."

"In case you need me."

"I don't."

"You might want me." He brushes my cheek with the back of his hand, like some goddamned leading man. His touch is both familiar and foreign. A forgotten handshake, a song.

I look into Glen's eyes. I am both here on the balcony and

ALI BRYAN • 94

there, inside him. A notch in his heart, an imprint, a feeling. I know, because he's also there on the balcony, and here inside me, cracking open my chest, filling me with joy and pain as only an ex-lover can, as only the father of your children can.

He had the regret, not I. It was he who took the midlife trip and found himself, and yet it's I who am standing here feeling lost. I didn't ask to go with him. Pedalling through the Taklamakan Desert, clinging to him like a parasitic twin.

Joan appears at the open balcony door. "My flat iron won't plug in here."

"There's an adapter in my suitcase," I tell her. "It'll make things work."

When she leaves, Glen says, "We can make things work."

Below, the pigeons have fled and the doorman removes what's left of the sandwich: a string of tomato, a wedge of ham. An obnoxious motorcycle rips down the street. A man wears red shoes.

"I don't have an adapter for that," I say, surprised by the sharpness of the words.

Glen moves closer so our bodies are pressed together, side by side as though we are in a crowd on the cusp of a surge, a stampede. Something dangerous and deadly. I think he might kiss me and that I'd probably kiss him back because Dan is right. I'm lonely. And now that I've admitted it, it's an image I can't unsee: a flogging, a beheading, a de-hearting.

I open my mouth to speak but the words don't form. They drift away as thoughts when the smoker tosses his cigarette butt to the sidewalk below, just missing Mona who's stepped out of West-End Hotel and planted herself on the sidewalk, chest to the sun. I see the rise and fall of her shoulders as if she's inhaled all of Paris in one glorious breath. It's exactly what Mom would have done.

sixteen

"THIS STUPID ADAPTER DOESN'T WORK," Joan hollers from inside the suite.

I glance at Glen. "Can you go find her one? Please? I'm sure they'll have one at the front desk."

He sighs, slipping back inside the room, which now resembles a Mt. Everest base camp. Clothes and gear and people are strewn everywhere. Glen fumbles for his wallet, ties on a pair of newly minted Lacoste sneakers, and leaves.

I peek in on my father, who is still fast asleep, flat on his back, corpselike. I did this regularly when he first moved in — checked on him. He'd alternated from prolonged bouts of insomnia to sleep marathons so incessant I'd have to make sure he was still breathing. We'd tried melatonin, white noise, weighted blankets, sleep tea. In the end, it was leaving the window open a crack — as my mom had — that seemed to balance things. He could feel her in the breeze.

I help Emma pick out an outfit and braid her hair. It's too early to FaceTime her mom so I set her up at a mid-century teak table with the activity book Dan bought her in the airport. Where is Dan?

Liam reads my mind. "He went to get towels."

I fold back the covers of the king-sized bed and climb in. A short rest, I tell myself. There are Petit Verts to find, a memorial to plan, cafés to haunt. Wine. I sink into the pillow and immediately smell Glen. He's never changed his cologne. He'd die and his bones would smell of Issey Miyake. I'm flooded with memories from my twenties. Tin-canned dinners, stand-up sex, road-trips to Montreal.

The bed is luxurious and hot. I rip off my sweater, sink deeper into the mattress and my memories. I think of one-night stands, shift work, bus routes. I remember a particularly terrible job interview for an entry-level sales position with a confectionary company. I was hungover, dressed in clothes I'd picked off the floor, my bra smelling of cigarette smoke, vodka, the Norwegian Navy. Typos in my resume, pauses in my responses. The disappointment on the HR lady's face. Like a mother's.

I wake up to Glen's hand on my shoulder. My head throbs and it takes a minute to register where I am.

"What's all over your face?" he asks.

I don't know what he means. I touch my cheeks, pat my forehead, feel nothing.

"Black shit."

I haul myself out of bed and into the bathroom where Dan is shaving. I look as though I've escaped from a collapsed mine, my left cheek blackened and marked. Numbered. I can make out a five and a three. Maybe a two? Felix's phone number has melted onto my cheek from my arm, branding me.

"Fuck," I whisper into the steamy mirror.

Dan rinses his razor in a sink of cloudy water. "What is that?"

"Some guy on the plane gave me his phone number."

"And you let him draw it on your face?"

I whack him. "You've seen me since we got off the plane, idiot. It just happened now." I show him my arm, the smudged digits.

"Creepy," he says, gliding the razor over his face, which resembles an old baseball, well played and worn. Reliable.

"Help me get it off."

"With my razor?"

"Soap or something."

He empties the sink and we examine the hotel's apothecary of toiletries. "Try this," he says, handing me a tiny bottle of lotion. "It has honey in it."

Does honey remove Sharpie? I could ask Wes but he got a sixty-five on his last chemistry test. He'd probably tell me to use Borax or battery acid. I massage the lotion onto my skin, but the stain spreads like a bruise. "Tell Joan I need her lip gloss remover."

Dan comes back minutes later with the tube. I rub the gel onto my cheek and the numbers lift like fingerprints. "There," I say, relieved. Then I check my arm. I can barely make out the original numbers. Panic must register on my face because Dan says, "why do you even care?"

I don't know why I care but I want the numbers. I want to hoard them like old cables or cords in case I need them someday, like tomorrow. There was more than a vacant seat between us in row forty-two. I use the colour-end of Joan's lip gloss to transfer the phone number onto a walking map of Paris someone's picked up from the lobby. I can't make out the last digit. A one? Seven? Nine?

Glen lightly knocks, doesn't wait for a response, edges his way into the bathroom. "You got it off," he says, noting my hot, blank cheek. "What was it? I thought Joan must've left makeup on the bed or something."

"A guy's phone number," Dan replies.

Glen looks at me to confirm and then scoffs. A jealous one, green and scathing. It ignites a little fire in my chest.

"What? You never exchanged numbers with a stranger?"

Glen grabs my arm, studies the numbers. "Not like this."

I pull away.

"Do you like him?" Glen asks.

"That's none of your business."

Dan tiptoes away, mumbling, and shuts the door. He's missed one of his side-burns.

"But do you?" he asks again.

"I only just met him. Why does it matter?"

"Because I came here for you. For us."

"I didn't ask you to. This whole trip is supposed to be about my mom. And here you are and there's the guy on the plane and Mona."

"I just want a chance."

"What does that even mean, Glen?"

"Let me in."

"You are in. You're here, right now. In my bathroom!"

It's his bathroom.

He takes my wrist, and holds my forearm to the bathroom lights, which are hazy and warm like the lights of an underground pool.

"Seven," he says, "The last number. Go ahead and call him. He will never love you the way I do."

His hand is still clutching my wrist. Unthreatening, because it's Glen. Threatening, because it is. This is how he'll get his chance. He gradually loosens his grip but his fingers linger, tracing my knuckles, the hot mess of veins on the back of my hand, my bare ring finger.

"Can we go somewhere?" Wes calls from the other side of the door.

"Yes," we shout in unison.

"Uncle Dan wants his razor."

Glen collects it from the side of the sink and leaves, taking the moment with him in a cloud of escaped steam.

I stare at the numbers on my forearm and do not wash them off. I squeeze toothpaste on Glen's toothbrush.

He will never love you the way I do.

And how is that? I think. Long? Intermittently? Hard? Hardly?

I brush my teeth until my gums bleed.

seventeen

PARIS, THREE O'CLOCK. We are huddled around a pair of wobbly tables on a café terrace, sharing green laminated menus. The air crackles with supernatural promise. Catnaps and showers have erased the initial shock of touching down in another continent.

Emma is begging Dan to go to Euro Disney. She stirs her hot chocolate, thick as pudding, with her finger, ignoring the quaint parfait spoon on her placemat. Drinks clutter the table: Beaujolais, Chardonnay, beer, Sprite. We order a variety of soups and sandwiches.

"I haven't been on a vacation in so long," Dan says, staring wistfully.

I follow his gaze to the market across the street, the bins of oranges and herbs and roses. Well-dressed children in proper shoes and slim jeans eat pastries beside a newsstand. At least Wes's Air Jordans are clean.

I'm happy for Dan. Maybe Paris will help him accept his amputated marriage, its unflattering and severed end. Its permanence. Next to Dan, Allison-Jean looked just like a music teacher, a tad weary and vaguely unfashionable, straight. Beside Cindy, she looks like a practiced lesbian, a trailblazer, a veteran. She looks like k. d. lang.

"I want to see Notre-Dame Cathedral," Dad says.

"Didn't that burn down?" Liam asks. The drinking age in France is eighteen and Dan's let him have a beer.

"Not to the ground," Mona replies. "They're fixing it."

"Your mom always wanted to see the bells."

I don't recall Mom having an affinity for church bells. I begin to wonder if Dad's making stuff up. If he's just listing things that he wants to see. Or that Mona does. But church sounds like a good place to start. We won't be able to go inside but maybe just standing below the stone sinners and saints, I'll find some deliverance.

Joan plugs the cathedral's coordinates into her phone. "We can walk from here," she says. "It's only about fifteen minutes."

Thirty with seniors. "Can you manage that, Dad?"

Dad seeks Mona's guidance. She nods.

"Okay," I say. "Let's do that and then we can take a river cruise."

Mona claps.

A server wearing an impeccable black apron begins plunking meals down at our tables. A second waiter follows. They're like a pit crew, but with nicer hair.

Emma's ordered a plate of fries. She complains about the ketchup tasting like tomatoes. Dan's face turns red and I give him a look.

"The ketchup's different here," I say. "Tomorrow we can try a grocery store and maybe we'll find one that tastes a little more like what you're used to."

"Add more salt," Joan encourages. "That always works for me."

Emma frowns but listens to her cousin and shakes enough salt to melt a frozen sidewalk onto her plate. Her eyes are red.

"We'll FaceTime your mom from the river cruise," I whisper.

She smiles and I burn my mouth on the onion soup.

Mona pays for lunch. When no one's looking, I take the rejected parfait spoon and slide it into my purse. It reminds me too much of a can-can dancer's lithe leg to leave behind.

Joan leads the way to Notre-Dame. I walk near the back, flashing hawk-eyed glances at the men, whose eyes linger on her svelte frame. She could be a can-can dancer. I want to suggest she wear onesies or ponchos for the rest of the trip. Baggy jeans. Those plastic bubbles they used to put immune deficient kids inside.

I catch Wes admiring a flock of schoolgirls in grey and burgundy uniforms. They put on a show when they notice Wes and Liam watching them through nervous Canadian side-eyes. The girls laugh, joke, bat their lashes, playfully shove each other, squeal. Wes is enchanted. He turns red when he notices me noticing.

A vagrant dressed like a garbage man kicks down the sidewalk muttering obscenities. He asks me for a cigarette, and tells me to go fuck myself when I shake my head that I don't have one.

We stop at the lights of a busy intersection. There's chaos ahead. Journalists, news trucks, and traffic police crowd the bottom steps of a hotel. At the top of the stairs, a podium has been set up, empty but for a sleek bendable mic.

"What's going on?" Emma asks.

"Looks like a news conference," Dad says, guiding his youngest granddaughter away from a particularly large cameraman in black fatigues.

We spill onto the street and walk single file. I catch the handwritten placard of a lone protestor: *Changeons le système, pas le CLIMAT!*

I try to read the hotel's swirly name but get jostled from behind, and bumped into a parked Peugeot. I wonder if Felix is somewhere inside the building, holed up in a conference room with other oceanographers discussing deoxygenation, acidification, currents, fish. How many of them know Sable Island?

I slow down. My family trudges along in a careful conga line toward the Seine. I wait long enough to see a stylish woman with sleek auburn hair and a practical suit step up to the podium. I gather she's a politician. I don't stay for her address, and Felix doesn't appear on the steps like a cooperative member of her team. I catch up to Wes.

"What do you think?"

"Of Paris?" he asks, as if I could possibly be referring to something else. "It's cool. I guess."

Ahead, someone is breakdancing in a Pikachu costume.

"And a bit weird," he adds.

"A touch," I reply, avoiding the glare of a gargoyle so foul I begin reciting the Lord's prayer in my head.

We are close to the cathedral. The bridges are dense with tourists, the skyline crowded with scaffolding. Street vendors hawking everything from candied nuts to watercolours line the walkways. An old-stock Parisian strides by in red pants and a beret.

"Are you and Dad getting back together?" Wes asks.

We are standing in the middle of the Petit Pont. The Seine is green. I pause to make sure I can still see Mona's Crayola-orange hair in the crowd of people making its pilgrimage across, before I reply.

"No."

"Then why's he here?" Wes shoves his hands in his pockets.

A black duck floats into view from under the·bridge. We watch for a minute before it flaps its way onto the stone bank and pecks for crumbs.

Someone has strung a coil of wire around a post, and it drapes with locks: brass, blue. Wes absentmindedly hooks his pinkie around one of the shackles.

"I guess your dad just wants . . ." I pause, unsure what to say. How.

"To get back together."

I ignore his statement, examine a tiny silver lock. "You know about these?"

Wes shakes his head.

"Love locks. Started on another bridge by the Louvre. Couples would attach a padlock to the rail as a gesture of their love and commitment to each other."

Wes frowns and I can't tell if he's moved or flustered.

"After a while there were too many, and part of the bridge's parapet collapsed due to the weight. They became so dangerous the city had to remove them. Imagine. More than a million locks."

"And these?" he says, touching the dull blue of the largest lock.

"Tourists, trying to recreate it. They'll probably be cut off by morning."

Joan's appeared out of nowhere. "Can you take my picture?"

She normally takes her own pictures, so the request surprises me.

"I can't get the right angle without getting the scaffolding. I need you to."

She fixes her hair, checks her makeup in the screen of her iPhone and then gives me directions on how to take the shot. Stand there. Move left. Why are you so close? Hold it lower. I take seven hundred pictures and Joan lets me and half of Paris know that I deserve to decay slowly in hell for my poor photography skills and also my nose, which she wishes I hadn't passed down.

Somewhere beneath me a chunk of the bridge falls away and sinks.

I leave Joan with Wes and Liam, who's now joined his cousins, and meet up with the others.

"There you are," Dad says. "I figured at each place we visited, we might say a few words about your mom."

I'm glad someone's thought this through. Mona stands at attention, hands crossed in front of her like a proper parishioner, and waits for Dad to continue.

Dan cuts in. "Any specific words?

"You know," Dad says, irritated. "Like a fond memory." He gestures towards one of the cathedral's rose windows. "Maybe a church one."

Dan nods in understanding, and rests his fist on his chin earnestly in thought.

I try to think of something lovely to say but the only church memory I have aside from my mom's funeral is the Easter Sunday I was fifteen and she leaned over to whisper that my eye makeup looked like a prostitute's. I start laughing.

"A funny memory!" Dad jests. "Claudia, please share."

"I'm not ready." I wave.

Dad shares a memory of a time my mom went to choir practice hungover. Dan and I exchange glances. Neither of us knew she sang in a choir and we certainly can't imagine her ever drinking enough to be hungover.

"I just remember her crying at Wes's baptism," Dan blurts.

"She cried?" I ask.

"That was because you and Glen weren't married," Dad explains. He turns to Mona like she needs clarification. "They had Wes out of wedlock. Janice was super disappointed Claudia and Glen chose to be common-law."

He says "common-law" as though we had chosen to have Ebola or bathe in hot garbage.

"But I never minded," Dad says. "Made it easier when Glen left. Speaking of which, why is he here?"

"Okay, wow," I say.

"He wants to get back together," Dan chirps. "Except Claudia met some dude on the plane."

"How lovely!" Mona exclaims.

"Nope, not lovely. Just enjoyed the conversation."

"Liam said you were holding hands."

The sun beats and I excuse myself to buy river cruise tickets to avoid pushing one of my family members over the bridge. I pass artists showing their work in orderly displays. Photos of Paris rooftops, milky landscapes, tight black-and-white drawings of city blocks and landmarks. The last artist sits cross-legged on the ground, paintings fanned around him. He rocks back and forth, chanting, face concealed by heavy metal hair. All of his paintings are of the Notre Dame cathedral on fire. There are flaming spires, blackened windows and charred bells. I buy two and carry on to the boat cruise sales window.

For the price of the river cruise, I could probably have purchased an entire fleet of paddleboats. I reluctantly tap my credit card and the tired student-aged attendant slides the tickets through the wicket. She points to the spot where we'll board the boat. I shove the square stubs into my purse and look back on the Petit Pont. In the centre of the bridge stands a circle of schoolgirls and in the centre of the circle: Wes.

eighteen

I CAN'T SLEEP. I'm jet legged, seasick, and buzzed. Wes is asleep on the pull-out couch without having made it into a bed, and Joan snores from the other queen with headphones on and a full face of makeup.

I pace the dark room, tripping over shoes, open luggage, and toiletry bags. Our hotel room doesn't have a balcony, so I peel back the heavy black-out drapes and check the view. An apartment building, modern, ten or so storeys. Most of the lights are off, but in the few windows that are lit up, there is nothing extraordinary to see. The glow of a TV. The frame of an elliptical. A man at a sink. If I strain my neck, I can catch a glimpse of the street that the front entrance of the hotel faces. It could be Detroit or Fredericton.

My phone chimes with an incoming text. I hope it's from Glen or someone interesting, but it's from Mona: *your father has forgotten his Voltaren.*

I reminded him three times to pack it. It was on the checklist. I'd specifically taken him to Shoppers Drug Mart to buy a fresh tube for the trip. Dad can't sleep without it. Before I can respond, I notice Mona's sent a group text. I haul myself up on the window ledge, watch the man at the sink in the neighboring building, and wait. Liam is old enough to stay in the room with Emma. Dan can go looking for Voltaren.

Instead of responding to the group text, Dan messages me directly: *can you go? I'm really tired.*

So am I, I text back.

Emma's homesick.

I can't leave my kids by themselves.

I'm already in my pajamas.

I bought him Voltaren in Halifax.

I'll pay you.

I stop texting, check on the man in the kitchen. He's finished washing the dishes. A lover comes into the room while he's putting something away in a high cupboard and slides his hands up the man's shirt.

I'm busy, I type.

Fine, Dan says. *We both go. Bring the kids here.*

He replies to the group text before I can protest. I rouse the kids. Wes grumbles, but he and Joan obediently file into Dan's next-door room. Emma's curled up with her iPad and Liam's wide awake watching TikTok videos.

"We'll be back in a bit," I say. "We're going to the pharmacy for Grandpa. Keep the door locked. If you need anything, text. Grandpa and Mona are across in the hall in 716.

"Can you bring back food?" Liam asks. "Chips or something."

"Yeah," Wes says. "I'm starving."

"You were asleep five minutes ago," I say.

He shrugs.

We're in the elevator before I notice Dan's wearing Liam's bright high-top sneakers.

"My shoes pinch," he says defensively.

I don't tell him how ridiculous the sneakers look, paired with his pleated chinos.

"Have you looked up a pharmacy?" he asks.

The elevator opens to the lobby and I go to the front desk,

test my French. The clerk is Sudanese, friendly and polished, in a black blazer and blue-red lipstick. She gives us two options in opposite directions. The closest one, near a bicycle repair shop, might not be open. She can't remember if it closes at 11. It's now quarter after. The further one is at least a twenty-minute walk, but it's open twenty-four hours. She's never heard of Voltaren but she's certain they will have it.

Dan and I debate the options as the hotel's automatic front doors quake open.

He looks in the direction of the nearest pharmacy, but the street is dark. Nothing looks open.

"Let's just do the far one," he says.

I agree.

The air has cooled since the river cruise but the temperature is still comfortable. We walk in silence past shuttered stores and quiet apartment buildings until we turn down a more populous street with a McDonald's and a string of noisy cafés. Bass from an invisible discotheque pounds the sidewalk.

At a fountain, where throngs of people are smoking, laughing, and kissing, we make another turn.

"Sorry I mentioned the plane guy in front of Glen," Dan says.

"Felix," I reply. "It's okay."

"I didn't think it was a big deal."

"It's not."

"Was to Glen."

We continue down the street, dodging revelers and lovers, dogwalkers and workers en route to night shifts. Occasionally, a rat darts out from some secret hideout and disappears into another. The mood shifts from quiet exasperation to somberness. I can feel Dan's thoughts as if we're twins. I know what he's going to say before he says it.

"I wish Allison-Jean had come here for me."

I put an arm around my brother. "I know."

The pharmacy comes into view with its potion-green sign and glass front. A bell rings above the door when we enter. The only other patron is a weary father fumbling his way through the children's painkillers.

We can't find Voltaren but the pharmacist speaks excellent English and recommends a French equivalent. Dan pays for the ointment and we head back into the cobbled street.

"We should pick up some snacks," I say, dragging my brother to the other side of the street, where I think I see a convenience store. "For the boys."

He stumbles on a storm drain, nearly dropping the inflammation cream. What I thought was an open convenience store is a closed grocery store. Beside it is the entrance to a second-storey nightclub.

"Bonjour." A well-dressed man in nightshades and a jet-black suit gestures toward the entrance. He stands in front of a pair of brass stanchions, linked by a red velvet rope. "Allons-y."

Dan doesn't hesitate. The man unclasps the rope and Dan allons-ys straight down the black carpet and up a narrow staircase.

"Wait," I holler, in shock. "What about the Voltaren?"

Behind me, snickering, a flight of rowdy American men half my age stands in a semicircle waiting for the handsome bouncer to let them in. I hear one of them mimic, *but what about the Voltaren?* I think about flicking them. Dan is gone. There's nowhere to go but after him.

I find my brother at the bar. "What the hell are you doing?"

"Getting a drink," he says. "What do you want?"

"I don't want anything. We have to get back to the hotel." Pink lights strobe from the dance floor, where couples grind and women kiss. The electronic music plays at such a high frequency

I can't tell if I'm having a stroke or if someone's welding a gate next door. I look back to make sure the Americans haven't been let in. They have not been.

"I already texted Mona and said they didn't have any at the first place and that we'd be a little longer."

A doll-faced bartender sets a whiskey in front of Dan. The glass is thick, artisanal. She raises her brows, signalling for me to order. "House wine," I shout. "White."

"And two shots of tequila," Dan adds.

Tequila? I haven't seen Dan drink tequila since his third year of university, when he got wasted and I had to pick him up downtown. One of his pant legs was missing.

The shot burns, and, chased with wine, tastes like a tool bench. I wince and order water that never comes.

"We should go," I yell over the throbbing base.

"Come on, Claud. We're in Paris. And you know what they say about Paris —"

He's slurring his words. I think out of grief more than alcohol, though he did have a few beers on the river cruise. At home, he rarely drinks.

"What do they say about Paris?" I reply.

"That you should —"

Before he finishes, a curvy woman with mousy bangs and chandelier earrings hauls my brother onto the dancefloor. She cradles the back of his head and shoves it into her chest, jolting him side to side in her cleavage. I turn away, order a martini, and find a cocktail table in the back of the club.

I pull out my phone and text Georgia: *I'm at a nightclub and Dan is motorboating.*

Ew, she replies. *Is she at least hot?*

I check her out. Dan and Allison-Jean briefly took up social dancing, which I realize now was probably Allison-Jean's attempt at saving their marriage, and Dan is spinning the woman around the dancefloor with authority, the neon orange tongues of Liam's sneakers flapping, his soles skidding, forehead shining.

She's okay, I reply.

And what about you? Have you met anyone? You know what they say about Paris . . .

No motorboating before midnight.

Glen's here.

The phone rings. I need to get to the washroom, though I'm sure it won't make a difference. The washrooms seem to be tucked down a hallway past the DJ booth and I have to cross the dance floor to get to them. As I do, I notice the French Voltaren on the floor. I get kneed in the head trying to retrieve it, crucified by a stiletto and then lightly spanked. I have no idea who's administered the spanking. Could be the hot Arab with the greased hair and crystal ear stud. The short Frenchman in the muscle shirt. The tiny woman with the pearl necklace. The bus boy?

I make it to the hallway and answer.

"GLEN'S THERE?" Georgia shrieks.

I explain the flowers, the surprise, Felix.

"And what are you going to do about it?" she asks.

"Nothing."

What's there to do? Take him back? Ignore him? Sleep with him? Slap him? Send him home? Pretend like I didn't spend the last decade loving and hating him?

Love him. I could. It would be easy, familiar. A bit rough, perhaps, but we were always rough. A hand-hewn beam. Sandpaper.

I peer down the hallway and see Dan at the side bar, a row of shots in front of him. Fuck.

"Gotta go," I say to Georgia. "Dan's going to get raped if I don't stop him."

I hang up before she can say anything inappropriate. By the time I make it back to Dan, only one of the six or however many shots were lined up is left on the bar. I snatch it from his greedy fingers, shoot it, and slam the tiny glass on the counter. Goldschläger. Now all I can think of is Oak Island, Mona's party, the Lagina Brothers, Sgt. Face Blown Off. Hope and despair.

I tug at Dan's sleeve and the woman he is with tugs on mine. She tries to pull me into her cleavage the way she did my brother.

"Non, merci," I say, ducking under her arm — a technique I learned in self-defence. Dan's bolted. I pay for our tab, and find him minutes later twirling on the other end of the dancefloor, alone. I push him toward the exit, march him down the stairs and through the door.

Dan feels his pockets. "What about the Voltaren?" he shouts, twisting back toward the club.

"I have it," I say discreetly, yanking him away, but Dan trips, lands on his face. Blood pools in the cobble cracks. A wave of panic. He lifts his head. Is that a tooth? I hover over him, examine his mouth, the ground. It's only a bit of paper, but he's put his tooth through his lip.

"Oh my God, Dan."

An elderly couple strolls the street opposite. They hold hands.

Dan rolls onto his back. "Best day ever," he says, blood dripping from the corner of his mouth, the tips of my mother's pewter prayer hands poking up from his breast pocket. He stares up at the sky, his shirt untucked and his limbs spread across the cool ground. Tears well in his eyes and his expression slowly turns from breezy to anguished. I look away.

The doorman holds up one of Liam's sneakers. I motion for him to toss it over.

"You need help?" the bouncer asks in perfect English.

"We're okay," I reply.

The streetlights reveal an iridescent sheen on Dan's forehead. Probably some bizarre cleavage cream he picked up from that woman. I rummage through my purse, find a Subway napkin, and press it into my brother's lip. He groans. Down the street, a small police car prowls.

"Get up," I whisper.

The bouncer recognizes the potential problem and stands in the middle of the sidewalk to block the view. I get Dan into a seated position, and brush the street debris from his back.

"You gotta get up. If you get arrested for public drunkenness in Paris, Allison-Jean will kill you."

Fear mobilizes him and he scrambles, using a planter he narrowly missed smashing into to stand up. I help him put on his shoe. He wavers.

"Can you walk?" I ask, not waiting for a response. "We have to walk this off."

Dan puts one foot in front of the other. He moves like the tin man. I think about opening the cream and rubbing it on his knees. At least he's moving. We almost reach the end of the block when he vomits beside a heap of garbage bags. I wipe his mouth and debate whether to hail a cab to take him back to the hotel where he can sleep in my room.

Dan straightens, takes a few steps, falls in the pile of garbage.

I call Glen.

"Dan doesn't even drink," Glen says. "Where are you?"

I send him a geotag.

"That's close."

I'm glad. The arrondissements look the same: arches, awnings, buttresses, beautiful people.

I sit Dan on a bench, find an open corner store, and buy a

bottle of water. A man outside asks me for spare change. Maybe. His accent was thick. He may have asked me for a banana, my hand in marriage. Some joint cream. I shake my head. "Désolé."

Ten minutes later, Glen comes around the corner. "What did he do to his mouth?"

"Put his tooth through his lip."

Glen helps Dan up and we walk-carry my brother to Glen's hotel.

"He can stay in the spare room."

"What do I tell the kids?" I ask, thinking out loud. "Emma's already missing her mom."

"Make something up."

Mona sends a text asking how much longer we're going to be. Dad's having trouble bending his legs.

So is Dan.

I text back that we're close, suggest applying a warm compress to each of Dad's knees.

Inside the lobby, Dan starts dry-heaving, piquing the interest of hotel staff and a group of Germans lingering in club chairs. I bat my eyelashes like the schoolgirls on the Petit Pont and rush the elevator.

By the time we get Dan to the fourth floor and inside Glen's hotel room, I need Voltaren.

I massage my shoulder. "Do you think he needs stitches?" I stare at my brother, now passed out spread eagle on the spare bed. He looks both young and old, relaxed and rigid. Hurt.

"Probably should," Glen says, leaning over Dan like a doctor.

What does he know about stitches? He sells speculums for a living.

His cologne drifts through the room like tiny invisible drones. He wipes sweat from his forehead, examines Dan's chin and mouth.

"Three or four," he concludes.

"Does Paris have walk-in clinics?"

"I can do it," he says.

"Since when can you do stitches?" He could not do stitches when Wes tripped and smashed his face on the coffee table, or when Joan fell into the fence at the petting zoo. He also wasn't there for either of those mishaps.

He pulls down the side of his jeans, the thick black band of underwear I've never seen and shows off his hip, sewn together like a rag doll's mouth, a baseball. I try to focus on the scar, the Halloween of it. So jagged. But it's hard not to notice the bareness of everything around it. The angles and shadows.

"Skidded off the road in Kyrgyzstan. Sliced it on a piece of metal. Cleaned it in an abandoned garage, stitched it up, kept going." He pauses. "There's ice in the wine chiller."

I wrap a few cubes in a cloth napkin that I find crumpled on a room service tray, and freeze Dan's lip. From the open bathroom, Glen threads a needle, eyes focused, posture serious.

"Yellow?" I say, staring at the thread dangling from the needle.

"It was a sixteen-thousand-kilometre trip. I went through a lot of thread."

We come at my brother from both sides. I hold Dan down by his forehead, kneeling on his wrist. Glen positions himself within inches of Dan's face, cleans the wound and pierces my brother's lip with an infallible touch.

Dan makes basement noises, battlefield groans. His legs twitch. Glen is quick, expert. Four stitches. I help him tie off the knots before he clips the end with a pair of sleek medical scissors. I gently run my finger across the sealed laceration and remember my mother. The starkness and horror of seeing her head shaven and stitched. Her closed eyes, the dank Cuban hospital room with the too-high beds. I get off my brother's pinned wrist. He groans.

Glen still kneels across from me, scissors in hand. It's the first time we've been in bed together in ten years. It's a peculiar reunion, depressing, septic and yet. The needle. It reminds me of the early years. The recklessness. Breaking onto the apartment building's roof to watch the stars. Skinny-dipping. Secluded campsites. Train hopping. Chipping teeth.

I lean forward, and over my brother's turned-out wilted knees, Glen and I kiss.

nineteen

"**I NEED MY VOLTAREN**," Dad yells into the receiver.

"Sounds urgent," the taxi driver says, eyeing me from his rear-view mirror. He's Eritrean, an immigrant, largely hated by the French populous. He told me so before we'd even left the 8th arrondissement.

"He's old," I explain.

"Old is a gift."

I smile, grateful for the reminder, and think of Rodney. Rodney on the dancefloor. Rodney serving Goldschläger. Rodney always in the moment. He doesn't need to be reminded that old is a gift. He sees it every time he looks down at his melted hands, or pulls a sweater over his disfigured face. He hears it in every joke he's missed. He hears it in the silence.

The cab driver pulls up to my hotel behind an idling older model Mercedes. When I go to pay, he waves me off. "The gentleman's already paid."

I never thought of Glen as a gentleman, though I've thought of him as a lot of things: a lover, a leaver, an asshole, a dad. At one point, a soulmate.

Digging for the Voltaren, I crash into a pretty girl with soft flared jeans and flushed cheeks. "Je m'excuse," I say, bypassing the elevators and heading for the stairs.

I go straight to my father's room to drop off the Voltaren. He's cranky. Hair curls from his ears, his lobes big as sand dollars.

Mona moves about in a purple satin nightie, a far cry from the ghostly dressing gowns my mom used to wear. The room's a mess. Mona has outfits sprawled over the backs of chairs and the contents of my dad's ancient toiletry bag are strewn about the counter.

"Goodnight," I say.

"Thanks," Mona whispers, seeing me out.

Just as she's about to close the door, I notice she's wearing a replica of Mom's ring. The setting is slightly different and the stones are smaller, but it's a decent match to the earrings. Has she gone and bought a knock-off to appease my father? Of course, she did. She knew how distraught he was after the wedding. I saw the way she cared for him on the plane. I feel like shit for not telling either of them that I'd already recovered it from the Tupperware during the Oak Island marathon: the only treasure found that day.

I tiptoe, flustered, to the kids' room. I took Dan's key from his pocket before I left Glen's and I wave it now over the flat door handle. It clicks open.

Emma is jumping on the bed and Joan is perched on the desk painting her toenails. Wes's hair looks . . . freshly gelled? He's staring out the window, hands cupped to the glass.

"You bring the chips?" Liam asks.

"There was a girl here," Emma blurts.

"Huh?"

"No there wasn't," Wes spits.

"There wasn't," Liam assures, coming to his cousin's aid. "We tried to order room service but it was closed so the front desk sent us these instead." He holds up a package of cookies.

I'm pretty sure the label says Air Canada.

I forgot the chips.

Emma stops jumping. "Where's my dad?"

"He's getting the chips. *But,*" I say dramatically, "he says you're supposed to be asleep. Why don't you come to my room with Joan and we'll have a girl's night? Let the boys sleep here. Joan can paint your nails. We can have our chips for breakfast."

"Is the nail polish non-toxic?" she asks.

"Of course," I lie, making a mental note to buy nail polish remover so Allison-Jean will never find out. "Joan, take Emma to our room."

Joan blows on her freshly painted big toe, climbs off the desk and walks on her heels. "Did you know that the world's oceans are heating up forty percent faster than scientists predicted?"

Oceans. Felix. I give her the room key. "I'll be there in a second," I whisper.

As soon as the door closes, I grill Wes. "Was there a girl here? A pretty one, with flared jeans?"

"Yo, he's so in love," Liam says, gesturing wildly like an SNL character.

"Wes?" I say trying to keep my face neutral.

"I love her," he says, and he does so with such purity and conviction I have to cover my mouth to stop myself from laughing.

"How could you love her? You just met her. Did you just meet her? How did you meet her?"

"He met her at church," Liam chides.

"On the bridge," Wes corrects. "By Notre-Dame."

The schoolgirls.

"How old is she? And what's she doing out on a school night, sneaking around at a hotel?"

A flicker of panic. Does Wes do these things? Will Joan?

"She's sixteen."

"You can't have girls coming here. It's not safe for her, or you. What would her parents think?"

"They just came to pick her up."

WTF, France. I throw up my hands. "We'll talk more in the

morning. Get some sleep." I tell Liam about Dan's accident, leaving out the drinking, motorboating and crying. I focus on the stitches and say goodnight.

By the time I change into pajamas and settle into my own room, Joan has managed to get Emma to sleep with all of three fingernails painted. She brings up the oceans again and talks about coastal flooding and coral bleaching. I should engage with my daughter. Her steep and sudden interest in climate change is a good thing because she's bored by so much, but all I can think about is moustache bleaching and the floodlight seeping through the gap in the black-out drapes.

I wonder if the men in the apartment across the street have had sex, what Glen thought of our kiss, whether my father's knees ache less.

I'm still pondering these things at three am when I get a LinkedIn notification. *Claudia, add Felix Davies to your network.* The word "network" reminds me that I have a job and direct reports and unread email, and a mission to scout out artisanal French grocers while I'm here.

I haul my laptop from the bedside table drawer and open LinkedIn. Felix Davies did a BSc (Honours) in Marine Biology at the University of Plymouth, an MS in Ocean Sciences at the University of California Santa Cruz and his PhD in Oceanography at the University of British Columbia. Many people endorse his skills. His picture implies he may have arrived in Canada in 1021. A Viking. He's lovely, and I get a jolt of nostalgia thinking about the flight, his hands, the way he looked at me, through me. The recklessness of scrawling his number on my arm.

I accept his invitation to connect and notice a slew of other invitations, none from people I recognize or have any obvious reason to connect with. A yoga instructor from Newfoundland. A man working at a pipeline integrity firm. Twelve life coaches.

The last invitation piques my interest: a recruiter.

I've been with EnerFoods for nearly fifteen years, drowning myself in planograms, hashtags and advertising campaigns, scouting influencers. I discovered early in my career that acquiring grocery chains provided consolation when I couldn't acquire men. I accept the recruiter's invitation to connect and note there's also a message from him in my inbox. Am I interested in an opportunity? Confidentiality guaranteed. Could we set up a chat?

A new message pops up from Felix: *I can't stop thinking about you.*

My heart flutters. I ignore it, for now, and focus on the recruiter. I explain that I'm currently satisfied with my job, am in Paris, but would be open to a meeting. I feel a twinge of excitement pressing SEND. Maybe a new career challenge is exactly what I need to bring some energy and focus into my life. Seems less risky than making out with Glen or engaging with Felix. There is familiarity in loneliness. Safety.

The recruiter gets back immediately, as recruiters do. It's only nine p.m. in Toronto. Excellent, he replies. The role is a with a global company. An innovator in food tech. The CEO has specifically sought me out. And she's a woman.

I digest the details and flip back to Felix's message. My phone chimes. I turn off the ringer before it disturbs the girls. It's from Glen: *I can't stop thinking about you.*

No one has been thinking about me for ten years. I sit cross-legged on the bed, the cream comforter puffed up around me, and revel in the moment. My mom would be happy about this. She hated me being a single mom. A single working mom at that. And not because of the stigma or the extra work or the absence of a fulltime father in my kids' lives. She worried that being alone would make me hard and cynical. That I'd become a drinker, a witch or a lesbian.

There's a bottle of white wine in the fridge. I don't know if it's complimentary or whether it was left behind by a previous guest, but it's unopened. I twist off the screw cap, and pour it into one of the hotel's paper bathroom cups. It's sweeter than I'm used to and pleasing. Appropriate, given how many people can't stop thinking about me. I drink quickly, unsure of the paper cup's life expectancy.

I imagine a new job, a new office. Staff I can handpick and develop. New conferences to attend in Riyadh and Ghent. I imagine coming home and discussing the takeaways with Felix over lentils and strawberries. He can take me to Sable Island, fold me tiny origami sharks, brand me with his hands, his virility. I then imagine coming home and discussing the takeaways with Glen over permission slips and pho. He can take me back in time, fold me tiny love notes, brand me with his mouth, his regret.

I down the remainder of my wine, click on Felix's message. *I can't stop thinking about you either.* Then I go to my cell phone and type the same thing to Glen. This is not what Cathy would do and it's certainly not what she would advise. But Georgia would. Georgia would send all the messages, open all the doors. Love, she once texted me from a beach in Phuket, is not a two-player game. The accompanying photo was of her lying on the beach with half a rugby team.

A new message displays in my LinkedIn inbox from the recruiter. He's persistent. The kind of person you want in your career corner. I should replace our current employment agency with this guy. He gets it. I open his message with anticipation. Perhaps there's more information about the position and the mysterious CEO who wants me on her team.

No. He's just sent punctuation. A question mark.

I've told the recruiter that I couldn't stop thinking about him. From the bowels of my purse the origami horse neighs.

twenty

WE'RE IN THE CATACOMBS underneath Paris. I'm hungover and tired, my mouth dry as the skull jutting from the wall behind me. Dan looks like Frankenstein's monster and Dad has twice mistaken the yellow thread keeping Dan's lip from falling off his face as egg yolk from his over-easy and otherwise gruelling breakfast.

Emma is repulsed by the bones and even more repulsed by her family for dragging her under the city. She's twice threatened Dan that she's going to tell her mom, as if we've taken her to a Trump rally or a shisha bar. Liam tells her to quit acting like a baby and she responds with a catlike attack, scratching his arms and face with her partially painted box-cutter nails. Liam's reaction to laugh only makes Emma crazier. She balls up her fists, stomps her tidy pink sneakers and calls her brother a little bitch.

It's Mona who steps between them, admonishing Emma for her violence and language, before pulling her into a fleshy, grandma hug — or restraint. Dan, unable to parent, stares open-mouthed at the wall of femurs as if their ancient marrow contains the secret to un-gaying his wife.

I make eyes at Liam, mouth for him to behave, and nudge Wes to keep walking. He's been pausing every ten bodies to text Célestine, and by text I mean sending her hearts: pink hearts, red hearts, double hearts, pulsing hearts, hearts wrapped in bows, hearts wrapped in hearts.

"Wes, Bud, you gotta keep moving. We paid a lot of money for this tour."

"But, it's all the same," he says, sweeping his arm from one side of the path to the other. "Bones."

"Not entirely," I reply. "There's a cross over there, and look," I point to a skull. "This guy looks like he might have had a run in with an axe." I show him a beautifully assembled section of pelvic bones, but his gaze is fixed back on his phone, as an explosion of hearts blows up his screen.

I give up on Wes and join Joan and Dad at the front of the group. The ground is uneven and Joan is quick to steady my dad when he stumbles. It's damp and earthy. I shiver and wish I'd brought a jacket. When we reach the end of the current tunnel, before the path curves to the right, Dad stops and waits for the rest of the family to catch up. No one's bothered to notice that Mona's limping and having a hard time navigating in the dim light. I go back for her, hook my arm in hers, and guide her to my father. She squeezes my hand.

Dad clears his throat. "This would be a good place to stop and say a few words about Janice."

I study the display of bones around us and wonder why Dad's chosen this particular spot as a good place to stop. Does one of these skulls remind him of my mother? Her strong cheekbones and meager forehead? Is it the large stone cross, blank and bleached and unclaimed on the wall? The compact stack of feminine bones behind his left shoulder? Or does my dad just need a rest, the spiral staircase we used to get down here having nearly done him in?

Wes looks up from his phone. "I remember the Halloween Mom was sick and Grandma had to take us trick-or-treating instead, and she didn't have time to make a costume, so she borrowed Dad's skeleton mask."

Dad smiles. "And she wore my black snowmobile suit," he says. "I helped her pin up the pants because they were too long."

I remember that Halloween. I'd eaten salmon I knew was probably off, but didn't want to throw out. We were on a budget and it was one of the rare times I bought salmon fresh instead of from a can. I didn't know the skull mask was Glen's. How had my mother known to call him?

"I remember when I broke my collarbone and Grandma came to the hospital and Mom said I couldn't have any sugar because my body needed to heal, but Grandma smuggled in a pint of ice cream and spoon-fed it to me every time my mom got up to speak to the nurse or check the clock in the hall."

Liam's told this entire story with his hand resting gently on his collarbone.

"This is no fair," Emma blurts. "I was just a baby. I have no memories."

Dan crouches in front of his daughter. "No," he says, tenderly. "You don't. But when your mom found out she was pregnant with you, the first person she told was Grandma and it was your grandma who took your mom to her first ultrasound appointment because I had a meeting I couldn't get out of."

"How little was I?"

"Eighteen weeks. The size of a grapefruit. And you know what a baby can do at eighteen weeks inside her mom's belly?"

Emma shakes her head. The catacombs are quiet.

"She can hear."

Emma's eyes widen.

"Which means, though you never met your grandma, you heard her, and that's incredibly special because your grandma had the most beautiful voice in the whole wide world."

Tears, smelling like last night, spill down my face. Mona dabs her eyes. Liam and Wes fidget. Joan smiles. My dad stands with his mouth open looking like he's seen a ghost, and then to everyone's surprise he breaks into song, Louis Armstrong's "What a Wonderful World," Mom's favourite lullaby.

Dad's voice is raspy, achy and pure. The catacombs fill with colour, the bones blurring into a mosaic of beautiful things: feathers, blankets, memories. Then comes the grief. It rises from my chest and explodes out of me in a silent cry, so excruciating I double-over, catching myself on my knees.

"I miss her," I choke and then my children's hands are on me. One each on my collapsed spine, and I feel her, my mother. Her love whistles through the gaps in the bones, and settles gently on the back of my neck.

When I finally return to standing, I'm surrounded by my entire family: Wes, Joan. Emma, Liam and Dan. Dad. Mona. I wipe my tears, follow the path toward the exit, climb the stairs to the land of the living.

From my purse I hear galloping hooves. I step into the light, the sun so intense I desperately pull my sunglasses over my face, and Glen is there with exactly what I need: a coffee and silence.

twenty-one

THE KIDS WANT TO GO SHOPPING. After a quick stop for baguettes, we take the Metro to the Champs-Élysées where they won't be able to afford anything. Dad and Mona are too tired to do any more walking, so they plant themselves at the edge of a café to slurp cappuccinos and watch people.

The boys want to split up and go on their own. I give Wes a hundred euro and tell him to spend it wisely. Joan wants a break from Emma. I want a break from Emma. I also want a break from Dan. I suggest he make it a father-daughter-day, buy her some lip gloss or a hip little French outfit, hair accessories, ice cream, a muzzle. She's been whining all morning, a low battery smoke detector.

That leaves Glen and me and Joan. She wants new soccer cleats, so we take her to Paris's flagship Adidas store, designed to look like the entrance of a stadium. We climb the indoor concrete steps. The shoes are showcased under blue lights and the mannequins are sleek and headless. Some have skipped leg day.

We watch our daughter examine a wall of cleats. Occasionally she'll pick one up, test the leather, study the toe box, run her hand along the studs.

"I'm pretty sure those are same ones we looked at at Sport Chek," Glen says, as she flips over a neon yellow shoe.

We find a bench while she uses hand gestures to ask a handsome sales associate in a puffy vest for sizes. He returns a few minutes later with a comical stack, seven boxes high. Joan gets to work, trying on each pair, planting and pushing off her toe, revering her profile in an angled ground-level mirror.

"Coach said he's moving her to midfield for indoor," Glen says.

"Since when? She's terrible at mid. She needs to be up front." How does Glen know this?

"We talked about it after her last practice. I think it's the right decision."

"She hates mid," I say.

"No, she doesn't."

Joan is tying on a pair of cleats that look spray-painted.

"You talked to the coach?"

"Is that a problem?"

"I talk to the coaches. That's my job. I am Coach-Talker."

Glen crosses his arms, gives me a look as though I'm being unreasonable. "I can talk to our kid's coach," he says.

"She shouldn't be playing midfield."

"Did you see her last exhibition game?"

"I've watched almost every one of her games since she started playing. How many of those have you watched? Because if you'd seen even half of them, you'd know she's a striker. That's her position."

The sales associate with the puffy vest glances over at us, his crystal earrings sparking in a beam of sunlight. He hands Joan another boot, this one glossy.

"She scored three times."

"That was one game."

Joan looks up mid-tie. "Are you guys serious?" she says, her cheeks flushing with embarrassment, rage. "You're going to sit here and fight about this?" She resumes tying her shoe, aggressively yanking the laces. "What are you guys even doing?"

Glen and I sit in silence, like a pair of scolded children. Joan tests the cleats, exchanges a few words with the sales associate, and eventually returns them to the box. He nods and collects the rejected pairs.

"It was me," she says when he's gone. Is she crying? "I asked to be moved to mid. I play better there. He agreed." She stuffs the box under her arm and starts texting. "Can we just go now?"

I look for the checkout. Glen goes to Joan. "I'll get them," he says, taking out his wallet. The sales associate is back and he gestures toward a minimalist counter with futuristic payment terminals. Glen taps his card. When we get back outside, Joan rushes ahead.

"Wait," I say, not wanting to be stuck with Glen.

"I'm meeting up with Wes."

"Let us walk you." Glen says.

She stops, turns around. "I don't want to be anywhere near either of you. You're separate. That's the way it is. You're my mom," she says, squaring her hips to face me. "And you're my dad. You're not my mom-and-dad."

Glen and I exchange glances. Neither of us speaks.

"Like, no offense, Dad, but I don't even know why you're here." She checks her phone, turns and crosses the busy street, dodging an array of attractive people and a less attractive poodle. We follow. A red Bugatti idles in an alleyway. When we catch up on the other side, Joan stops again. "You left when I was in preschool," she says to Glen. "*Pre*school." Then quieter. "Mom doesn't want you."

I open my mouth to speak. I find myself wanting to defend him because her words are a mace, bludgeoning and cruel and true and false. I want, I don't want. Last night, I wanted more.

"Mom met a guy on the plane and they held hands."

Glen looks at me, hurt. It's in his eyes. I can barely stomach it.

"You held hands?" he asks.

"Does it matter?"

"You bet it does," he says. "You love *me*."

Is he serious right now?

A table at a nearby café breaks into applause. I am starring in a terrible American film. I look for the cameras. I hear the horse thumping in my purse, pounding against the zipper, trying to get out. And a few feet away, Joan has been replaced with a mime. A real one with suspenders and a striped shirt and a chalk-white face. He's turning us into his act, pretending to eavesdrop, nodding, crying real tears.

A crowd gathers and the mime pulls out a pair of handcuffs, motions that he'd like to cuff us together. I shake my head but Glen offers his wrist like some kind of sister wife or Manson girl.

"What are you doing?" I say, as the mime snaps the cuff onto Glen's wrist.

"It's just an act," he says, nodding at my arm. "Just play along."

I don't want to play along. I've been chained to Glen for a decade, as single mothers are to the fathers of their children. The mime is winking, begging with his ugly bowtie pout for me to cooperate. When I don't flinch, he pulls out a gold badge and a small book. He's writing us a ticket. The audience, which seems comprised mostly of round and enthusiastic Americans, laughs. It starts to rain.

From the corner of my eye, I see Joan. She's met up with her brother and Liam, who sip drinks from McDonald's cups. They take cover under an awning. Wes gapes. Distracted by my kids, I've missed whatever the mime was miming, but the crowd is clapping. I could walk away. Excuse myself from this ridiculous Parisian horror. The mime can give Glen a ticket. All the tickets. One for each offense: leaving, coming, talking to the coach.

The rain is falling harder now, fat, steady drops, and the

audience is chanting. A bald man in a Duck Dynasty T-shirt and Wranglers is yelling *Lock her up!* And that's exactly what Glen does. He swings the free end of the handcuffs, catches it, and clamps it around my wrist. The ratchet teeth sound like farm equipment. A prison door locking. Glen bows, the mime bows, and a roar of delight rises from the crowd. He's cuffed my right hand.

The show's over. Umbrellas go off like airbags and tourists flee for cover inside shops and restaurants. The underground. I fumble for my phone, check the time. We are meeting at the Arc de Triomphe at four. It's now five to.

I storm toward the monument like an occupying soldier, dragging Glen behind me. The handcuffs are in fact plastic, not metal, but they work.

"Where's the key?" I murmur, dodging a bus tour.

"Here," Glen says, pinching the end of it.

I see the Arc in the middle of a roundabout. Is it even accessible? It must be. A solemn row of tourists in ponchos stands atop it, umbrellas and disappointment activated. We're almost there.

"Claudia, wait!" Glen shouts. "My shoe!"

His shoe has fallen off. It's landed six feet back in a puddle upside down like it's been blown off his foot in a terrorist attack. He hops hopelessly on one leg, the sock so blue and pitiful, shin so vulnerable, I want to run from him.

Instead, he pulls me into a tree branch, poking my eye. Searing pain. I press my palm into my face, squinting through my good eye while the rain drips down my back. When we reach the puddle, the shoe is gone. A stranger has picked it up. The horse in my purse bucks.

"Claudia?"

Felix looks deep into my eyes, into my rattled soul, my refurbished heart. He stares at the handcuffs, and passes Glen his shoe.

twenty-two

WAIT. THE WORD FORMS, but it stays in my mouth. Felix takes a few staggering steps back as if he needs to reassess the situation in full screen. I will him to see something different. Just me, and no Glen. Like Joan said: separate. I will Glen to dissolve, evaporate, but he stands tall, doesn't even put his shoe back on. He just stares at me watching Felix because it's something to see. Our connection is real. You can feel it in the air like an impending weather event, spectacular and a touch threatening. You can almost hear the buzz and crackle. The coupling.

"You know him." Glen says, a statement not a question.

I nod, my gaze still fixed on Felix. He's wearing the same shirt from the plane, but it's partially concealed by a rain coat, fisherman's yellow. His face is stubbled, his eyes recessed and dark, as if he's stayed up all night trying to solve for "x." Ex.

"Alright then," Felix says, swallows. "Carry on." He smiles in that proper ministerial way and continues down the Champs, away from Glen and me, away from the Arc de Defeat. Felix, leaving.

"The guy from the plane," Glen says, like it's not obvious. "The one who wrote his number on your arm."

He says it in a way that implies wrongness over romance. I stare at my arm. Where there was a seven, there's now a cuff. Glen hastily slips his foot back inside his shoe and yells, "Wait!"

"What are you doing?" I say, my eye still stinging. I push the branch away from my face. Glen starts chasing Felix. I dig my heels into the sidewalk to stop him. "The frig are you doing?"

"I wanna ask him something."

"He has nothing to do with you."

"It'll only take a second."

"Have you lost your mind? Give me the key."

"Please, Claudia. I have to do this."

I tug him toward the Arc. He pulls me toward Felix. Felix, who's now two stores and an Italian restaurant ahead. The handcuff key drops to the ground. We both dive to get it, clashing heads. We nearly topple. Glen grabs the key, and I try to wrestle it from his fingers.

"Give it to me," I say. We're too close to the curb. Too close to the swirly manhole cover.

"I need to ask him something," Glen insists, scrambling back to his feet.

By the time I haul myself up after him, Felix is gone. Ducked into a café, slipped away into the underground. Church bells like fog horns mark the hour: four o'clock. We're late. A group of protestors with noisemakers and whistles moves towards us. They carry white banners with bloody letters and sloppy globes. *ALERTE! Sauvons la TERRE.* They're forced to go around us. They stare at our wet clothes and cuffed hands as if we too are in protest, in demonstration. They look for signs of what we're trying to save.

Glen drops the key again. It clinks against the manhole cover, but doesn't fall. This time I retrieve it, poke it deep into my pocket with my mother's ring, and head toward the Arc. Glen lags behind. I can't see, but I can tell he's looking back, looking for Felix. The reedy lament of an accordion plays in some distant café and my poked eye weeps.

"Wait," Glen calls.

We've caught up to the protestors, drumming, chanting. Glen ducks under a drooping sign fixed to a pair of dowels and leads me into a dark cobbled sidestreet that seems too narrow for cars, too narrow for us.

"Claudia," he says, holding my face, the small plastic chain of the cuffs — grey, not silver — dangling between us. I study the links. If I pull hard enough, they'll break.

"Everyone's waiting for us."

"Us," he repeats.

I fumble for the key. "Me. They're waiting for me. This whole trip is supposed to be about my family, my mom. We're supposed to be remembering her. Do you have any idea what the past ten years have been like? First you leave and then Mom. She had a lover here — in Paris! — and I didn't even know. There's so much I don't know about her and she's gone and it's too late and instead of remembering her, I'm remembering us. I don't want to remember us!"

"Fine!" Glen shouts. "Forget us." He shakes our cuffed hands, jerking me away from the building I'm using to hold myself up. Water drips from shuttered windows and leafy plants. At the far end of the street, another couple, young and unshackled, stumble into the alley. They are laughing, throwing their heads back, tasting the rain. When they see us, they retreat as though we're an omen. A premonition. As though we are them. We are them. Were.

"Give me the key," Glen says, beckoning with his free hand. His eyes are hard now. Serious. As though he's said *give me the gun*. And that's what it feels like, the key in my hand. Lethal. It's barely out of my pocket, when Glen snatches it, jams it into the keyhole, and starts twisting. His hands are trembling.

"I came all this way," he says through gritted teeth.

"You also left."

The key breaks. I shove his hand out of the way, hoping my French manicured nails will be long enough to pinch the broken shaft. They aren't.

"On three," Glen says, grasping at his cuffed wrist and bracing himself against the wall.

We count, perfectly in sync, and pull. The cuffs snap. I'm left with the chain.

"There," he says, staggering, breathing as if the cuffs were made of something much heavier: granite or lead or regret. "You got what you want." He fiddles with the remaining plastic looped around his wrist. He looks back toward the Champs, still bustling with tourists and Parisians, despite the rain, and then toward the end of the narrow street.

This is the direction he goes. Glen, leaving. He blows by back doors, a smoking chef, a tiny set of stairs that leads nowhere. The street bends and his footsteps lengthen. He reaches the spot where the couple just stood.

"Wait!" I call after him.

He doesn't wait, doesn't look back. The chef blows a smoke ring. I watch it rise, bloom, shift, disappear. It's now quarter after four. My phone buzzes from my pocket.

Wes: *where r u?*

I type *I'm coming.*

"Pardon," I say to the chef, lifting my cuffed wrist over my head. "M'aidez?" Mayday.

The chef, aproned and weary, sucks another drag from his cigarette, crushes the butt under a clogged foot and waves me over. The door is small and we have to duck to get inside. The corridor is dank and narrow, the walls cracked as if they've been shot up. He leads me to the edge of a bustling kitchen and grabs a knife from a prep table. He takes my wrist with such tenderness that I start to cry. Curious kitchen staff glare.

When I'm free, he dangles the broken cuff over a garbage can heaping with vegetable peels. I shake my head, take it from him and bury it in my purse. A souvenir. "Merci," I say, massaging my arm. I turn to go, and then pause. "How do you get to the top of the Arc? You can go up there?"

"You need a ticket," he says. "Many steps. Beaucoup, beaucoup."

I nod, skid down the restaurant's crumbled doorstep and head back to the main road. There are beaucoup de people. I see the placards of the protestors waving in the distance. Schoolgirls, a basketball team? A wave of Chinese tourists. I stare up at the Arc and think I see Dad's umbrella, Mona's hair, a beacon.

I reach the roundabout. Impossible. Cars and buses enter and exit at a dizzying pace. Where the hell are the steps? I follow a tour group that's edging its way around the circle. The guide holds a quaint red megaphone. She walks efficiently, barks short melodic orders, hustles everyone to a set of stairs leading to an underground passageway. I follow, overtake the shuffling tourists, climb the steps to the other side, and there he is. The goddamned mime.

twenty-three

WHEN THE MIME SEES ME, he makes a face. *Quelle surprise!*
Quelle fuck off.

I run. Back down the stairs, through the tour group with their matching red lanyards and jolly faces, and up the steps. I turn mid-flight to see if the mime's following. He is, *was.* The tour group is now mauling him. The guide can't believe her luck.

When I get back outside, I find the least busy street corner and call Dan from a bus stop.

"We're all waiting for you," my brother says, irritated. "It's raining up here."

"A mime is chasing me."

Is that Claudia? Dad in the background. *Why isn't she here? We said four o'clock. She's the one who decided on that time. We're getting soaked. Why would a grown man dye his hair purple? I need to take my medication. I think those people are protesting something. Mona? What do their signs say? Is it about the round-about? There's no way to cross! Damn near got us killed.*

"You hear that?" Dan says. "Plus, he got his pants wet and forced Liam to hold his legs up to a hand dryer in a public wash-room. Hurry up."

"There he is!"

"Who?" Dan replies.

"The mime."

"I think Dad needs his knees replaced. Or his hips. We've done way too many stairs today. He's moving like a stilt walker. I think maybe we should rent him a scooter. I thought he had a referral to see an orthopedic surgeon."

"Can you just get everybody back to the hotel? Glen and I got into a fight."

"What about dinner? The kids are starving."

"We can order in or eat at the hotel. I don't care. I just need to get away from the mime. Can you see him from up there?"

"New plan," Dan yells, slightly muffled. "Claudia's ditching us. We're going back to the hotel."

But what about the Eiffel Tower? Dad complains.

I hang up the phone, tuck behind a bus and cross the street. I land at a café with wicker chairs, and tables adorned with chunky glass ashtrays. Pots of weighty red geraniums crowd the entrance.

"Pour un," I say, lifting a sad digit, the cuff marks on my wrist still a shameful hot pink. "À l'intérieur." I want to be unseen. The host guides me to a table in the corner near the kitchen. It's dark and damp. I rub my arms to get warm while an Edith Piaf ballad trickles like rainwater from a ceiling speaker. It's a bit gloomy. An unlove song. From the kitchen, invisible cooks sing along to Aerosmith.

I order a glass of Burgundy and a hot chocolate. There are mostly tourists here: families sprawled across chairs, knees touching, shopping bags clustered at their feet, phones in hand. American couples, foreign students, a foursome of women in their sixties on a trip of a lifetime. One of them could be my mom. I feel both my aloneness, and the consequences of my choices. Work over love. Playgroups over friend groups. Glen over Felix. My mother's choices: love over work, mostly. Gerald over friends. Gerald, over Paris. Gerald over easy, over everything, over her. I move my chair closer to the women.

The server brings me a small basket of bread even though I haven't ordered food. I dip a piece in the hot chocolate because Paris wants me to fall apart. I'm halfway through my wine and a second basket of bread when Dan texts from the hotel.

Joan and I are going out for steak. Dad and Mona are ordering room service and having Emma for a sleepover. Liam wants sushi. Told him he could go without me as long as he goes with Wes.

Okay, I reply, wondering why he's telling me this. *I don't mind if Wes goes for sushi. I gave him money earlier. He should still have enough.*

K, well tell him to hurry. Liam's hungry.

I put my phone down for a minute. What does he mean by *tell him to hurry?* Why can't Dan tell him that himself? Or Liam?

I take too big a sip of wine and it dribbles down my chin. The foursome of ladies is holding hands like they're about to conduct a séance. The one across from me has her eyes closed. After a few seconds she bursts into reckless laughter. The others follow. I smile. *Why don't you just tell him?* I text back.

He's not answering his texts.

The waiter refills my glass.

Then go to his room.

Can you just ask him please??? I promised Joan we'd go in five minutes. I don't think you give her enough iron.

My brother, who hasn't homecooked a meal since Allison-Jean left, giving me nutritional advice. The ladies have ordered fondue and I watch them take turns swirling their elongated forks in the cheese. Behind them, a couple practically sits on top of each other at a single tiny table end. They eat nothing. Then it occurs to me: Dan thinks Wes is with me. It's the kind of lie

Wes would tell. The kind of lie you tell when you're young and desperately in love and you *have* to see someone. A life-or-death have to. A never-love-again have to. Such a gorgeous and dangerous feeling. How I felt on the plane with Felix, how I feel with Glen even when I simultaneously hate him. For a moment, as I stare at the couple across from me, their undrunk wine and touching bodies, I feel a tinge of envy more than outrage. But only for a moment.

I down my hot chocolate, which is nearly solid, and text Wes: *where are you??*

I stare at my phone screen, watch the familiar blinking ellipses that indicates a response is in progress, and wait.

And wait.

And wait.

One of the ladies has proposed a toast and the women hold their glasses up in anticipation. The waiter, about to dump another serving of bread on their cluttered table, pauses theatrically, a hand behind his back. I can't hear what or who is being toasted. A new beginning? An end? Maybe nothing. Perhaps they are raising a glass to all the moments that make up a life in between: the messy commutes, stitched lips, and disheveled relationships, the miracles and mistakes, the Hail Marys, the bad haircuts, the hail.

After a few minutes, the ellipses vanish. Wes never replies. He is there, here, but also not.

Hello??? I type, hoping he'll reconsider, but this time, nothing.

The toast is over and the women all slurp their wine. I hastily pick up my glass and mimic them, splashing Burgundy on my phone. *To missing children,* I think as I motion to the waiter for my bill. I dab my screen with a napkin and log in to the find-my-phone app. I will track Wes, scold him, ground him, take a picture of him and Célestine and then drag him back to the hotel by his heart. Except his device is not on the find-my-phone app. Glen bought him a new one in August and I forgot to register it.

I pay for my "meal" and send one more text to Wes: *just tell me you're safe.*

He replies with a thumbs-up emoji.

No response when I ask: *where are you?*

Of course I know where he is. The Eiffel Tower. Where we'd planned to go this evening. Travel bloggers recommended going at night when it's all lit up. Wes would have told Célestine our plan. He wouldn't have told her it changed.

Outside it's dusky and warm, the sky still dense with rain-clouds and crows and the longings of a thousand strangers navigating the city's grey sidewalks. Garbage trucks careen through narrow streets. The only children are tourists, over-tired and practically dressed. Half-eaten bags of cotton candy spill from stroller crevasses. The soft coo of a pigeon sooths the growing tension in my neck. In the distance, more protestors and the flash of a yellow coat. Felix is all I think. The look on his face when he held up Glen's shoe. Something on the spectrum of hope and despair.

I don't even know what arrondissement I'm in. I follow a crowd down the stairs of the nearest entrance to the Metro and check the wall map. Without asking, a man halts beside me, taps at the Eiffel Tower stop on the line, Champ de Mars, and then carries on. I never see his face. I know I don't look French in my faded romper but I hate that I look so stereotypical.

It takes me five minutes to buy a ticket, on account of trying to swipe my Tim Horton's Rewards card instead of my Visa. Rattled, I blunder the turnstile, and clothesline myself. On the train, I tell Dan that Wes might be a while and suggest he take Liam with him to get steak because he too is probably iron-deficient.

The trip is short. Only three stops. I exit, walk along the river toward the unlit tower. The top third is blanketed in mist. In the glow of the surrounding streetlights, it looks robust and industrial. A worksite at night. Spectacular.

I search for Wes but am distracted by the air. It crackles with anticipation. It's almost nine o'clock and people around the tower pace and shift, waiting for it to light up, their necks craned and hands squeezed. I squeeze my own hand, take my mother's ring from my pocket and slip it on my finger. She would have loved this.

I break from the crowd and weave my way to the other side of the tower's edge. The foursome of ladies from the restaurant is off to the side, sprawled on the grass, untroubled and unshoed. Their belongings are scattered around them, thoughtlessly. One uses her purse as a pillow, hands crossed over her stomach, gazing at the clouds. The four of them look like troops who've returned from battle and found pretty girls, candy bars and cigarettes in their tents. The grass is wet.

I check my phone. 8:59 p.m. The crowd is loud now. No words, just undiscernible noise. Like the ocean on a January morning. I spin, hopelessly searching for Wes between the rows of tour busses and patches of grass and squares of cool concrete.

I stop to catch my breath below the centre of the tower, when it lights up. The crowd ooohs. I gasp. It's overwhelming and frenetic and there's no one here to witness it with me. This seemingly benign fact breaks my heart and I find myself crying. "Oh, Mom," I whisper, closing my eyes. I strain to feel her presence but sense only my pulse, the hot flare of tears on my cheeks and the tension in my jaw. The space around me.

I wipe my face, exhale, and resume searching for Wes.

The tower lights continue to flicker, tourists stroll and then I see them: Wes and Célestine, standing face to face, holding hands in the light of a hot dog cart. My son, in love and nearly unrecognizable, softened like a sandcastle touched by the tide.

"Wes!" I holler.

Wes looks up, makes eye contact, looks at Célestine. They run.

twenty-four

MY SON, THE ROMANTIC, fleeing with Célestine like some kind of schoolboy Casanova. Some kind of Glen. Some kind of asshole. My instinct is to call or text him. He's not going to answer. He's going to have one night in Paris and spend the rest of the trip paying for it. I have to call Glen.

I dial, half-jogging. A group of men whistle and catcall in some foreign language. I should be appalled. I should tell them to smile or frig off, but the truth is, I enjoy it. I need people to believe in me right now. Give me all the whistles.

Wes and Célestine get caught up in a group of seniors boarding a tour bus. A French woman in a fall coat yells at me, raising a wooden cane. Wes looks back and then disappears with Célestine behind a shiny black bus.

"Hello?" Glen answers.

"It's me," I say, huffing.

"I can't talk right now."

"Wes is making me chase him. He lied and said he was with me but he met this girl at the Cathedral and I caught them having a secret date near the Eiffel Tower. Just a second . . . Wes, stop! He's not stopping. Oh, for fuck's sake. They're crossing a bridge. I need your help."

In the background, a voice asks: *is that her?*

I stop in the middle of the street, plug my free ear, and listen. "Glen?"

Silence. A motorcycle rips around me, its driver bearded, leather-chapped and temperamental. He gestures with a gloved hand and I can't tell if he wants to drive over my forehead or bend me over his bike. I cross the street toward the bridge.

"Glen, where are you?"

I hear her again in the background. Extra French, likely petite, probably not wearing a bra. She's close enough to Glen's phone I can distinguish her breath from his. Taut as a tightrope.

"I'm at a friend's," he says.

Do we have friends in Paris? Does Glen? And is she a friend as in *friend* or a friend as in "friend"?

"Did you even hear what I said? Wes is not answering his phone and he's running around Paris like some lovesick criminal."

"So, love is a crime now?"

Christ almighty. "I dunno, Glen. The handcuff mark on my wrist would suggest it is."

There's a long pause and I use the interval to search for Wes. The bridge isn't as crowded as I expected. A few people linger along the ornate railing, but most are on the move, tall Europeans in the lead, puny travellers at the back, and a single wheelchair cruising up the midline.

"God, Claudia, you've changed. Just let Wes be. It's one night of his life. Love that makes you crazy doesn't come around that often. The last thing he needs right now is for you to wreck it for him."

"He's fifteen. In a foreign country!" A duck cuts in front of me to get first dibs on a shattered waffle cone. "This is ridiculous," I mumble. "Maybe if you'd stuck around, you'd know the shittiness of your parenting right now. We know nothing about this girl. Not her address, not her phone number — we don't even know her last name."

"Le Roux," Glen says, cool as a charlatan. "Her family's from Brittany. She plays basketball and has a pet rat. She's into astronomy, Hollywood movies, and if it isn't obvious, our son."

"A pet rat?" Wes hates rodents.

"Named Bebe."

"Bebe," I yell into the entrails of a stranger's cigarette smoke. "That's the stupidest name I've ever heard."

"Her parents are quite lovely."

"You met her parents?" I'm shouting on a bridge in Paris. The group of men who'd catcalled me earlier have migrated in my direction. They think I'm crazy and dodge my gaze. "Tell me I'm pretty now!" I holler. The oldest of the crew turns his back. Hands and words fly in conversation as a lone pigeon pecks at the street, searching for its reflection.

"I'll bring him back to your hotel," Glen says. "Give him 'til midnight."

"Great. You do that. In fact, why don't you bring them all back? The whole family: Célestine, her parents, Bebe. They can all stay the night. Won't that be fun? I've come to Paris to have a sleepover with a rat!"

"You had other options," Glen says.

"It sounds like you still do."

I hang up before Glen has a chance to say anything else. Wes and Célestine are gone again. I drag myself to the last place I saw them, at the centre of the bridge. I know exactly the spot because there's a fresh lock fastened to the rail. A gold one, Sharpied with their initials W H + C L and the most precious heart I've ever seen. They've left the Sharpie behind. I pick it up, replace the lid, and head back to the tower.

I don't want to know who Glen is with, or why Wes has told me nothing about Célestine. Why he only told his father. Of course Wes knows I would set rules and boundaries and curfews. I would caution him about falling in love with a girl he'll never see again. I'd remind him we're here to commemorate his grandma's memory. I'd say no. I would help him see the truth of the situation. The real world. I would absolutely wreck things.

I pass the Eiffel Tower and head toward Trocadero. There are lamplights and fountains. Hulking statues, tiny birds. I climb the stairs to the square. A rat tiptoes along a wall, camouflaged by leaves and vines. Maybe it's Bebe. The rain has turned to a milky drizzle. From up here, the view of the Eiffel Tower is luxurious and golden.

I see the women from the restaurant strolling the promenade below. They stop to take pictures with the statues. Foolish ones. Their laughter floats through the night sky like a hot air balloon. I imagine one of the women is my mom. The quiet one in the back, clutching her purse out of hyper-vigilance. She would have read about pickpockets and petty thieves. Her friends urge her to squish in for a picture but they are too close to a set of high-pressure fountains resembling gatling guns and she fears getting wet. She fears her hair falling flat and her shoes not drying out before tomorrow's walking tour of Versailles.

I whisper, "It's too late, Mom."

Her friends have already climbed into the fountain. They wade like disciples hungry for deliverance, miracles, mercy, touch. One of them dunks herself and comes back up, rolling and gasping for air. Not my mom. She stands in the shallow pool, away from the spray and her galivanting peers, sopping but contented. I hope they get arrested. Mom never had the chance.

"You should join them." A street vender nods. He's taken a break from packing up his garbage souvenirs to watch the women. He shakes his head at the debauchery.

"You think?" I ask.

He bundles a heap of figurines in tired bubble wrap, secures the lump with a cinching strap. "I think," he replies, with a smile that is equal parts wise and boyish.

I want him to tell me why. Does he think I'm as old as the women in the fountain and that I belong on their "last chance" trip and should be doing last chance things? Zany and vaguely naughty and not-at-all noteworthy things? Flirting with much younger men, wearing outrageous clothing: neon, mesh, beads the size of baseballs, waxing on about sex — no — waxing on about *fucking*. I'm too young for that.

Maybe it's that I look bored or cautious, or uptight. Like my mother. Maybe he believes I'm depressed and thinks should I drown myself.

The vender stuffs the remainder of the souvenirs — a few sparkling keychains and a collection of handheld fans — into a duffel bag. He heaves the bag over his shoulder and flinches from its weight.

"Bonne chance," he says, with a wave. Below, one of the women howls. I peer down at them. Their age and the alcohol have caught up with them. Instead of frolicking, they're now wading, stumbling, dragging themselves as though the water has turned to sludge.

I look back at the vendor heading into the night and wonder if he made enough money to pay his rent. I should have bought a souvenir. I should have bought all of them.

"Wait!" I call out. "I want a souvenir."

He turns and hesitates, as if contemplating whether the sale of a single souvenir is worth the bother of dismantling his duffel bag and consequently missing the next train, or kissing his son goodnight.

"How much for the Eiffel Towers?"

"Two euro."

"How many do you have?"

"Je ne sais pas. Maybe twenty?"

"I'll take them all."

I pay, and he packs the Eiffel Towers in a tattered paper bag. He thanks me and I wish him good luck because sometimes, more than hard work and goodwill and thoughts and prayers and patience, luck is what we need.

It's ten o'clock and Trocadero is eerily quiet. I call Glen under the guise of confirming that he'll bring Wes back at midnight. But it's her voice I want to hear. Whoever she is.

"I'll get him home by midnight," Glen says.

I strain to hear her in the background: a peep, a pardon, a je m'excuse. Worse, I hear her laugh and it's so full of life and hijinks, I almost trip down the stairs.

By the time I hang up with Glen and reach the fountains, the foursome of women is gone, recovering probably at some hotel one of them got a good deal on. I find a Holiday Inn key card on the ground, a wet stick of gum, a bent box of corn removers.

I kick the remnants of their shenanigans aside and sit on the pool's edge, dipping my pinkie in the cool water and wondering where Wes is now. He's probably making out on the subway or having sex in Célestine's bedroom. Her parents are probably feeding them strawberries and oysters. Ew. They better not be making bébés.

I shake the thought from my head and text Dan an update: *Wes is with Glen.*

We're in my room, Dan replies. *Liam and Joan are playing cards. Where are you?*

At the Eiffel Tower.

Why?

'Cause I'm in Paris.

Come back to the hotel and have a drink with me, my brother says and I find the invitation both endearing and appealing. I'm glad he's here.

It's not like you have any options, he adds.

I check the time on my phone. One hundred and twelve minutes until midnight.

I do have options, I reply.

Like what?

Not *what,* I think, but *who.* I open LinkedIn and find Felix's message. Because Glen's right: Love that makes you crazy doesn't come around that often.

And as luck would have it, I have options.

twenty-five

I WAIT AT THE FOUNTAIN FOR A RESPONSE, but nothing comes. Scientists probably don't sign up for notifications. I try texting instead, crossing my fingers that I've transcribed his number from my arm correctly. I stare at my phone. My reflection looks desperate. I splash water on my face and immediately regret it. It's probably filthy. Tinged with bleach or bacteria or bird. Contaminated with lost wishes and the regrets of the dying. I'm drying my cheeks on my sleeve when my phone chimes with a response. It's not from Felix. It's Cody from Joggins. More specifically, his dick. It's a helluva of a pic. Like he might have taken it in the woods after building a cabin with his bare hands, or wrestling a bear. I delete the text and block the number. I touch my wrist where Felix's phone number was once inked into my skin. Of course the last digit wasn't a seven. That would have been lucky. There's nowhere to go but back to the hotel.

I hail a taxi from the Eiffel Tower. The driver is an old-growth forest. Hair sprouts from his ears and shoulders. A Serbian flag spins from a cord on his rear-view mirror.

"You doing what in Paris?" he asks, his accent thick, austere.

His question catches me off guard, though it probably shouldn't. It's the exact question I'd ask if I were driving a cab in Paris, if I were driving a cab anywhere. But for a second, I don't know why I'm in Paris, in this cab, clutching a bag of trinkets.

He eyes me in the rear-view mirror, waiting for a response. "I don't know."

He furls his brows. "You don't know?"

"No idea." I start to laugh.

He taps the steering wheel, gently nodding as though processing my response. A bus cuts us off. The driver swerves, causing the dangling Serbian flag to spin. On the backside of it is a poorly-laminated photograph.

"Your family?" I ask, pointing to the picture.

We pass a pharmacy with an electric green sign. We're close to the hotel.

The cab driver cups the photo in his hand, while gunning through an amber light.

"My mother," he replies.

"I guess that's why I'm here," I say. "My mom."

A tram, lit up like a display window, lumbers by cradling weary passengers. Shift workers and hustlers. Teens. I can't help but think of Wes. I don't want think of Wes.

A passenger van is parked in front of the hotel. A sports team with matching duffel bags and tracksuits spills out. My driver waits for the chaos to clear and then pulls over to the curb.

"How much?" I ask, gathering my belongings.

He waves, like he can't be bothered to collect the fare. I dig down in my purse for cash, but I've spent it all on souvenirs.

"Twenty-nine years since I see my mother," he says quietly.

"Ten for me," I say, edging toward the door.

"And yet I still remember her voice. Very serious," he says, smiling, "like mine."

I sit back with the understanding I'll be here for a while, paying my fare with commiseration.

"My mother liked to sing," I say. "You know ABBA?"

He chuckles. "Dancing Queen."

"That, she was not."

We both laugh. We both sit. The cab, an older model Citroen, idles and laces the air with the faint smell of gasoline. The driver takes a drink from a thermos wedged into the cup holder. *Petit Vert* is etched into the metal.

"I'm also here for work," I say.

The driver turns in his seat, sizes me up. "What do you do?"

"I'm in the grocery business."

"That's good, yes? Everybody eats." He pats his stomach.

A staticky call comes in over his radio, the directions indiscernible to me, but he shifts the car into drive. He gestures for me to leave. I reach through the centre console and give him an Eiffel Tower, a grey one to match his ancient sweater. I pause to look at the picture of his mother.

"You look like her," I say.

He swallows and I exit the cab. I watch him pull away. He makes a U-turn, and disappears onto a darkened side street. With him, thoughts of our mothers dissipate like tailpipe exhaust.

I amble past the sports team toward the elevators, but stop short of pressing the UP button. Mona's hunched at the bar alone, sipping a spring break drink in a curvy glass. Her hair is pulled back, revealing a bald spot. She doesn't see me right away. When I call her name, she jumps.

"Claudia!" She taps the barstool beside her. "Have a seat. Your dad fell asleep reading to Emma."

My father's signature move. A thousand times I've shaken him awake, shown him to his room amidst a debris field of picture books, shucked socks, reading glasses.

"You want a drink? Try something fun." Mona waves down the bartender.

I should be checking in with Joan. I haven't seen her since the Adidas store but the idea of drinking fun is more appealing. I want to swallow a carnival. Mona points to something on the menu, and orders for me. The bartender, a handsome woman with dainty spectacles and swirly braids, gets to work, lining up shot glasses and opening cans of soda water and lemonade.

I tell Mona about Wes's disappearing act at the Eiffel Tower. I want her to worry the way my mom would, but she just stirs her drink, a mischievous smile on her face like she too is on his side, on Glen's.

The bartender sets my drink on a leather coaster. A flayed strawberry floats on the surface. "He's just like his father," I say. "Reckless and inconsiderate."

"Some would call that romantic." Mona rests her sagging face in her hand. "I mean, Glen just dropped everything to surprise you in Paris. And Wes —" she pauses to pluck a cherry from her glass, "he's young and in love. You're only in your forties, Claudia. Don't tell me you've already forgotten how that feels?"

"The last time Glen dropped everything, *I* was everything. He dropped me." I kick off my shoes and they fall to the floor like cement bricks. "Makes it easy to forget."

"What about the guy on the plane? According to Joan you were holding hands as though one of you was being shipped off to war."

Did Joan tell all of France that Felix and I had held hands? She probably put it on TikTok. My face reddens. I ditch the straw from my drink and take a sports fan slug. The strawberry gets caught in my throat. I think back to the plane. It already feels like years ago, not days. A fizz of pleasure fills my chest. And then I remember Cody from Joggins. His reptilian cock, maroon ball sack and boreal thighs, thick and nocturnal. I start coughing and then, as always, my thoughts return to Glen, like a homing pigeon.

"He's with another woman," I say with a prick of rage. "Right now."

"Glen?"

"Yes, Glen."

Mona orders us another round and I swing my legs from the barstool as though I'm on a Ferris wheel.

"I betcha it's the woman from his bike trip. Don't worry though. She's a lesbian. You really should have gone to his talk at the library. Did you know he almost died in Kosovo?"

Mona went to Glen's talk at the library? I shrug.

"My youngest served there," she says, wiping a drink spill with her shawl.

I wonder if it was Rodney, but remember he's the oldest, not the baby of the family. I want to ask her what happened to him, but how can I talk about mortar shells and IEDs and amputated fingers when she's dressed like happiness? When she's dressed to forget?

I change the subject. "I tried texting Felix."

She bats my arm. "Good for you," she says, a proud father. "You took a little risk."

"It was the wrong number."

"Maybe Wes is more like you than you think."

I shake my head. "He's all Glen."

"Or maybe," she says, beady-eyed and almost jubilant. "Maybe he takes after your mother."

"My mother?" I shoot back from the bar and laugh. It's a quarter 'til midnight. Fifteen minutes until this frigging day can end. The paper bag of Eiffel Towers spontaneously tips and the figurines tumble out like piñata candy. My heads spins. A boozy tilt-a-whirl. "How on earth could Wes be anything like my mother? I mean, besides the obvious." Same nose, same penchant for rain and bread. French lovers. For fuck's sake. The word "lovers" doesn't even sound right. Too mature for Wes, too scandalous for Mom. "They enjoy French people, so what?"

The bartender glances up from a tray of glasses, and the tall German at the other end of the bar says something in German. I can't tell if he's agreeing with me or mocking me. The other customers don't seem to notice. They drink wine and discuss things over opened laptops, oblivious to the hour. They are plugged into the real world, the tangible one with tasks and responsibilities. Spreadsheets, wire transfers, freight. I don't even remember my job title.

Mona whispers, "I found emails."

"What emails?" I'm louder than I mean to be. I lower my voice. "What emails?"

"From Émile. To your mom."

"My mother's been dead for ten years." I tell Mona as if she's a stranger. Based on the looks of the other patrons, I've told them too. I try again to lower my voice.

"Your dad's computer wasn't working. You know the old desktop he kept in the guestroom?"

I nod. It had barely survived the hoard.

"I was fixing it and stumbled across some old emails."

How does one digitally stumble? Did the mouse trip? Or did Mona open every last one of my parents' files?

"You read my mom's emails?" The glass in my hand might shatter.

"I know I shouldn't have," she says, her eyes pleading and apologetic. Despite my fury I can't help but notice the charm of her eye colour: candy floss blue. "But I couldn't help it. They were beautiful."

"My mom loved my dad." My throat catches.

"Oh yes, she did. And he loved her. Still does," she smiles, almost wistfully. "But so did Émile."

I let this sink in. I don't want to know anymore. I want out of Paris. I want back in the real world of deadlines and meal prep. Soccer practice, chores, runs in the park.

"The heart can love more than one," Mona says. She's matter-of-fact now, like we're discussing something domestic, or mechanical. The multiple uses of coconut oil or a Leatherman. "I mean, no one disputes that when we talk about children. I have five boys. I love them all. It's no different with romantic love. Your mom knew it. So does Glen."

Does my dad? I wonder.

As if she's read my mind, Mona says, "I never showed Gerald. But I did fix the computer."

Mona sounds like Georgia. My nose tingles with emotion so complex I can't even discern what. Sorrow, joy, regret, curiosity. It all feels the same: heavy.

Mona noisily hoovers the remains of her drink: pulp, ice shavings, secrets. Then her eyes widen and she gestures towards the hotel lobby.

I turn to see Wes and Glen standing by the front desk. They're the same height. Wes looks starstruck, a faraway smile on his face, as if he's travelled to heaven and back. Glen waves, raises a finger as if to say *one minute* and then nudges Wes onto the elevator. I resist the urge to disobey and follow.

Beside me, Mona touches up her lipstick. Nestled in her palm is a purple compact shaped like a seashell. When she's finished, she snaps the compact shut and slides it back into her purse.

"I didn't always dress like this," she says, tying her shawl loosely around her neck.

I'm not sure what she means. Tacky?

"Colourful," she continues. "The military turned my boys grey and right along with them: me." She shudders. "You remember the opening of the *Wizard of Oz*, how it's all drab and dreary and you got the tornado and Toto and everyone's running around desperate. It's real depressing. And then the house lands and the movie switches to colour and even though Dorothy is completely lost, the colour kind of makes everything just a little more tolerable. It makes things better."

I nod.

"I know it can be a bit much — the ladies at the pool always joke that my bathing suit is gonna give them all a seizure, but after Rodney's accident, I just couldn't take any more grey. Except for the wedding — your dad *insisted* on a grey suit."

"What happened to Rodney?" I ask. The question comes out like a bullet I can't take back.

"A training accident," she says. "Imagine. He can't even blame it on war. Well, at least not directly. Lost three fingers, part of his ear, his hearing on his left side, half of his face . . ." her voice trails off and she covers her eyes as though hiding from the memory. "It really messed him up. Took years to get him help."

"Dad, too."

Mona fans a wad of euros across the bar and then rests her hand on the top of my knee. "The thing is, Claudia, life *is* a training accident. You can't plan for what you don't know's gonna happen. Wouldn't hurt you to live a little more like Wes. Or," she nods toward the elevators behind me. "Like Glen."

She goes to pull away but I stop her, pinning her hand under my own. I don't want her to leave. I want her leopard print and party beads. Her carnival drinks and festive earrings. I want her orange. I want her neon. I want her motherhood; I want her grey.

I can smell Glen approaching.

"He went to see the world," she whispers, reciting his blog.

"But what he saw was himself," I finish with a tinge of sarcasm. "I know."

"No," she sighs, shaking her head. "What he saw was you."

She slides off her stool and gathers her purse. There's lipstick on her teeth.

twenty-six

GLEN ORDERS A DRINK. "Before you say anything," he says, throwing down his credit card. "I already grounded him."

"For a month, I hope, at least. The hell was he thinking?" I stare at Glen's drink and wonder when he switched to scotch.

"He wasn't." He takes a sip, swallows as though he drank a serious document and is processing its meaning.

"Where'd you find him?"

"The wall of I Love Yous."

"Never heard of it."

Glen nods, unsurprised. Like I'm incapable of believing such a place exists.

"It's exactly as it sounds. A wall with *I Love You* written in more than three hundred languages. I had a hunch he'd go there."

I pour myself a glass of water from an elegant jug at the end of the bar. "How did he know about it? He didn't even know where our fuse box was."

"I showed him." He stops, looks into my soul in the way that he does and in the way that I hate. "I wanted to take you there." Then he resumes drinking. "My friend Vivienne agreed that was probably where they'd end up."

Vivienne. I wonder if she's a real lesbian, or just pretending. Maybe she used her sexuality as a safe space for Glen to come over and hide, only to seduce him with her hetero legs and lips. I hate her.

"So that's it? You found them at a wall?"

"Célestine's dad met me there and then drove us home."

"It's over now?"

"For tonight."

"You said you grounded him."

"Love doesn't just end, Claudia. God." He slams down his glass, making me flinch. "You know," he says, almost thoughtfully, "maybe I was wrong about you. About us." He tugs my shirt, right in the centre of my chest. Instead of rage, I feel the hot flick of arousal. I snatch his scotch, take a sip, my teeth crashing into the glass.

The elevator dings behind me. Probably the German marching back to his room to engineer something.

"What are you guys doing down here?"

It's Joan, standing there in pajama pants and a hoodie, her hair piled on the top of her head, an erupted volcano. She crosses her arms.

"Your dad just brought Wes home."

"What are *you* doing down here?" Glen pushes his scotch behind a tent-card menu as if Joan's a recovering alcoholic.

"Uncle Dan wanted a Shirley Temple."

I roll my eyes. He's regressing one menu item from each year of his failed marriage.

Glen orders the Shirley Temple and motions Joan over. I open my arms for a hug. She declines.

"There's a protest on Saturday," she says, electric. "I'm going."

Glen and I exchange glances.

"What kind of protest?"

"A climate one," she says, like we're the thickest humans in the room, maybe not even human. I stare at the stuffed rooster behind the bar. The bartender has disappeared, probably hiding in case our dysfunction is contagious.

"That's our last day here," I say. "I don't know if a climate protest is the way to cap off Grandma's memorial trip."

"And you and Dad playing house is? Or Uncle Dan having a nervous breakdown or Wes running around like a lovesick idiot?"

"My brother's having a nervous breakdown?"

"He cried at the restaurant," Joan says. "Because the garlic mashed potatoes tasted like Allison-Jean."

I cringe.

"And on the bus, the subway, the elevator. He's crying up there now."

"I can take you," Glen says to Joan.

I glare at him.

"If your mom says it's okay."

"I don't know what our plans are yet. I was kind of leaving it up to Dad."

Tears well in Joan's eyes. It's the first indication that the protest might be important to her. That climate change might be more than a reason to get out of fifth period for a school walk out.

"Grandma died when she was flying over the ocean. She cared about the environment. Don't you remember she got me that little bracelet to support the Sea Turtle Conservancy? And she used to pick up garbage every time she took me to the playground. And she never wasted water! She always turned the tap off when she brushed her teeth. You don't even do that," she yells at me. Wipes her face.

A Shirley Temple has materialized on the lip of the bar. Joan swipes it and storms back toward the elevators, pressing the UP button with her knee.

"We can talk about it!" I call after her. "The protest."

"Talking won't save the planet," she hollers back before the elevators quake shut and she ascends to the seventh floor like a saint.

"What's wrong with your brother?" Glen asks.

"His wife left him."

"He's taking it pretty hard."

"What did you just say to me, Glen? Love doesn't just end."

He clutches his scotch. We sit at the bar, hunched, shoulder-to-shoulder, a pair of order-pickers preparing for the night shift. I sign the tab to my room, slide off the stool in slow motion and stumble into my shoes.

"I have to check on my brother."

"Maybe I should talk to him," Glen offers, suddenly alert. He straightens his spine. He downs the remainder of his scotch, pays the bill.

Maybe he should, I think. My shoulders are weary from carrying the load, the woes a sack of Eiffel Towers. We ride the elevator to the seventh floor. The kids are in Dan's room. Wes and Liam are both asleep, mouths open, phones in hand. Joan sits cross-legged in the middle of one of the beds with her tablet. She scratches numbers on a hotel notepad. The remains of a charcoal face-peel litter the bedside table along with half a dozen bottles of water.

"I refilled those," she says before either of us can judge. "Uncle Dan's in our room. I told him he can sleep there."

I nod and hope that my brother hasn't chosen my bed to have a meltdown in. Joan eyes us curiously, wondering why her dad is still here.

"I'm going to talk to him," Glen says. "Check on his stitches."

Joan spreads a Paris street map across the bed. "You're a doctor now?"

Glen ignores her, turns to me. "You have the room key?" He kisses Joan on the forehead and heads for the door. "Don't stay up too late," he calls over his shoulder. Joan slides her project to the end of the bed and rearranges the pillows. "I'm sleeping here."

When I open the door to my room, Dan is not in bed where I expect him. He's perched on the sill, staring out the window at the apartment complex across the street. The lights are dim, the air eerie and sour, as if we've been living here for a month.

"You need anything?" Glen asks.

"There was a couple up there playing piano together." He gestures, presses his cheek against the glass. "Allison-Jean offered to teach me, but I said no. Never had the time. Can't read music. And now all I can think about is that maybe I should have said yes. Maybe that was her way of trying to connect and I just completely ignored it. Cindy plays piano. Emma said they spend hours together playing. That's what they do."

I pull my hair off my face. "But that's not why she left."

"I see it now," he says. "I ignored it then, but I see it now."

I have no idea what he's talking about. I'm watching Glen, who's taken off his shoes and tossed his jacket on the bed. Does he think he's staying?

"She was always trying to find ways to connect and I ignored them. And if I'm really being truthful? I found it annoying. I didn't want to go snowshoeing or to poetry readings or learn how to cook Italian or play piano. I wouldn't even go for walks with her. The most basic activity and I refused. It's all my fault."

"Even if that's true," I reply, knowing it is, "it wouldn't have changed things now that she's a lesbian."

Dan jumps from the sill. "But maybe we could have worked things out? Maybe we could have stayed together. As a family. And she could have seen Cindy on the side. There might have been ways we could have made it work. Emma's only ten."

"Maybe you still can?" I shrug.

"They could have the master, and I can live in the basement. Turn it into a suite. We can all live in the same house."

"Worth a shot," Glen replies.

"You think?" Dan knocks back his Shirley Temple. Glen examines Dan's stitches, mumbles something under his breath while I lie face down on the bed, Glen's jacket scrunched under my nose smelling like rain. A minute later, he tugs it from underneath me and says goodnight.

Glen, leaving.

I lift my head and see my brother spread across Wes's bed. The pillows are on the floor. He stares at the ceiling.

"Claudia?" he says.

I roll onto my side.

"I think you should give Glen another chance." He closes his eyes. In ten minutes, he's snoring so loud I collect the discarded pillows from the floor and bury myself. It doesn't help. I get out of bed, climb onto the windowsill and search the apartment building for signs of the piano unit, but all the blinds are drawn. Even the gays from the other night have gone to bed.

I'm about to retreat when a child pulls back the curtain in the apartment directly across from me. She is big-eyed and big-haired. A stuffed animal is cradled under her arm. She sees me, so I wave and then close the blinds. I wonder about her. How many parents, how many siblings, how many people are jammed under that roof of hers trying to be a family. Maybe she lives with her dad. Maybe she lives with two. Maybe her parents are in love, or she lives with her grandmother and she only sees her dad on weekends. Maybe her mom sends emails to the man she loves in another country.

I text Glen: *I'd like you to take me to the wall.*

A LinkedIn message notification pings. Another life coach wants to connect. I decline and open my conversation with Felix. There's a new message I've missed. Probably sent when I was chasing Wes around the Eiffel Tower.

Dinner?

twenty-seven

WE ARE STANDING IN FRONT OF the staggeringly opulent Châ-teau de Versailles. All of the kids are restless except for Liam, who finds the grounds inspiring. So much so, that he pauses, breathes it in, opens an investment app, and makes a trade. Or five. Virtual confetti flutters on his screen. He thinks GameStop will earn him a palatial lifestyle. It probably will.

"Why are we at a stupid castle?" Emma asks. Mona's styled Emma's hair into a high ponytail, so severe her face is tight as a drum, and she's wearing worn pedicure-grade flip-flops, imprac-tical and ill-fitting. The kind a mother wouldn't pack. I'll give her an hour before she starts complaining.

"I thought you liked princesses?" Dan replies, playfully tug-ging the tip of her ponytail. He looks like a meth dealer at a golf tournament.

"I like witches."

"Oh, I'm sure this place has housed a few of those too." Mona winks, takes Emma's hand, and marches her forward toward the admissions queue. Dad lurches behind them. It's hard to tell if it's his back or his knees making him move like the subject in a stop-motion film.

"You should take melatonin," I tell Dan. "It'll help you sleep."

"I don't sleep," he says, nudging Liam forward.

Joan snaps a pouty selfie in front of the Chateau's golden gate and I'm comforted by the familiar gesture. Instagram Joan is easier to manage than Climate Activist Joan. Now would be a good time to tell her one person can't change the world. It's just after nine and I'm already exhausted. My coffee's burnt and I have a virtual interview this evening with the recruiter and the food tech CEO who is "desperate to meet me." I should have stayed up last night to do some research. Instead, I googled face serums, Sylvester Stallone, the wall of I Love Yous, polygamy, and a what-would-I-look-like-with-bangs simulator. The answer is Jim Carrey.

We plod through the gates to the main square, where pigeons criss-cross the plaza like courtiers. Tourists are already posing for pictures. Emma is already complaining about her feet.

"Is there food?" Wes asks.

We haven't spoken much since last night. Despite numerous prods, he missed the hotel breakfast and didn't comb his hair. It seems he also forgot to put on deodorant. He smells like Louis XIV.

"We'll eat at lunch," I reply.

He shoots the remains of a Monster energy drink he opened on the train ride here and then gazes at me in hopes I'll direct him to the garbage or recycling bin. I don't. He can figure this one out on his own.

We're about to join the back of the line, when Mona bursts from the crowd, an arthritic jester, and motions us toward a concave man wearing a striped shirt and aerodynamic sunglasses. Beside him, an array of bikes with coppery leather seats and Wizard of Oz baskets. No helmets.

Oh.

No.

"Surprise!" Mona half-squeaks, half-squawks. "I booked us a private bike tour and brunch!"

Dan and I exchange glances and then we both look at Dad. Mona doesn't know. These are the drawbacks of a four-month courtship and marrying a man in his seventies. The last time Dad rode a bike he drove it off a wharf into the harbour, and had to get rescued by a tugboat with googly eyes and its own TV show.

"At least it's a private tour," Dan mumbles.

Mona's waiting for a reaction, so I force a smile. Only Joan seems enthused. Probably because the bikes don't emit harmful emissions or clog up the ocean.

"After Glen's talk at the library," Mona says, "I thought we might try our own little adventure. You know what they say: life is better on a bike."

Dan whispers, "No one says that."

I elbow my brother. "Show some gratitude or something."

Dan jumps forward and reaches for a gun metal green bike with a round basket fixed to the handlebars, wide enough to carry his regrets. Thankfully, Emma is enchanted by the lavender-coloured child's bike. The dark-eyed guide adjusts her seat and she climbs onto it with aplomb. I look away when her garbage flip-flops fall to the ground. Dan stares at my feet. Oh, hell no.

"Claud," he starts, "would you trade shoes? Just for the cycling part?"

"It's a bike tour, Dan. The whole thing is 'the cycling part.'"

"I don't think we're allowed to take the bikes inside the chateau," Mona says.

Dad stands beside an ivory bicycle that resembles something out of a wedding magazine shoot. He thumbs the bell and it produces a lovely tinny sound. The kind of you'd associate with Mary Poppins or a general store stocked with bolts of fabric and oats.

"Do you know what to do?" I ask my dad.

His mouth falls open and his eyes turn the colour of a man who's found sand in his car.

"Of course I know what to do," he says, indignantly. "It's a bike. Why the hell else do you think they came up with the expression 'it's just like riding a bike.' Because it's easy. You don't forget how." With that, he heaves up a leg, an audible grunt escaping his mouth, and catches his shin on the seat. The bike falls and crashes into Dan.

Liam is unintentionally taunting us, driving in circles, too close, like he wants us to buy drugs off him. Wes is texting. I threaten to take away his phone if he doesn't hurry up and get on a bike. People are looking. Joan waits patiently, her long tanned legs resting comfortably on either side of the frame. Mona in her headscarf is an elderly ET.

"I can't get my shoes on!" Emma whines.

Dan gives me a pleading look.

Oh for fuck's sake, I think. "They're going to be too big for her," I holler, untying my laces with a seventeenth-century violence. I carry my shoes to my niece and soften my tone. "Emma, honey. Try these."

Emma doesn't hesitate. She has Allison-Jean's gargantuan feet and though my sneakers are two sizes too big, when double-knotted, they manage to stay on.

The cement plaza is cold beneath my bare feet. A quick survey of our group reveals that most of us are underdressed. The temperatures have been unseasonably warm for September, but today is cloudy and grey and a breeze that felt refreshing when I stepped off the train now feels menacing. Mom would know if it was going to rain.

Our guide introduces himself as Ben, which is disappointing. I was expecting a Fabrice or Jean-Luc. He mounts his bike and says, "Welcome to Versailles," with a sweep of his long, graffitied arm.

I try to listen to his speech but the green flip-flops *are* pedicure-grade, disposable. I'm wearing lettuce. I do my best to secure my feet, but the toe straps are dangerously thin. My seat is too high, but it's too late to make adjustments. Ben has already started pedalling with Dan and Joan hovering behind him, followed by Emma, Mona and the boys. I file in at the rear, behind Dad.

Our tour begins outside, around the gardens and orange groves, away from the front gates. Goosebumps stipple the backs of my arms. Dad wobbles, meandering in and out of my way at regular and irritating intervals. Within a few minutes we are so far behind the rest of the group, we'll need a tugboat to catch up.

"Stay to the left!" I shout, as his giant wedding bike starts careening into the narrow part of the lane that I've managed to carve for myself.

"What?" he hollers, glancing over his shoulder at me.

Oh my God. "Watch the road!"

"Well, I was, until you started shouting at me."

"You keep cutting me off."

"Claudia," he says, gripping the handlebars, "when's the last time *you* rode a bike? Look how far behind we are. Keep up."

I move further to the shoulder, take a deep breath, and focus on riding in a straight line. I try to appreciate the elegant statuary and beautifully mapped gardens sprawling from either side of the path, but every time I look to the side, my heel slips from the pedal, which causes the pedal to maniacally spin and shred the back of my ankle. I feel a warm trickle of blood, followed by a piercing drop of rain, and then another.

Ahead, my father is talking. I can't hear him. He lifts a hand to point to some landmark in the distance.

"Watch where you're going!" I yell, as he once again starts drifting into my lane, forcing me onto the cobbles.

"What?" he calls.

He's on me now. I try to brake, but his pedal is caught in the spokes of my front wheel, my handlebars hitched to his fanny pack. We are attached.

"Claudia!" my dad yells. "You can't crash into me."

I try to pedal with one foot. A parade of bicycles is approaching from the other direction. I attempt to ring my bell, but it's buried under the fanny pack. Dad steers with the accuracy of a toddler. A potato could do better. The oncoming stream of cyclists whizzes by. We jump the path, sail on top of the grass and crash spectacularly. A fresh crack runs the length of my phone screen. Dad's horrible hat with the ear flaps is pinned under my bike.

I climb out from under the mess and reach for Dad's hand. He trembles, wears a look of worry so pronounced I feel a sort of woozy despair. "Are you hurt?" I ask.

Blood seeps through his pants at the knees. He cradles an elbow. "I can't ride a bike anymore," he says with a ghastly expression as though stunned by his own revelation.

I'm equally stunned. He literally drove a bike off a wharf, into the ocean. How is he surprised by this mishap? Did he think the first accident was an isolated incident? A fluke?

"You can," I say, despite the obvious. "You just need to focus on what you're doing."

"I'm old."

It is both a fact and a declaration. I take his arm and gently haul him to his feet. He assesses his wounds while I dismantle the wreckage, resetting the bikes on the pavement, collecting euros, which are scattered through the grass like forgotten shell casings, Dad's room key and tube of Voltaren.

I blow the stardust of glass from my shattered screen and tuck my phone back inside my pocket. People ride by us unperturbed. I brush dirt from my father's hat, tear the flip-flop from the wheel spokes. I tape it back together with a handful of Band-Aids.

The rain is light, but steady. I help Dad remove his rain poncho, which has managed to stay tucked into the corner of his fanny pack. Together, we drape it over his head. I survey the crash site once more, as if it's a hotel we're about to check out of. A glint in the grass. I bend to examine the object, assuming it's a missed coin or lost button.

"What is it?" Dad asks, gripping his handlebars for support, the bloodspots on his pants blooming like ink poppies.

I pinch the item between my fingers and hold it up between us. It's a shell: plain, common, cloudy, the size of my thumbnail, exactly the kind Mom used to collect. The kind we used to paint or stack or glue to tiny wooden boxes. There's still one in Wes's room, in the back of his bedside table drawer, with a minefield of forgotten relics: elastic bands from when he wore braces, parts of a geometry set (mismatched because we buy a new one every year), wrestling figurines, a petrified Sour Patch Kid.

Dad takes the shell and turns it in his palm, running his finger over the fan of ridges. He says nothing, but I can tell by the look on his face that he's remembered something. Something private. Something specific. Something special.

The sky opens ceremoniously. Dad clamps his hand around the shell and slips it into his pocket. Side by side, we walk our bikes down the path, shaking the rain from our hair.

twenty-eight

HAVE YOU GOTTEN LAID YET? Georgia texts.

I don't tell her that the only people in our party getting laid are the septuagenarians. And maybe Wes. Fuh.

I'm in Versailles, I text back

Perfect. Maybe you can find a man to tie you up in the King's room, coronate you in the guardhouse, canonize you in the hall of mirrors.

The last thing I want is to be "canonized" in the Hall of Mirrors. No one needs to see me without armour and the only men in the vicinity are a grizzled tourist in a MAGA hat and a painting of a Royal draped in so many robes he could be hiding a passel of pigs beneath them. Plus, he probably has syphilis. Or lice. Likely both.

We are midway through the tour of the Chateau's interior and I've stopped to decompress in the washroom. Mona's cleaned up Dad's road rash and sorted his coins. The kids, to my surprise, are enchanted by Versailles. By its over-the-topness, its size and arrogance, its daring. They gaze at chandelier planets, run fingers over forbidden furniture, marvel at the details: pheasants hidden in the wallpaper, sin in the drapery, tiny embroidered rosettes, the finely chiseled cheekbones and the swirling ears of sculpted boys and men. In Nova Scotia, treasure hunters have razed an entire island in search of treasure. In France, you just walk through a gate.

No sex, I finally reply to Georgia and instead tell her about my upcoming interview with the recruiter and the CEO. She asks how I'm feeling about that; the idea of starting a new job and it catches me off guard. I pause in the Hall of Mirrors, en route to our family meeting spot outdoors, to consider it. How do I *feel?* That is the horror of this place. Paris is making me feel: lonely and for God's sakes, frightened. I need my recognizable self back. I need familiar, I need boring, I need predictable. I need safe. I want roosters in my kitchen, and Sunlight. The happy basset hound I see walking by the strip mall on my morning commute. The ancient pictures on my office bulletin board. My robe. My aloneness.

The Hall of Mirrors is crowded. The sun must have come back out because it leaks through the windows, casting people in golden chessboard squares. They move in and out of the light, taking it all in, or perhaps ignoring it completely. The rumours of this place. The luxury and deceit. The debauchery.

I weave through tour groups and families, note things I missed on my first pass through. Pedestals, trumpeters, gilded leaves. Maybe I should accept the job. Why choose Glen or Felix when I can have a new office, a new title by my name. An excuse to buy a beautiful new suit, soft and exquisitely tailored. Maybe I'll buy it here, in the fashion capital of the world.

I'm lonely.

I traipse down the stairs, toward the sun. My stomach aches with hunger. For the next part of the tour, we are riding to the local market and having a picnic brunch by a canal. I'll ride shotgun with Mona, and make Dan ride with Dad in the rear.

A rustling in my purse. Hooves, the pleasing scratch of paper. The origami horse, sensing my want. Worse, sensing my *need.* For a man. And it feels shameful, anti-feminist, archaic. This is why I like Georgia. Also why I desperately miss Cathy.

Cathy, who could work a chisel, parkour a park bench, fix a door. So practical. I imagine her texting me now: *of course, you should take the job! Glen wants to get back together? Hard NO. A guy on a plane? Seriously, Claud?* She would not be asking if I got laid on my mother's memorial trip.

Ben, the guide, is straddling his bike when I re-join my family. The lines outside Versailles are airport long and I'm grateful Mona booked the private tour, even if it's cost me my shoes and my dignity. Bruises are already forming where Dad and his bicycle bowled me over.

I debrief Dan, nodding toward my father. "He can't pedal in a straight line."

"He said *you* cut *him* off."

Oh my God. I can't even. "Just remind him to keep his eyes on the road."

"Kind of defeats the purpose of a tour if you can't view the sights, no?"

"Whatever. I don't care what you do. It's your turn. With him."

Dan shrugs and I mount my bike.

Mona pedals with surprising vigour, her scarf flapping daintily in the breeze. Her poncho is a pleasing yellow and matches Dad's blue one. She wears a cheerful expression and it makes me want to seize the lushness of the moment. The colour. Teen children whom I adore cycling at my heels, a high-limit credit card in my wallet, strong legs, green grass. I glide with my feet off the pedals, then with no hands. I feel giddy and childish. Alive.

"Auntie Claudia," Emma cries behind me. "Watch out!"

I hit the brakes and skid. Someone's dropped a backpack. I crank my handlebars and bump Ben's back tire with my front one.

"Sorry," I holler, coming to a full stop.

He gives a little wave. The backpack's owner has returned to retrieve it. He apologizes in another language, swipes it from the ground.

"Neither Mom nor Grandpa knows how to ride a bike," Wes says behind me.

I resume pedalling with a scowl.

Ahead of me, Ben clears his throat. I'm driving in the wrong lane. I tug on the handlebars to correct course. Oh. I'm driving down a hill. Ducks in my path flee.

"Brake!" Mona yells.

Too hard. The bike stops and I skim the handlebars with my face.

"Wow," Ben remarks.

I dismount and drag the bike uphill. "These aren't normal bikes."

"The end of your nose is bleeding," Liam points.

Great. The recruiter will think I have impetigo or fucking nose shingles. "Where is the canal?" I yell to Ben.

"You nearly rode into it," he says. "Market's just up here. Five more minutes."

I ride the remainder of the trip in silence and stroll the market alone. I buy a little cup of freshly squeezed orange juice and immediately think of Mom. I understand now why Dan cried in the restaurant over garlic mashed potatoes. I can almost smell her. The powdery scent of her drugstore makeup, the earthy aroma of her fingertips when she braided my hair after gardening, her scandalous fur vest.

The picnic spread is lovely. Wine, sausages, cheeses of all persuasions, baguettes, honeyed pastries, sparkling water, pastel petits-fours.

"We saved you a seat," Wes says, motioning to a luscious

patch of grass facing the Grand Canal. I join my brood cross-legged and begin assembling a plate. Everything tastes rich, cared for, important. I stuff myself like a bourgeois, ignore that the grass is wet, and lift my face to the sun. All that food and all I remember is the orange juice. All I feel is her.

twenty-nine

"**HOLD STILL.**" Joan grips my chin like it's a buffet plate, her other hand waving a makeup brush dangerously close to my skinned nose.

"Don't press too hard," I caution, squinting.

"I have to press hard if I'm going to cover it," she sighs, swirling the brush in a blob of concealer she's squirted onto the inside of her forearm.

I close my eyes and she gets to work, dabbing, stroking. She switches brushes, uses her fingertip, a Q-tip, a tissue. After a solid ten minutes, she finally says, "There," and spins me roughly in the hotel room's office chair to face the mirror.

I lean forward, examine her work. Still a bit pink, but not nearly as embarrassing as when we started. I've kicked Wes out to get ready for my interview. Mona's gone for a pedicure and Dad's offered to take the kids out for dinner. To McDonald's.

Joan wipes the remaining dollop of concealer from her arm and changes into baggy jogging pants and a crop top. Before leaving for her cousins' room, she fixes a lock of my hair. "Good luck," she says, halfway out the door. "And don't forget to talk to Grandpa about the protest."

I'd forgotten about the protest. "You can talk to him," I call after her, unsure whether she's too far away to hear. Dad would appreciate the ask coming directly from her.

I wear a simple black blazer, a white shirt, and a scarf I picked up in Versailles. I contemplated pulling my hair back into a chic low bun, but Joan said that would accentuate my "giant nose."

I slide lip gloss and eye shadow palettes off the desk and open my laptop. Thirty minutes. I check that I have the latest version of Zoom downloaded on my computer. I creep the CEO's personal Instagram account. I skim key words in every article written about food tech in the last thirty days. I open and close my mouth like a singer preparing to take the stage.

Fifteen minutes. Check mole for cancer, teeth for pulp. Apply another smattering of deodorant. Test the lighting in the room. Search for a pen. Read the abstract of an academic paper titled: *Plant-based and cell-based animal product alternatives: An assessment and agenda for food tech justice.* An incoming FaceTime from Glen. Why is he FaceTiming? I'm suddenly self-conscious. Unsure about the scarf, ashamed of my nose, my age, my penchant for Wagon Wheels and Justin Bieber. I know it's ridiculous. Glen having seen the mangled remains of my crotch, as if I'd given birth both times to a tank battalion instead of a baby.

I accept his call.

"What's wrong your nose?" he asks.

For fuck's sake. "Is it that bad?"

"Looks raw."

I wait for him to tell me why he's calling. It better not be on behalf of Wes, and a campaign for another bender with Célestine.

"I'd like to take the kids out, tonight. If you don't mind. There's a game at the Stade. Vivienne has a friend who can get us tickets."

I used to hate these offers. Glen always had a friend who could get him tickets. Box seats. Skip-the-line. Front row. Fast-pass. Free flights. And the kids would always come home exhausted, happy, and souvenired.

I took them to the library. Or the cold city pool.

"Yeah," I say, with a prick of envy. "They'd love that."

"Wes said you had a big interview tonight. Thought it might help."

"Interview's in ten minutes," I reply, examining my nose in the mirror. "Gotta go. Just make arrangements with Dad. He's taking them to McDonald's."

We hang up. I clear the room of visible debris and reset my laptop. The normal protocol would've been to meet independently with the recruiter first, then interview with the CEO second. Alone. But here we are, having a threesome.

The CEO is quirky and charming. From the UAE via Cornwall, England, according to the recruiter's last email. She surfs and keeps bees. Cats instead of kids. We hit it off. She has a background in food retail, knows my current employer, has shopped at Petit Vert. She speaks passionately about her company's ethos, scope, and vision. She explains in great detail the role she is recruiting for, and why she thinks I'll be a good fit. The recruiter looks like he might whack off because it's going so well. A rare chemistry.

"The position would be in Rotterdam," the CEO says and the screen immediately freezes, all of us locked and pixelated. The recruiter's a Minecraft character, the CEO a hologram, and I look as though I've been caught mid-colonoscopy.

Rotterdam? Did the recruiter not think this was an important detail to share? I adjust the volume on my computer to make it appear as though I'm doing something to solve an unsolvable problem, and my head moves across the screen, a disembodied Marie Antoinette. I wonder if I've somehow got myself into a recruiter's version of a catfishing scheme.

The call resumes, the audio skips and then resolves.

"I hope that wasn't a sign," the CEO says, referring to the glitch. "We have an office in Toronto, but I'd want you here."

I don't know Rotterdam, but if it's anything like the rest of Europe, if it's anything like Paris, I'm not sure I could cope. The population density, the "oldness," the psychology of it all. The risk. I can't imagine moving to Rotterdam. Can't even fathom it.

I catch a glimpse of my skinned nose in the mirror, and worse, my posture. I'm slumping. I never slump and then a sudden thought: I'm a coward. I want familiar, low stakes, same-as-yesterday. Is this why I also want Glen?

The CEO continues on about key initiatives, markets, and major projects. She rattles off some stats on plant-based food technology, I'm pretty sure from the same abstract I'd reviewed prior to the meeting. The recruiter interrupts with a comment. A joke I've missed. They both laugh. I smile and listen intently as the CEO continues, but I'm still thinking about Glen and is this what he meant when he'd said I'd *changed*? Was I, at one time, adventurous? Did I used to take chances? Maybe. But also, maybe *he* took that spark away from me when he left. I couldn't take risks as a single mom of two young kids. I stayed in the same neighbourhood, and same house, stayed with the same company.

"I hope that's not a dealbreaker," the CEO says. "Wanting you here. In Rotterdam."

Of course it is. "Not at all," I lie.

The recruiter is gleeful.

The CEO leans into the screen. Her skin is lovely. Radiant. And then, to my horror, she points up at her nose. "We have a product," she says. "It'll heal that right up."

A hot surge of embarrassment blows up my cheeks.

"I've had some pretty bad run-ins with coral, shoals, my board." She points to her cheek. "You name it."

Right. Surfing. I muster a smile.

"I'll send you a list of places you can find it in Paris."

Plans for a follow-up meeting are discussed, and we finish our conversation.

I close Zoom.

I open LinkedIn.

I open Felix's invitation to dinner.

I type: *Yes*.

thirty

I KNOCK ON THE DOOR to my dad's room. When he opens it, I'm surprised to find him standing in swim trunks, his blue legs glowing, torso and chest covered in a froth of white hair. Remnants of McDonald's litter the overflowing garbage can, side tables, and desk. A half-eaten box of nuggets sits in the middle of the bed. Evidence of Emma is everywhere: gobs of ketchup, donut-themed Band-Aids, fidget toys, markers, half-finished sketches.

"Need some help cleaning up?"

He waves a dismissive hand.

"Let me at least tie-off the garbage."

There's ketchup and McChicken sauce all over the can, and the ends of the trash bag have disappeared. I have to dig to retrieve them. When I remove my hand, there's a pickle on my wrist. I knot the bag and toss it beside the door.

"I'm going for a swim," Dad declares, windmilling his arms. "Wanna come? Mona's still at the spa. She's getting a massage once her pedicure dries."

"Is there a hot tub?"

"And a sauna," Dad replies.

"Kids got off okay?"

"Glen took all of 'em. And your brother!"

"I'll grab my suit."

It was nice of Glen to include Dan. He's not much of a

soccer fan, he's not much of an anything fan, but he could use the camaraderie, the bright lights, a few stadium beers. I head back to my room, change into my bathing suit, and meet Dad in the hallway. Shiny black goggles dangle from his wrist. He looks weary.

"You okay?" I ask as he presses the elevator DOWN button. The bruises from his bike accident are in full bloom.

He pulls back one of the bandages from his knee. "Tore off the skin."

"No kidding," I poke around the crude pink edges. "You know what Mom would say —"

"Keep it clean," he finishes.

We ride the elevator to the second floor in silence. The pool is empty but there's a large family marinating in the hot tub, and judging by the location of several pairs of sandals, a convention in the sauna. I take Dad's elbow and ease him down the stairs into the pool's shallow end. The lights are hazy, the tiles a tropical blue. There's a Biblical warmth to the water. I wade until I'm up to my neck, float on my back. Dad bobs beside me, both of us gazing up at the ceiling, which is curved and dark as a mountain tunnel.

I try to force a memory of Mom in keeping with the trip's theme, but the chlorine reminds me of Dan. The hours we spent as kids at the outdoor pool, diving for rings, racing, jack-knifing off the diving board. The long bike rides home, our towels unfurling and dragging behind us, the stop at the white clapboard corner store for ice cream sandwiches or New York Seltzers.

Dan used to be fun. When did he stop? It was long before Allison-Jean left him. Maybe it was the anxiety of being a father, a provider. The incessant worry over whether the kids were getting enough potassium, or too much screen time. Whether he'd put enough money away for RESPs and would they be able to fix the roof if any more shingles blew off and is that *mould* in the bathroom? And God only knows what went on in their marriage. They seemed to have their shit together. Date nights (scheduled), chores (divided), driving responsibilities (shared), gifts (exchanged). But did they care about each other? Did they really *see* each other? Could they distinguish between indigestion and resentment? An unfinished task and despair? An empty linen closet and a lack of fulfillment?

Dad's floated over to the deep end. I flip onto my stomach and swim to join him. I want to talk about Dan. Ask Dad what he thinks about Dan's idea to live with Allison-Jean and Cindy. What that might look like if he were to meet someone new. Would she move into the basement with him? But Dad looks like he's in a coma. Eyes closed, mouth open, palms up as if waiting to be baptized.

There's a ruckus in the hot tub. School-aged siblings pinching each other. Their parents become reluctant referees. It goes on for several minutes before one of the children is evicted, a boy about Emma's age. He wraps himself in a pool towel and sulks on a sleek deck chair, black curls dripping.

"Your mother loved another man." Dad kicks, triggering a tiny tsunami so that when I open my mouth to respond, I swallow the deep end. I scramble to find my footing on the pool's smooth bottom, and sputter. I can't derive any sort of tone or intent from Dad's statement, so I focus on draining the water from my ears. "Émile," I eventually say.

"He was a lawyer. Real ugly fella."

I feel an odd desire to defend my mother's former lover from my father. It's as if by insulting Émile, he's insulting her. Also, Dad is no Emmanuel Macron. I look at him now: wooden nose, spotty complexion and ruined knees.

"Maybe it was his accent," I offer, thinking of Felix.

Dad smiles. "It never bothered me," he says. "Your mother loved me. We had a good marriage." He drags his fingertips across the water, back and forth, creating ripples. "But sometimes I wonder if they weren't a better match." He looks beyond me, wistful, contemplative, and I let the comment sink between us.

There's so much I want to ask but I tread lightly because the direction of this conversation is still a mystery and is equal parts horrifying and scintillating. I say nothing, focus on my dad's gargantuan hands, like baseball gloves, paddling the water, while the family vacates the hot tub and files out of the pool, shrink-wrapped and in single-file.

"I gave your mom an ultimatum," Dad blurts. "I wasn't even ready to get married. I just wanted her to choose." His voice croaks to a whisper. "I wanted to win."

What to do with this information?

I kick onto my back so that I'm once again staring up at the dark ceiling. My head dips below the surface, my ears fill and Dad says something I miss. What I really want to know is, where is this coming from? Guilt? Regret? Did he read the emails? Is Mona his Émile? Was my parents' entire marriage just two people making the best of a very large mistake?

"Not a good reason to get married," I finally say, more thinking aloud than deliberately chastising my father for admitting that their "happily ever after" was born of some egotistical misplaced bravado. "Did you even love her?"

"Claudia," Dad says, indignantly. "Of course I loved her. I still love her."

"Then why are you telling me this?"

"The thing about swimming is that you often can't see the bottom, can't make out what's below the surface. I'm getting old, Claudia. I'm trying to show you what's on the bottom."

The sauna door opens and a stream of lithe men in Speedos tumbles out. Each wrestles for his sandals, while clinging to the towel knotted around his waist. They speak Dutch and I think for a second about the job interview and the wild prospect of uprooting my life and moving to Rotterdam just as Glen has decided to come out of parental retirement, a quarterback in a midlife crisis, and as my father before me floats towards the menacing pool drain contemplating his life choices, as he moves closer to the end.

"I used to think your mother and I met at exactly the right time. Both of us had just finished school. I was already apprenticing and she got a job teaching grade one. Your mom was so different than anyone I'd ever met. She was introspective. In tune with the little things I never even noticed: crickets, chickadees, the plants that used to climb up the side of the house. She loved art and yet we never bought any." He pauses to tug the rubber strap of his goggles. "And now, when I look back, I think the opposite. That maybe we met at exactly the wrong time and she settled because I wanted her all to myself."

With that, he ungracefully suctions his goggles to his face and launches into a rheumatic front crawl. I watch him swim to the far wall, touch and then throw himself back in, slapping the water with the recklessness of a whale, all sound and big splash.

I consider the possibility that Glen and I too met at exactly the wrong time. It's such a bewildering concept that I have to steady myself on the pool's sloping brass ladder. Would things have worked out differently if we'd met in our thirties? Our seventies? Now? Does it even matter? We're so entangled and yet there's something oddly comforting about the possibility of blaming our failed coupling on something intangible: time.

Dad is charging toward me on a diagonal. I pull myself half-way up the ladder to get out of his way, but he still manages to swipe the backs of my legs. He stops to assess what's happened and looks annoyed when he sees me clinging to the ladder, as though it's my fault he can't do anything, other than marriage, in a straight line.

"You're in the way, Claudia," he scolds.

I heave myself up another rung as Mona appears at the pool door dressed for a cruise. Bold floral suit, fuchsia sandals, a sheer cover-up with fringe and beading. She waves, before barrelling through the heavy door, shoulder first.

"What's Émile's last name?" I ask, wiping my face.

Dad eyes me suspiciously and then says, "Fontaine," before he dunks under the water, only to resurface and slick back his gnarly hair.

Mona heaps her belongings on a lounger, removes her shoes, and then limp-runs across the deck, cannonballing herself into the deep end. Freezing, I tiptoe to the sauna, shutting the door firmly behind me. Through the opaque window, I watch Dad and Mona embrace.

thirty-one

IT SEEMS GLEN WASN'T the only one who was able to get tickets to last night's game. Wes has a hickey on his neck. A red card. He's asleep on the pull-out. I tug the comforter to cover him. Joan is sprawled in the other bed snoring lightly, her phone at her fingertips playing YouTube videos. They've been playing all night. Clip after clip of climate films. I scroll her screen. Emaciated polar bears, koalas burnt to a crisp, trash flotillas. I toss her phone back on her bed screen-side down, beside her new cleats, which are untied in a lump beside her pillow. Next to them, a crumpled souvenir jersey. I check the tag still attached to the neckline: one hundred forty euros. Glen's not fucking around.

I dismantle a still-warm croissant purchased this morning from a bakery two streets over. It's moist and flaky, nothing like the lard crescents we mass-produce back home. The coffee's a bit sketch, but I sip it anyway, catching up on work and sending emails to the recruiter and the CEO, thanking them for their time. No commitment, other than a follow-up meeting when I return to Nova Scotia. My counterpart at Petit Vert is in Japan this week, but Marcus has arranged for me to meet with their sales and marketing manager at a hotel in the 5th arrondissement this afternoon. I plug the coordinates into my phone and prepare a list of questions. Executed precisely, a Canadian version of Petit Vert could be a crowning achievement in my career. One more decade of intense output, and then I can coast to the finish line. That, or move to Rotterdam.

I check my phone. In fifteen minutes, I have to wake the kids because we're going to Disneyland Paris. I would rather be handcuffed to a mime than go to Disneyland, but Dan is determined to make it happen. As a new member of the recently-separated parent club, he needs to get Emma to Disney before Allison-Jean does. He needs to win. And as sad and spiteful as it sounds, I understand. When you can't give your child a second parent you load them up with mouse ears and magic, fireworks and best-days-ever. Tickets to a football game in Paris. Box seats. Dan will eventually learn these things don't matter. That his kids will remember the stuff we perceive as insignificant: hanging around to read one more chapter, making them hot chocolate after a shitty day at school, cleaning their bedroom for them after their first major break-up. But for now, glass slippers.

While they sleep, I eat another croissant, and google "Émile Fontaine" "lawyer" "Paris." I click on a website for Chalamet Avocats.

Hmm. He's . . . interesting looking. A small face stretched thin as a shoreline. Olive-skinned, dressed practically in a grey suit, and the most spectacular eyebrows I've ever seen. They look embroidered. His eyes are dark, more slate than brown, but there's an undeniable warmth in his gaze, surprising for a legal portrait, and yet so endearing, so capable. The kind of man that, if he was a doctor, you'd trust to perform your child's surgery. If he were a hair stylist, you'd tell him to do what he wanted. And if he told you he loved you, you'd know it was sincere and forever.

My heart seizes. A quick, hard contraction that sends a wave of emotion through my body so potent I nearly see it travel beneath my skin. It climbs my spine, pricks the back of my neck, stings my nose. I know this feeling: grief. I inhale, my breath ragged as a shift worker, and close my eyes. I can't pinpoint exactly why I'm crying. Whether the grief circulating through me is mine, or Mom's, or Émile's, or someone else's entirely, but it's acute and I wait, bare and unmoving, until it passes.

When I open my eyes, Wes is awake, sitting up, headphones wrapped around his neck, a pillow on his lap, watching me curiously through the mirror. He does not know what to say. All of his life when he's caught his mother in these moments, crying alone in the middle of the night, or on the drive home or standing in line at the grocery store, an endless silent film, he has never known what to say, but he always knows what to do. He shoves the blankets aside, pads across the hotel's jewel-toned carpet, and hugs me.

And now it's me who doesn't know what to say because I want everything for him. I want him to experience all the love, but in that wish, I'm simultaneously condemning him to a life of pain, and I can barely cope with that idea. In less than seventy-two hours he will have to say good-bye to Célestine, and he will experience a supernatural grief. The grief of love.

I hand him a croissant and he finishes it in three bites, helps himself to another.

"You can see her tonight," I say. "If your dad agrees. And with some rules. But," I caution, "rules."

He's already texting her. I nudge Joan awake and then jump in the shower with a sudden attitude change toward spending the day at Disney. How will Paris Disney differ from American Disney? I doubt there will be fathers of unusual size wearing NFL shirts and gnawing turkey legs as if their survival depended on it. Fewer mothers with rhinestone sunglasses, NASCAR strollers and cleavage you could plant a tree in. Besides, if it's horrible at least I get to leave early for my meeting.

I squirt shaving foam onto my legs, perch my foot on the soap dish. I haven't told anyone that after my Petit Vert meeting, I'm having dinner with Felix. I haven't told anyone what he wrote when I'd accepted his invitation. Not even Georgia, with whom I would normally share these details. By keeping it private, his response grows more reckless in my heart. Like thistle.

I meet my family in the hotel lobby, each of us carrying a kingdom-friendly backpack. Mona's raided the hotel breakfast. Bread and oranges jut out from the unzipped top of her bag. Dad wears a California Raisins T-shirt from 1986, his hair slicked back like a vampire's. Dan and I both stare. The hairstyle has given him the appearance of an entirely different man.

Emma is beside herself, talking incessantly, scrawling things in a cheetah-print notebook, her shirt starched and stiff as a Hitler Youth's. At least she's wearing shoes and not lettuce wraps.

"I thought she didn't like princesses?" I whisper to Dan.

"She doesn't. She's made a list of villains she wants to get autographs from."

We bus, and then board a train for the short trip to Chessy. From the station it's only a five-minute walk to the gates. Our first stop inside the park is the scooter rental hut, a surprise courtesy of Dan. Dad is initially insulted.

"I don't need a scooter," he protests while simultaneously stroking the machine's metallic blue chrome.

"Gerald," Mona interrupts, pushing a squat splayed hand onto the seat of the smaller model she's been presented with. "Feel how comfortable." I notice the imposter ring, which has been absent the last few days, gleaming from her hand.

Dad relents, mounts the scooter as though it's a skittish horse that might take off without him, and places his backpack in the machine's handy basket. "What would the guys think of this?" he says with a geriatric harumph.

"What 'guys'?" I reply. "Harold can barely walk and George's in a wheelchair."

"Melvin would never be caught dead on a scooter and neither would Grant."

Dad's curling friends. I roll my eyes. "Melvin's only in his sixties and Grant's had so many surgeries he's pretty much half-scooter. Let's go."

Dan signs sixty-three different waivers and then we gather outside to study the park map. Sleeping Beauty's iconic pink castle looms in the distance. This can't excite the locals. Not when they have real castles with turrets and towers and moats and gatehouses. Instead, they should have something completely foreign to gawk at: a trailer strung with patio lanterns and a trans-am on the lawn, a brownstone with rich people fighting inside it, a bungalow with a mugshot rooster border in the kitchen.

Emma turns a cartwheel. The older kids ask to separate but Dan and I say no. We've made the decision to stay together as a family, at least until I have to leave for my meeting. Our first stop is The Twilight Zone Tower of Terror.

"Janice would've hated this," Dad says, stepping into the "service" elevator.

This is true. Mom got stuck in an elevator with a dozen of her students on a field trip to the Parliament Buildings. It was her first and last year teaching junior high. They were trapped for only two-and-a-half hours, but that was long enough for her to apply for a transfer back to elementary school. She was well into her fifties before she rode an elevator again.

Dad screams for the entire duration of the ride. The elevator shoots up and down, periodically flinging open its doors to reveal some kind of horror: a possessed doll or tortured ghost, and every single time Emma yells, "Is that all you got, bitch?" to which Dan responds with threats.

This is how our morning continues to unfold. Dad screams, Emma swears, Dan threatens. Mona's having the time of her life, and the teens experience each attraction with a Swiss neutrality. Space Mountain's got nothing on Gen Z, on Wes or Joan or Liam, who've consumed between them probably a billion TikToks and YouTubes videos of real humans pushing real limits. Yosemite base jumps, Himalayan free climbs, Dominican free dives, Niagara fallers, wing-walkers, Mars rovers. They get off every ride with "meh" expressions.

Dad wants a burger, Emma more stimulation, so we head for a late lunch at the Rainforest Café, which is damp and sour. Once we've received our drink order, Dad proposes a toast. It's three simple words. "To new beginnings."

I'm fumbling for my glass of muscadet when I see a text from Glen. Also simple and all in lowercase letters:

wall of i love yous. you and me

I raise my glass, though I'm not sure I'm ready to toast new beginnings. We're here for Janice, not for life without her. Or are we?

"What are we doing here?" I blurt.

"Chicken fingers," Emma replies. She's pressing so hard on the red crayon she's been given to colour with that it snaps in half, loud as a cap gun. I jump.

The teens put down their glasses, assuming the toast is over, and return to their phones. Dan's looking at me inquisitively and I can't decide if it's because he doesn't know why we're here either, or doesn't know why I'm ruining the toast.

"What?" I say. "You don't want new beginnings. You told me you wanted to move back home with Allison-Jean and live in the basement."

Emma, now death-gripping a green crayon, pauses. She looks at me, and then at her dad. "Is that true?" she asks, her voice small, split open.

Dan opens his mouth but the glass of Sprite he's been holding for the toast slips from his hand and crashes to the table. Joan, sitting next to him, grabs both their phones and pushes away from the table. Mona hauls wads of Kleenex from her purse and begins sopping up the mess.

"Dad?" Emma says. "Are you moving back home?" A tear, crystalline and plump, whirls down her cheek.

"I —" Dan explodes from the table and takes off. On cue, the automaton animals lurking in the restaurant's palm frond décor and canopy ceiling, come alive. They gyrate and flap. They pound their chests and snap their beaks. They growl and hoot.

"Nice one, Mom," Wes says as Liam gets up and goes after his dad.

"I didn't mean . . ."

"It doesn't matter what you meant," Joan says. She's gone around to the other side of the table and has hoisted Emma onto her lap.

"Claudia," Dad says pleadingly. "She's only just left him."

It's been six months. Mona continues to sop up the Sprite, thieving place settings and cutlery from the adjacent booth.

I turn my gaze to Emma. "I'm sorry, sweetheart. I didn't mean to upset you. Your dad just —"

My own father raises his hand to stop me saying anything further, as a pair of servers arrive with appetizers. One of them dumps a basket of cheese sticks in front of me.

"Excuse me," I say, extricating myself from the table. I follow the path Dan and then Liam took toward the washrooms, and knock on the men's room door. No answer. I head outside.

Dan and Liam are sitting side by side on a rock wall. Above them leans a giant stone mushroom with a red cap. Liam looks both relieved and pissed off to see me. I motion for him to go back inside.

Seeing my brother hunched on the wall, I feel empathy. But I'm surprised that I also feel a sharp barb of resentment. He wasn't there for me when Glen left. He didn't offer to take the kids for a sleepover, or to help me change the furnace filters. Never once did he say "It'll be okay." Instead, he acted like my failed relationship with Glen, my broken family, was a disease, incurable and fatal. So, I only apologize for one thing. "I shouldn't have said that in front of Emma."

Dan wipes his eyes. "I brought it up with Allison-Jean last night," he says, sniffing. "We have enough money to do a proper renovation. We could even put in a separate entrance and you know what she said? She said, *you left a couple of your books in the living room, so I boxed them up. Cindy'll drop 'em off when you get back.* It's over, Claud. I don't know why I had it in my head that things could go back to the way they were and if not the way they were, that we could move forward somehow, whatever that looked like, but it's over. It's really over."

"Hope," I say, patting him on the back. "It gets you through until you realize it's time to move on. Hope waits until you're capable, and then nudges you forward."

"To what?" he asks, flatly.

"To new beginnings."

thirty-two

I HAVE TIME TO KILL before my Petit Vert meeting, so I seek out a health food store and buy some of the CEO-recommended healing balm. The packaging is quaint and clean. I tuck it in my purse and buy a cappuccino at a café that borders a cemetery. Across the street, is a row of elegant sandstone buildings, each with intricate filigree balconies and imposing doors. Offices. Etched into a simple black sign directly across from me: Chalamet Avocats. I choke on my cappuccino foam.

I fix my gaze on the building's amber oak door just as it swings open and a pair of lawyers, to judge by the way they're dressed, steps out, he in a smart wine-coloured sport coat, she in a shift dress and perfect black heels. They are lovely and young. I rest by elbows on the table, cradling my mug. Adrenaline zips through me like a flight of swallows.

I'm going in there.

Before I have a chance to talk myself out of such a ridiculous move, I pay my server in cash and cross the street. Only when I'm at the foot of the greyed stairs do I wonder what the hell I'm doing here, the same thought I had in the Rainforest Café, the same thought I've had every minute since touching down in Paris.

A man sits behind the reception desk.

"Je m'excuse," I say.

The man waits for me to continue, but I've lost my French.

I think he wants to know if I have an appointment. *Qui*, he says. Who am I here to see? And that's when I see the photo on the wall, framed beside half a dozen others. I point to Émile Fontaine.

"Ah, Monsieur Fontaine. Il est retraité."

Retired. "Oui, je sais." The man stares at me awkwardly, waiting for our exchange to end. "Do you speak English?" I ask.

"A leetle," he says in that French-man-speaking-English kind of way that's equal parts sexy and babyish. A linguistic centaur.

I gesture again toward the photograph. "He knew my mother. I was just . . ." my voice trails. What was I wondering? "I was wondering if there's anyone still working here who knew him."

An older man with Hitchcock jowls and a portly frame appears from a doorway down the hall. "May I help?" he asks in impeccable English.

The receptionist gestures for me to go. The sign on the portly man's office door reads Cedric Chalamet.

"Monsieur Fontaine knew my mother. They were pen pals. They met while he was an exchange student in Canada."

"Is your mother here?" Cedric asks, his eyes wide and as bright as a billboard.

"She died ten years ago."

Cedric leans back in his expensive chair, drawing his hands behind his head for support. His office is neat. Books and binders stacked with Egyptian precision. A glass ornament, a pear, sparkles from the credenza lining the back wall, where just beyond, a pigeon roosts.

"I'm sorry for your loss," Cedric says, leaning his large body over his desk. "I never knew your mother, but Émile did speak of a woman in Canada." He crosses his hands and says, "He never married, Monsieur Fontaine," and then he removes a pen from his desk drawer, scrawls a phone number on his legal pad, tears off the page, and hands it to me. "Should you need to get in touch," he says.

"Merci," I say, rising. I stare at the looping handwriting, the accent over the E in Émile's name, a checkmark.

Cedric shows me out. I fold the number inside my purse and walk toward the hotel, where I'm scheduled to meet Petit Vert's sales and marketing manager, Cornelle Ibrahim. A block out, there's commotion. Cars honk, and pedestrians wielding signs criss-cross the road without so much as a glance in either direction. Another protest. A news van is parked meters from the hotel steps, and just as I try to make my way through the bustling crowd, a tall black man, thick in the shoulders and wearing a tight floral shirt, tugs me to the side.

"Too dangerous," he says. "I'm Cornelle. You must be Claudia." He sighs, shakes his head at the flock of demonstrators, and slips on a pair of champagne-coloured sunglasses. "There's a pub around the corner. We can chat there."

"Great," I reply, trying to keep up as Cornelle weaves through the throng of pissed-off drivers, reporters, and protestors. We pass a fire truck with lights spinning, but no obvious emergency. The firefighters lean on the back of the truck, irritated, as if their card game had been interrupted.

"Every day," Cornelle says, opening the door to an English-style pub with a die-cut sign shaped like a barrel. He gestures for me to go inside. "Always protesting something."

"I noticed."

We grab a booth and Cornelle orders a lager.

"Is it always climate related?"

"No," he says, wiping the table with his sleeve. "But tomorrow there's a big one. All week that's what they've been preparing for."

I don't tell him Joan's intent on going.

"Don't get me wrong," Cornelle explains. "We need robust climate policy, and I support the right to protest, but last week, protestors blocked the exit to the car park and my son missed his fencing class."

Once our drinks arrive, we get down to business. Cornelle talks about his company's entrance strategy, the first Petit Vert and how they expanded, the challenges of a small-batch enterprise and rising transportation costs, guerilla marketing. I take notes, ask questions, try to imagine how Petit Vert could be adapted for the Canadian market. I have doubts about the feasibility, at least in the smaller regions.

A game is on TV and Cornelle stops to watch a penalty kick. He cheers with the other patrons when the ball is rocketed into the top left corner of the net. It's a helluva shot. I've seen Joan make that kind and for a second I long to be back home, watching her play. Cornelle is clapping, exchanging commentary with a fan who's plugged in to the booth across from us, staring down a plate of moules-frites.

"My favourite player." Cornelle gestures towards the TV, flashes a boyish grin. His teeth are stunning. When he excuses himself to go to the washroom, I check in with Dan. He sends me a photo of Dad and Mona on their scooters. Olaf is in the foreground. I imagine my father mowing him down. Next, Dan sends a picture of Liam and Wes posing with Darth Vader. Both Liam and Wes stand like men: chests proud, chins up, feet wide. But they smile like boys, and a streak of nostalgia zips through me as I remember little Wes. His scrawny shoulders, Pixar pyjamas and twin bed. His big eyes and small fists. The way he could curl himself into a knot and fit on a single couch cushion.

Cornelle returns and glances at his watch. It's a fine instrument. Gold and intricate. A detail I've noticed here: men still wear watches. They keep time close. I instinctively reach for my wrist. The indents from the handcuffs are no longer visible but I can still feel them in my fingertips. I can feel the attachment. Glen.

I flag down the waiter to pay the bill, but Cornelle's already taken care of it. We exchange business cards and shake hands. Outside, the mob of protestors has thinned. Cornelle hails me a cab and then disappears into the Paris underground.

I watch from the cab window, a plane flying overhead. I can tell from its trajectory, and the sweeping arc its flying, that it's just left the airport. Some of the passengers will be returning home. In a few days I will be one of them. Perhaps then I will know why I'm here.

thirty-three

FELIX AND I MEET AT Le Clown Bar, a "monument historique," which has been juggling cuisine since the time of steam trains, suffragettes and the Second Boer War. The colour palette is mustard and green, a touch of wine, all muted like an over-exposed photo, a circus tent left out too long in the sun. It has a vaudevillian charm and with my red nose, I fit right in.

Felix is seated at a corner table and stands when he sees me. I'm not sure what kind of greeting he expects. A hug? A handshake? La bise? The last time he saw me I was shackled to Glen, so perhaps he's expecting something radical. I could grab a knife from the table, throw it so it just misses his head and pierces the lithograph hanging behind him. Pull silk scarves from my mouth, a rabbit from my hat. Alas, I have no hat, nor rabbits, just the paper horse nickering in my purse.

As I approach, Felix comes around the table and reaches, cupping my face with an earnest grip and a look of such deep-seated longing that it makes me blush. It's the first time in my life I feel beheld, like I'm some kind of natural wonder, a masterpiece. I kiss him on the cheek and then glide into my seat. I'm a goddamn glacier.

A server approaches, haggard, as if he's just come from his day job shovelling coal into a furnace, and yet his recessed eyes and sad curls match the harlequin décor. He's lean as a tight-rope. He presents a wine menu, offers suggestions. Felix eyes me expectantly and I'm struck by the brazenness of this date. How it feels both like a first date and the date to end all dates. A date at the end of the world. The atmosphere is electric and I half-expect the forks to start levitating or for an elephant to stroll in wearing a fancy cap and a saddle.

We choose a Syrah.

"Claudia," Felix says before the waiter's even left the table, "I haven't stopped thinking about you. Not since the plane." He takes my hand. "Maybe even before that. I know I probably shouldn't have reached out given that . . ." He pauses, clears his throat. *Given, Glen,* I think.

I glance around the restaurant to see if anyone's listening. Felix isn't exactly whispering. The table of men beside us aren't paying attention, neither is the lone female diner with the grey dreadlocks nestled in the corner. The bartender, polishing a glass, is.

Felix fiddles with his place setting as though each piece is a thought he's trying to reorganize. "Even after I saw you hand-cuffed to your ex, which is totally fucked up by the way, I haven't stopped. In fact, if I'm being honest, that only made me think about you more. Because I saw it. I recognized my feelings for you. In Glen."

When I was eight years old, I astral-projected. I floated out of my body on a Tuesday night in the kind of high-necked night-gown preferred by Edwardian women and Ebenezer Scrooge. It's how I learned about consciousness before I knew about con-sciousness. It's how I feel now. Like my consciousness has been shot out of a canon and landed here in this three-ring circus. I haven't been on a proper date in years but I'm certain it's too early to be discussing feelings. We haven't even ordered. If this were a classic seven-course French meal, feelings should come around the four-and-a-half mark; between the main course and the salad. The wine hasn't even arrived to drink the feelings away.

Also, does he not see the awkwardness of comparing his heart to Glen's? Glen is a Leaver. And what to do about his passion? It's rising out of him, a tornadic waterspout spitting out of the Aegean Sea. Passion belongs to male figure skaters and renaissance painters. I need someone more concrete. A bricklayer or an engineer. A toll-booth operator. I need practical Cathy to tell me to get out now before Felix locks me in a wooden box and saws me in half.

I've left Felix hanging, like an unread snap, but the waiter's returned with the wine. He asks who will be sampling the Syrah and Felix gestures that it will be me. The waiter pours and I give the glass a little swirl before bringing it to my lips. Lovely. I nod, and the waiter pours. We order, and by the time the waiter's tucked the menus under his brilliant white shirt, I've forgotten my selections.

"I want you," Felix says.

This is very un-British of him. I'm expecting Hugh Grant in a Hugh Grant movie: self-deprecating, bumbling, nervous hands, a stutter. *Notting Hill* bullshit. And now the bartender is leaning in, and not under the guise of performing a task. He's full-on eavesdropping. My phone rings. I frantically dig through my purse, retrieve it, and switch off the ringer without even looking to see who's called, which I immediately regret. It could be an emergency. Maybe Wes has run off again or Joan's chained herself to a tree. Heaven forbid the Voltaren's been lost.

"Sorry," I say to Felix. "Could be my kids."

He gestures for me to take the call. He does not look the least bit offended, which is endearing. Most people without kids would find this interruption inappropriate, even in a clown bar. The missed call is from Wes. I fire off a quick text asking him if everything's okay. He wants money. Célestine has come to Disneyland and he'd like to buy her something. Correction: he'd like *me* to buy her something.

Ask your dad, I text back. *I'm in a meeting.*

He's on the Tea Cups with Joan.

Glen's there? Glen hates the Tea Cups. Glen hates tea. Roundabouts make him dizzy. And 3-D? Forget it.

How much?

Hundred bucks?

What the fuck is he planning to buy her? Mickey's index finger? I quickly EMT the money and apologise to Felix. I expect this is just the interruption we need to steer the conversation into a more pragmatic direction: hobbies, favourite movies, a smattering of stories from work or childhood, but before I can say anything, the bartender asks, "Do you want him too?" and instead of Felix or the dreadlocked-woman or anyone else in earshot condemning the bartender for his rudeness, the audacity of posing such a question, the whole restaurant falls silent and waits for my reply.

I gulp my wine and stare into Felix's eyes. I feel a spinning in my chest, like the oversized wheels of a bank vault. I very much wanted him on the plane. I slide my hand across the table and he takes hold of both my wrists. It's a bold and dominant grip, as if I'm dangling from a trapeze. And then, I ever so slightly dig the tips of my fingernails into his forearms.

"Well?" the bartender says, rimming a glass. "Do you?"

A fatherly thing my mother used to say: *you buy the ticket, you take the ride.* And here I am, strapped in. The elephant's already left the big top.

"I do," I say, shooting my wine. "I want."

Mussels in sake arrive and the mood shifts to something lighter, even though I can still see the faint indent of my fingernails on his right forearm. We talk about his work here in Paris, my attempts to memorialize my mother in the Catacombs and Versailles. I tell him about Émile and Mona and Célestine. As the courses progress, we dig deeper into each other, removing layer upon layer of face paint, costumes, masks.

I barely think about Glen. But I am thinking about Glen spinning in a teacup. We've been stuck on this ride for ten years.

"Why didn't you remarry?" I ask Felix as a magnificent tart au citron arrives with a razor-sharp lemon leaf garnish. He mentioned his divorce on the plane. He's been single longer than I have. Fifteen years.

"I couldn't have kids," Felix says. "That's why my marriage ended. I tried dating, but kids were what most women wanted back then. After that I poured myself into my work." He pours himself another glass of wine.

"That's it?"

"I was briefly engaged to a woman twenty years my senior, but she changed her mind. Picked up and bought a condo in Tucson instead." He forks the scorched surface of his crème brûlée and it shatters like puddle ice. "I kind of swore off relationships after that."

The bartender freezes, mid-pour. "Pourquoi?"

Yes, I think. *Pourquoi?*

Felix doesn't respond. At least not verbally. He just gives a melancholy shrug and dives into his dessert. My phone buzzes from my purse. I discreetly check my messages, concealing my screen beneath my napkin.

Joan: *are you almost done your meeting*

Soon, I reply. *Do you need something?*

Dad was asking.

I ignore this and wait for the message-in-progress.

Grandpa said we could go to the protest.

Felix pushes his plate aside. "Claudia, would you like to come back to my hotel?"

The dreadlocked women raises her brow. She's dressed like a cocky bird. I admire her.

"You should go," says the bartender.

"I have to get back to my kids," I say.

"You don't have to stay the night. In fact, you don't even have to come to my room. We can just continue our conversation in the hotel bar." He motions for the bill.

I don't offer to pay for half. I pretend for a minute it's 1902. He's more than welcome to fetch the bill, my coat, push me up against a wall and force his hand up my skirt, slip his fingers between my blouse buttons. I check the time. Still early. Disney's not shutting down for another hour.

"Why don't we walk and talk?"

He nods, slips a wad of bills from his wallet, tucks them into the billfold.

Outside the air has that dreamy autumn quality of new beginnings. We stroll toward Boulevard Voltaire until we reach a small city park with cobbles and gardens. The walkways are graffitied, the playground equipment tired. We sit on a bench.

"If you swore off relationships," I say, watching a sparrow hopscotch across a cement block, "why this?"

"Fate," he replies, his hands in anxious fists.

"That's dramatic."

"Completely," he agrees. "But what were the odds of you getting switched into the seat next to me on the plane?"

"Odd."

"Exactly."

"And so that's it?" I don't expect this kind of talk from a scientist, but then nothing about Felix has been predictable. I'm antsy and stand. I need to move. He follows and we continue down the pathway, streetlights and pigeons blinking around us. A skateboarder swerves by. Just outside the park, a woman laden down with a month's worth of groceries hobbles toward a bus stop.

I pause, note that we're standing across from the Bataclan Theatre. All of the romance bleeds away. A short gasp. Felix recognizes it too. The death. It's out there mingling with the stonework and the sidewalks. It lingers on the naked trees and cracked monuments. A sudden image of my mom's shaved head, her stitches red as fire alarms, slices into my mind's eye. And yet neither Felix nor I can look away.

The chatter of a squirrel interrupts my free-falling thoughts. I started out this morning at the "happiest place on Earth." I stand here now at the site of a terrorist attack, with a stranger with whom I feel an almost Godly connection. Is this what happens when you meet on a plane? Your relationship becomes unearthly? Spiritual? Supernatural? Unnatural? Is this why the origami is alive in my purse? Why my cell phone suddenly has no service?

Felix turns around, his back to the Bataclan. We stand like this for a minute, shoulder to shoulder, but facing opposite directions. I think of all the life cut short in that theatre. They were mostly kids, really, not much older than Harrison or Liam. Not much older than Wes. I feel the strangest desire to live in the moment. Like Rodney. Like Glen. To really *live*. For them, for Mom. There's terror in that, too.

I tilt my head towards Felix's ear. He smells like a magic trick. "Let's go back to your hotel," I whisper. When I pull away, I touch my face. My cheek is damp.

"Felix?" I say, now stepping back so we are face to face.

A tear drips from his face. He swallows. "I'm sick," he says.

"Sick?" I reply.

The streetlight flickers and I feel the teeth of a ghost saw touching down on my abdomen. Back and forth it goes, long rhythmic strokes, sawing me in half. Claudia, in pieces.

thirty-four

I WANT TO ÇO HOME. I don't want to live in the moment. I don't want sick people or Leavers. I want to be single for the rest of my life. Like Georgia. Like Cathy. No more husbands, or partners. No more dates. I'll surround myself with family and friends and coworkers and pets. I'll make lonely, wretched love to myself. Maybe I'll never have sex again. I could sell my clitoris on Kijiji: *excellent used condition, no longer need, best offer.*

I don't ask what kind of "sick." I know enough that it's not just a cold.

"You're an asshole," I say.

Felix abruptly stops fiddling with the sleeve he's been using to wipe his face. "You can't call a sick person an asshole."

"You can't go on dates with healthy people."

"I just did."

Tears gather behind my eyes like drops of lava as the wind picks up and begins whipping the trees and debris. Leaves and litter scatter. A bus pulls over and swallows the woman with the groceries.

"You can't love a sick man?" Felix shouts.

"Absolutely not."

Felix steps into me, as a leaf blows onto my face and catches on my lip. I try to spit it off, hiss the dirt from my tongue, but Felix plucks it away, releases it back into the wind where it loops and skitters. We watch. He's millimetres from my face.

His heart knocks against mine. I smell Syrah, brown sugar, dominance.

"You can't love a sick man," he says, teeth on my ear lobe, "but can you fuck one?"

Oh boy. This is . . . what is this? Can forty-somethings *fuck?* Can mothers? Can sick people? My mind blusters, flatlines. I imagine broken joints and stents and seizures and vomit. Gurneys, gauze, pins. But my body intervenes. *Give me your tired, your poor, your tumorous masses.* My body, it seems, is here for the sick. I drive into him, my tongue a dark web, and we kiss and kiss and kiss. It's crude and triumphant; an astronomer spying a black hole. A mathematical proof.

The origami horse bursts from my purse and gallops down the street. Felix and I pull away from each other. He fist pumps the air as if we'd just made the discovery of a lifetime and it's over now. We can go home. Our work here is done. He takes my hand, brings it to his mouth, kisses it over and over. Gratitude. My body twitches.

"I don't remember a kiss ever feeling that wonderful," he says. We pass a homeless woman, bent like a vowel over a cardboard sign. Felix removes a hundred euro from his wallet and drops it on her blanketed lap. Then we pass a weary couple with twins — triplets? Felix pats each child on the head in succession, a walking duck-duck-goose. The parents don't seem to notice, and the kids don't mind. Only the last one, the short one, turns around in search of meaning.

My body still wants his sick, but the moment's blown away. We're too old to be making out in a park. Too old for one-night stands.

Aren't we?

I don't know where we're going. We reach a huge intersection. Cars move like schools of fish, swerving, zooming. An ambulance honks, its sirens keening. A late-night tour group shuffles on a crosswalk into a headwind. I check the time on my phone. My family will be on its way home now. On the corner, an entrance to the underground. They may be beneath me right now, their bags stuffed with funnel cake and souvenirs. I wonder if Glen is with them.

"Claudia," Felix says, stopping in front of a military statue. "Thank you. I've been wanting to kiss you like that since the plane. It was even more than I imagined."

"Why didn't you tell me you were sick?"

"I wanted to, but I didn't think I'd see you again. I didn't think I'd have to." He starts walking. "Besides, you didn't tell me your ex was going to be in Paris."

"Neither did he."

I want to go back to Felix's room, ask him if he's dying and if so, how long he has to live. What does a man who knows he's going to die think about? I don't think my mother knew she was going to die when she had the stroke on the flight home from Cuba. There may have been a moment when she was recovering in hospital from the banana boat accident, but likely not on the blue carpeted floor of the airbus, where she was flanked by emergency lights, pretzel dust and the discarded shoes of squirmy passengers. When Dad hovered over her, did she see him? Did she wish he was Émile? Or was she thinking about her grandkids, the running toilet that needed fixing in the ensuite or the mole on her back that had recently changed colour?

Felix hails a cab. A bronze Peugeot slams on its brakes, performs a reckless U-turn, and pulls over, bumping the curb. Felix leans in the window, gives instructions to the driver that I can't hear. I freeze on the sidewalk.

"Will you come with me?" he asks.

I shift, uncomfortably. It'll be a matter of minutes before the texts start: *where r u? when r u coming home? how was your meeting?* Then the requests: *can I download a movie/have twenty bucks/ buy this game/eat these chips on the dresser/switch math classes.*

"Where?"

"I want to show you something."

"Is it far?"

He leans back through the cab window. The driver puffs out his lip, shakes his head no. Soca music plays from his stereo. He's a fan, or he's a long way from home. Like me.

"Twenty minutes," he says. "We could walk it, but . . ."

His voice trails. But he's sick.

Spirit Cathy hollers over my shoulder to just go home already, to my kids. So practical. So right. Imaginary Georgia makes popcorn, takes a seat, crosses her legs. "I don't have long," I say.

Felix looks me dead in the eyes. "Neither do I."

I climb into the back seat. The cab makes another u-turn and I feel the Clown Bar tilt-a-whirl in my stomach. Felix rests his hand on my knee. His hand doesn't look sick. It looks strong. I open my legs a whoreish inch, as the first text signals from my purse.

"Sorry," I mutter, cheeks flushed.

"All good." He plays with a lock of my hair and the intimacy of his fingertips grazing my neck is almost too much. I want to be both his nursemaid and his concubine. I want to gag on his fingers and also wrap them tenderly in a splint. I feel like the kind of man who whacks off during a Zoom meeting. I finally fish out my phone, doing my best to shield the screen.

How was your meeting?

Glen.

Good thanks, I type.

Felix places his hand back on my leg. Higher this time.

Mid-thigh. His pinkie dangles dangerously on the inside, a leg over a cliff.

I've arranged for Dan to watch the kids. Come meet me.

The next thing that arrives is a geotag, a dropped pin. All I can make out when I zoom in is a hat shop and a creperie.

Can't right now. On my way back. Felix's mouth is on the back of my neck. I like it there. The taxi turns onto a busy street. Protesters with placards are shaking street signs and climbing on statuary. I have no idea where we are. A square? I catch a glimpse of a sign being waved by an elderly man with a ponytail. *Le climat c'est comme la bière: c'est pas bon chaud!* I thought this was supposed to be happening tomorrow. The cabbie watches me from the rear-view mirror. "They are practicing," he confirms. "For tomorrow." Red and blue lights. He speeds up for a hundred metres, then peels off on a narrow one-way street.

I'll wait, Glen replies.

I stuff the phone back in my purse. Felix still has his hand on my leg but he's looking away from me now, out his window. He points to the moon. "Almost full," he says.

"And almost there," the cabbie adds.

I still don't know where "there" is. We pass gothic churches with pointy spires and complicated steeples, bustling cafés and balconied buildings. We may have crossed a few bridges. We could be driving in circles. We pass a woman, maybe a tourist or an expat, based on her hiking boots and cropped hair standing with a group of kids, finger-reading the menu outside a restaurant with a royal blue awning. Cue the guilt. I should be back at the hotel with Wes and Joan. I should be researching strategies for safe protest, checking in with the kids' teachers, Joan's soccer coach. She's done none of the hotel-friendly fitness drills her coach had suggested she do to stay in shape.

"Here," Felix says as the taxi comes to a halt. He pays in cash. *Here* is another park, not unlike the last. Cobbles, benches, and garden plots tucked behind fences and throngs of people. Unsurprising — it's Friday night. We stroll past leggy trees and squat tourists. I hear soundbites of German, opera, Tagalog, reggae. Laughter.

Felix slows to a stop. "Close your eyes," he says. I don't want to close my eyes. I want my safe, boring life back. The one I can see with my eyes closed: the two kids, the kitchen roosters, the kingless king bed. But I oblige because I bought the ticket and the ride isn't over.

I sense the buzz of oncoming pedestrian traffic. The graze of an elbow, the clip of a knapsack, a woman's loose hair. Jubilant voices, inflections, whispers. Somewhere, a baby cries.

"Okay," Felix says, halting me, his un-sick hands bearing down on my shoulders, his scent on my neck. "Open your eyes."

The Wall of I Love Yous. We're too far to read the tiles. From where we stand, behind the crowds, the words are indiscernible. An umlaut here, a serif there, a stroke of Cyrillic, but at the edge of the wall, something familiar. Someone.

Glen.

thirty-five

FELIX STANDS WITH HIS HANDS on his hips, chin cocked and chest proud, a realtor assessing the curb appeal of a new listing. "Would you look at that," he says, sizing up the wall. "It's much smaller than I imagined. What do you think?"

I think nothing because I'm crouching behind a garbage can, between a tiny black mouse with Swiss Army claws and a scrap of dessert crepe. I can't let Glen see me. I raise my head high enough to catch Felix's troubled face searching for me in the crowd. A child in a red windbreaker and rubber boots stares at me, bewildered, but also thrilled with the discovery. Seeing as he's been dragged to a wall that doesn't do anything, doesn't light up, doesn't change shape, warp, crumble or collapse, finding an adult hiding behind a garbage can, is something. I bring my finger to my lips. *Shhh.*

Felix calls my name, first as a question and then with the urgency of a parent who's lost his child in a Walcrotch parking lot. A few tourists look behind them, though most keep their gaze fixed on the glazed tiles. Except for Glen. I see him, still at the wall's edge, neck strained, brow furled.

"Hide-and-go-seek?"

The kid in the windbreaker won't leave. He squats beside me, a cat-squirrel, clinging to the garbage can's rim. I nod. Sure, hide-and-go-seek. This is why I've come to Paris. To simultaneously hide from and seek myself. Come to think of it, I've been playing this game my whole life.

I remove a tiny thorn from my fingertip. The boy slaps his hot dog fingers over his eyes and starts counting, loudly. "One, two, three . . ." Kid doesn't even know how to play.

I whisper, "You already found me."

"Six, seven, eight . . ."

I half-stand and bolt, breaking to the right. I find refuge behind an old tree further from the wall than the rubbish bin, but still too close to Felix, to Glen. My phone rings. Something from inside the crepe is smeared on my purse and gets on my arm. Jam? Sadness? I wipe it on my pants.

"Hello?"

Wes. "Why are you whispering?"

"I'm on the subway."

"Can we order a pizza?"

"Yes, gotta go." End call.

"Ready or not, here I come."

Fuck off.

Across from me, at the edge of the park, a man is pissing on a flower bed and a young couple is strolling toward me as if they've just come from a church picnic, gay and innocent. I pretend I'm out of shape and am using the tree to catch my breath, which is senseless, given that the wall doesn't require any physical exertion.

I steal a cautious glance behind me and there's Felix, hands cupped around his mouth, his back to the blue tiles, head tilted to the sky, a herald trumpeter. "Claudia," he hollers. *Fanfare for a Runaway Date.* And then it happens. Glen maneuvers himself through the crowd, dodging selfies and strollers, the boy in the windbreaker. He taps Felix on the shoulder.

A text chimes from my phone, which I'm clutching like it's a detonator.

Dan: *are you almost back?*

Ignore.

Have an upset stomach. Diarrhea. Want to go to bed.

I reply, *That sucks.*

Glen and Felix are talking. Do they recognize each other? It appears they do.

"Found you!"

I jump.

"See?" The kid says to a couple, presumably his parents, as he points. "Hide-and-go-seek."

They frown, take the child by the arm. The mother tightens her grip on the boy's sibling, who's strapped to her chest as if the Tree Pervert might come for her baby, too. I try to explain. "We were just playing."

The couple scowls, turns, hurries down the cobbles. A red balloon, tied to the father's wrist, bobs and jerks. The boy looks back, waving. I watch the balloon drag across the night sky until it pops.

Felix and Glen have agreed to split up. I contemplate climbing the tree, but it has the girth of a linebacker and barnacle bark. Get me out of this stupid park. A man, dressed as a train conductor, with a nose resembling a child's fist, pads by in prison boots. "The park ees closing een ten meenutes," he says.

I race to the far side of the yard, to what I guess is an exit. It's a locked gate. *Propriété Privée.*

A text from my father: *Dan has diarrhea.*

What does he expect me to do? Uber back to the hotel so I can wipe my brother's bum? Fuck.

I type: *thoughts and prayers.*

Claudia, Dad replies, *he needs Ginger-Ale!!!*

Then go down to the bar and get him some!!!

"Claudia!" My name, being sung by no less than three men: Glen, Felix and the park patroller.

Glen: *we know you're here.*

We.

Dad FaceTimes. I reluctantly answer. He's holding the screen so close to his face all I see is his great spotted forehead, and the tips of his brows, coarse and white as a wool sweater.

"Where are you?"

"I'm hiding."

"From whom?"

Mona's face appears in the screen. She's taken off her make-up and looks a bit like the garden crepe, enjoyed and discarded.

"Glen," I whisper.

"Why are you hiding from Glen? I thought you had a work meeting."

"I was on a date."

"Oohhh!" Mona squeals, clapping her meaty hands.

"You're dating a man from work?"

"No."

"Maybe Glen can get the ginger ale?"

I hang up, and slide my phone back in my purse. If I follow the park perimeter, I should find an alternate exit to the front gates, where Felix and Glen are now headed. What am I doing? Going on dates with sick men, abandoning my kids at hotels, having anything to do with Glen. My mother is gone and this is how I honour her. With a midlife crisis, subtitled in French. At my feet, a swatch of the red balloon. I pick it up. I'm nearly clear of the park when I sense a bold feminine presence: Mom. She does not guide me out, she hauls me back, toward the wall. I hear her voice, clear as a flight announcement: *This is why you came here.*

Because of Felix? I wonder. He's technically why I'm here.

He set this up. Set me up. And yet in a moment of shattering loneliness, I asked Glen also to bring me to the Wall of I Love Yous, and he obliged. He's here too. We're all here.

The wall is navy blue, the colour of veins and transatlantic crossings. Of moons and herons. Flames and forget-me-nots. The I-Love-Yous are white. I scan the blocks for a familiar language, but fail to recognize anything in the dim light, my eyes drawn to the seemingly random red shapes scattered across the enamel.

Above the wall is an unbecoming painting of a woman in a blue dress. A Hollywood dame, vampy and bitter. Beside her, an etching of another woman: faceless, vaguely shaped. A ghost.

Mom.

I touch the etching, the blackened lines and the words painted beneath it:

aimer c'est du désordre . . . alors aimons!

Love is disorder . . . and so we love.

A commotion outside the park gate. I see the outlines of Felix and Glen, the peak of the park patroller's hat, tourists moving away in droves, back to their Airbnbs, villas and hotels. A tiny swirl of wind startles me and yet I still feel my mother's warmth in the worn cobbles, the curbs, the drowsy flowers and the night birds. In the disorder.

thirty-six

I REACH THE EXIT with a ready-or-not-here-I-come gait just as Felix collapses. He hits the sidewalk half-pinning Glen who seems to have broken his fall, preventing Felix from smashing his head off the concrete or the shoes of passing pedestrians. The park patroller squats beside them, an old-school radio in his hand, jacket flapping in the breeze. A small crowd has gathered. A woman smoking a Marlboro offers Felix a bottle of water. He accepts, and Glen helps Felix take a few sips before he moves him into a recovery position.

Paramedics arrive and treat Felix on the sidewalk. They take his vitals, give him oxygen, juice. They move him to a bench. Within minutes, he is lively and talkative, dismissive of the attention. He waves people away. *All part of my condition,* he seems to say with the casualness of a man whose knee's just given out, and not of a man who's lost consciousness on a Paris boulevard.

I watch, frozen, from a bus stop fifteen feet away.

"Well, go to him," Glen says, lightly shoving me from behind. I didn't even see him coming. He was just there, mauling Felix, conversing with the EMTs or whatever you call them in France, and now he's here and I can smell them both, mostly Glen, but a touch of Felix, a cocktail of gym bag and shower sex.

"He's not mine," I protest, as if Felix is an item that's fallen out of a shopping bag looking to be reunited with its owner. Something embarrassing. Something unclaimable.

"You're the closest one here to a next of kin," Glen says, wearily brushing sidewalk debris from his sleeves. "Go see if he's alright."

"I barely know him. We just had din —"

"I could smell you on his neck, Claud. When I caught him." He spits, paces. "How could you have brought him here, to the goddamn wall, *the* wall, when you knew I was going to be here? Do you think this is all some sort of joke? That I came all this way to show you I can't live without you, and I'd all but given up until you texted." He angrily grabs his phone from his pocket, scrolls it like a madman. "Here. It says *I'd like you to take me to the wall.*" He shoves his phone in my face, hand trembling. "I was supposed to fly home today, but I stayed. I stayed because of this text, because you said you wanted me to take you here. Me," he shouts. "Not him."

A single text. The difference between hope and despair. Like a tiny piece of gold, a tooth, to the Lagina Brothers, to every Oak Island treasure hunter. A reason to keep digging, keep drilling. Order the caissons! Blow up the swamp! Money the money pit! Stay in Paris.

"But you *can* live without me," I calmly reply. "You can and you have. For ten years. And you even had the nerve to make it look easy, with your clean condo, and nice clothes, and your goddamn Jules Verne road trip. Do you have any idea what it's like trying to bring a man home when there's my father in the kitchen, salsa on the carpet, Sharpie on the coffee table and two a.m. nightmares?" I clear my throat, lower my voice. "And would this be different, Glen, if Kara could've had kids? With you? If you had been able to successfully build a second family, would you be here right now, trying to reclaim your first? You know what happens to those people who drop some used trinket off at Value Village and only realize later that it was valuable? They never get it back."

Glen rubs his face. "Did you fuck him?"

"Are you serious? That's what you want to know right now? A, that's messed up and B, that's none of your business." I peer at the bench where Felix is listening, recovering, hunched over a bottle of water, his camel-hair coat rumpled beside him. He pushes a lock of hair from his face.

"I would have liked her to," Felix says, shrugging.

We stare at him. Felix stands, pauses as if to check that his legs are still attached, and then swipes his coat up from the bench. A family with identical-looking boys of varying heights, swoops in and takes his place. The father distributes forks. In succession, the sons open takeout containers and begin to feast.

"Sorry to interrupt," Felix says, placing one hand on each of mine and Glen's shoulders. "I should get back to my hotel." He reaches for Glen's hand. "Thanks for catching me, back there," he says, gesturing behind him. "I have a big day tomorrow. Couldn't do it if I was concussed. Appreciate it."

Then Felix turns to me. "Thank you," he says. "Hadn't been on a date in years and as weird as this is right now, it was all worth it. You're worth it."

My phone rings. I let it go to voicemail. It rings again. "Would you excuse me for one minute?"

Dad shouts into the phone. "You brother's diarrhea's real bad. Did you find that ginger ale? We tried Sprite but it wasn't helping. It's the ginger that does the trick."

Click.

I mumble "sorry" and then Felix leans in, right in front of Glen, and kisses me ravenously on the mouth.

Glen watches.

"Sorry," Felix says, backing away. "I don't have ten years. Goodnight." And then he's gone. A few measured steps, a hand in the air, a black cab, taillights in September. All that's left is the disorder. A broken umbrella in a garbage can, a blue medical glove at the edge of a storm drain, faded constellations. Me and Glen.

The drugstore carries three brands of ginger ale. I buy them all, overpriced Imodium and an emergency travel pack of adult diapers. Glen calls an Uber. We cram in to the back of a Prius and ride to my hotel in silence, the bag of Depends quelling any possibility of romance or reconciliation. Of anything at all.

When the Uber pulls up to the hotel, I'm quick to exit. I can't handle any more phone calls or texts about diarrhea. Glen stays in the Prius and a jolt of disappointment roughs up my chest. I'm halfway through the lobby when I hear him: "Wait!"

I turn, keeping the pharmacy bag behind my back.

"Did you actually *see* the wall?" Glen asks.

"I saw it," I reply. "I mean for . . . a minute, I didn't study it or anything,"

"But you saw the red splashes on the tiles?"

I did, and they made no sense. I think of the shred of red balloon in my pocket.

"The splashes represent fragments of a broken heart," Glen says. "Gathered together, they form a full heart. That's why I wanted to take you to the wall."

I nod, step into the open elevator, press the floor number. The doors quake shut and I see my reflection in the brass. A lovely sentiment, I think, the red splashes. But it only works — you can only put something back together — if you have all the pieces.

thirty-seven

WHEN I ENTER MY HOTEL ROOM, all the kids are inside.

"What are you guys doing here?" I set down my pharmacy bag and fix my gaze on Emma, who's doing a handstand against the headboard of my bed, her feet inches away from a framed photograph of Mont-Saint-Michel.

"My dad destroyed our room," Liam says without looking up from his phone. I can see his screen in the mirror. He's trading again. Kid never stops. He's either going to be rich or Dan'll wake up one day to find his accounts drained and his house repossessed.

"My dad shit his pants," Emma says.

Bits of Disney clutter the room. Mouse ears, ticket stubs, glossy shopping bags, foil balloons.

"Emma, honey. You should not be using that type of language. You're ten. You're too young to swear. What happened to the little girl who was the first to volunteer to say grace at Thanksgiving? The girl who started a veterans' food drive last Christmas? You used to make cards for the garbage men and the crossing guards. Where's that nice little girl?"

Joan, gripping a thick black marker that she's somehow acquired, along with what appears to be several sheets of bulletin board, stops colouring. "Haven't you heard the expression *well-behaved women seldom make history?*"

"Yes, Joan, I've heard of that, but before you run off and put that on a T-shirt, you should know that quote has been taken out of context. What Laurel Thatcher was implying was that well-behaved women *should* be making history. Her intent was not to suggest that we all rebel and behave poorly to make it."

"What's this have to do with my dad shitting his pants?" Emma asks.

"Just stop swearing," Liam replies, setting his phone on the bedside table. He glances at the pharmacy bag. "Did you buy . . . diapers? Does my dad need diapers?"

"No," I reassure him. "It was a bit of a joke, though maybe . . ." Maybe Dad could use them. Or Felix. Fuck. I hope whatever sick he is, he doesn't need diapers. If I ever see him again. I want to see him again.

"That's kind of mean," Wes says. "The Depends."

"Well, I guess I won't be making history tonight."

Joan smooths the bulletin board with her hand and then holds it up. In English: REBUILD THIS CATHEDRAL! She's drawn the Earth and below it, a cartoon of Notre Dame. A fat red arrow points to the Earth. No doubt she copied it from something she's seen online, but still, it's clever.

"I will tomorrow," she says. "Make history." There's a flicker of darkness in her eyes, an unsettling confidence that both terrifies me and makes me proud.

"Just remember the proper context of that quote." I gather the bag. "It's a good protest sign," I say to Joan. To Liam and Emma, "I'm taking this stuff to your dad."

I'm halfway out the door when I think to grab my laptop.

"Take this," Liam says, tossing me a shirt.

"What for?"

"To wrap around your face."

I take the shirt to the bathroom. It smells like sweat and

Doritos. Who gets traveller's diarrhea in France? What next, cholera? I secure the tee over my mouth and nose, a coroner en route to an unreachable neighbourhood ten days after an earthquake. I slip out of the room and down the hall to Dan's, knock twice. An indiscernible grunt in response.

"It's me," I shout.

A groan and then the shuffling of feet. The lock clicks open. The air is green.

"Why didn't you put the fan on?"

"Broken," he mumbles stumbling back to bed. He curls into himself, a cooked shrimp, tucking a bolster pillow between his knees.

I want to suggest he ditch the bolster. Georgia cleaned rooms at the Chateau Lake Louise for a summer between degrees. People do all kinds of things to bolster pillows. She referred to them as crime-scene pillows.

"Was it something you ate?" I ask.

"Billy Bob's Country Western Saloon," he slurs.

Did he eat Billy? I open the first bottle of ginger ale. "Sit up a bit." He rolls onto his back and shimmies himself against the headboard. "Slow," I caution as soon as he starts gulping. "Want an Imodium?"

He shakes his head. "Diarrhea is the body's way of purging sickness."

"Also, your children." And any shred of dignity you still have after forty. "I'm not saying it'll cure you, but it might offer you some relief."

He relents, opens his palm. I pop two pills from the blister pack. He dry swallows, gags. I hand him another ginger ale and attempt to open the room's only window. Sealed shut. I climb into bed beside him where I can plug in my laptop. We catch each other up on the day's events and as I share the details of my meeting with Cornelle and my date with Felix, I realize I've put in a forty-eight-hour day.

"Harrison got his hair cut." Dan haphazardly throws his arm toward the bedside table to grab his phone, nearly tipping the ginger ale. He opens his messages, scrolls, turns the screen toward me. Harrison's cut a mullet. He looks a bit like Ricky from *Trailer Park Boys*. It definitely gives him a more masculine edge, and compliments his neck tattoo, but I still see Hannah in his cheeks, which are pink and round as candy apples, as Allison-Jean's.

"Mom's former lover was a lawyer. I went to his office."

Dan sits up taller. "You met him?"

"No. He's retired. I just wanted to see if anyone knew him."

"How'd you find him?"

"It was an accident, really. Or fate, if you want. Dad told me his last name and I looked him up. His office was across from the hotel where I was meeting Cornelle. Wanna see him?"

My brother crosses his arms over his chest. I field-kick the bolster pillow from the bed. It hits the window. I flip open my laptop and bring up Chalamet Avocats.

"There's our man," I say, tilting the screen toward my brother. His stomach makes a noise akin to a gravel truck crossing a bridge.

"Kinda looks like Mr. Bean," Dan says.

"A little," I agree. "But warm."

He nods.

"Dad gave Mom an ultimatum." I divulge my conversation with my father in the pool in detail. Line for line, lap for lap. Dan stares pensively at the ceiling the whole time I'm talking. "Isn't that disappointing?" I finish.

He points. "There's a spider on the ceiling."

There is. We watch it glide across the ceiling like a float plane.

Dan sighs. "Love usually is."

"Is what?"

"Disappointing. Look at us." He gestures toward our reflection in the framed slab mirror drilled into the wall. Dan is chalk-faced and rotting. My makeup's worn off and my nose has the high shine of a museum Cadillac. I have the scent of two men on my neck, which makes me feel simultaneously slutty and victorious, seventy-six unread emails in my inbox, a teen next door who never wants to leave Paris, and another who quite possibly wants to blow it up.

"I love two people." The words come out as a tiny squeak but they topple like a confession.

"That's okay," Dan says.

Is it, though? In theory, sure. But what about reality, where you have to make actual decisions about where you will sleep and what kind of mustard or brand of beer you'll buy, and who you'll invite to your boss's Christmas party. Invitations never ask for a "plus two."

Felix: *I don't have ten years.*

How many does he have?

"Here," my brother says, slipping the prayer hands from his chest pocket. "You need them now."

"I don't know what to pray."

"Just put 'em in your pocket." My brother turns on his side, flips off the bedside lamp. In minutes he's snoring. The spider's changed course and tiptoes across the ceiling toward the open closet. I glance back at Émile, still locked on my screen, his sincere eyes and finely-fitted shirt, the blur of book spines on the shelf behind him, the chestnut leather portfolio on his lap. And then I see it: the ring. The muted gold band, the ruby. A perfect match for my mother's.

thirty-eight

"THEY'RE THE SAME MAN," Georgia shouts over the Peloton instructor prophesying in her home studio. "That's why you can't choose."

The kids are at the pool, but I still cover the speaker and tuck underneath the comforter.

"If you pick Felix," Georgia continues through laboured breaths, "you're still picking Glen. You're hardwired for those kinds of men."

"What's that supposed to mean?" Am I hardwired for Leavers?

"Passionate ones. The kind that'll fly you to the moon and then leave you there."

I think of the red shards splattered across the wall of I Love Yous.

"I mean, come on, Claud," Georgia says. "Glen flew to Paris to surprise you and Felix wants you even though he saw you handcuffed to your ex. I'd tell you to go find someone placid, a librarian or a translator or a landscaper, but you'd never make it. You'd lose interest at the first hint of safety."

"That's not true."

"What about the guy you met in Calgary that time? What was his name? Clark? Earl?"

Oh my God, Carl. Hung like a grandfather clock. I haven't thought of his slippery forehead and mitten hands in years. I shiver.

"Wasn't he a tax accountant or something?"

A manatee. "That wasn't my fault."

"My point is, whoever you pick — which by the way, I think is ridiculous, the very idea of choosing, I mean honestly, who says you have to choose? I'd have 'em both — the result will be the same."

They'll both leave?

I hear the Peloton instructor imploring Georgia to go faster. It's the final sprint, the last day in Paris. Georgia exhales a strained *fuck you*. The spider from Dan's room is now in mine. It lingers in the corner with its bayonet legs.

"As for the job," Georgia says. "Negotiate. No one *needs* you to be anywhere. Unless you're guarding a prison or amputating a leg, you can probably work from home and just go to the office a few times a quarter. Think of all the side trips you can make to Paris."

"I'm never coming back here," I say. "Paris slits you open, then leaves you in the sun to bleed out."

"It's teaching you how to love," Georgia replies.

"Or grieve."

"Same thing." There's a moment of silence before she adds, "If you do end up choosing someone tonight, I want the details. All of them."

"I'm afraid I've already chosen the climate." I grab the remote from the bedside table and flick on the TV. "Joan wants to go to a protest. She's been planning all week. That's how we're spending our last night in Paris."

"When in France," Georgia sighs. "Be careful, though. I feel as though I've already seen it on the news."

I open the TV menu, turn subtitles on and watch a cooking show. The chef is mixing pine needles with hair gel. I flip to the news: Vladimir Putin, intubated man, and placards even though the protest doesn't start until seven, late if you ask me. I'm not sure of the purpose of an evening demonstration, but nothing is done in Paris without intention, from makeup to menus, poetry to punishment.

I land on *The Curse of Oak Island,* and feel a pang of homesickness. Nova Scotia, here, in Paris. I sit up in bed, and crank the volume. Rick and Marty have found a cribbing spike belonging to Jesus. They bag it and then bulldoze a tree. I imagine all the other things they could be doing right now besides treasure-hunting: making someone a cup of a tea, holding a grandchild and watching a squirrel tree-hop from their bay window, splinting a loved one's broken finger. The show's camera operator zooms in on the memorial commemorating the six men who died searching for the Oak Island treasure.

I think of Mona. *Life is a training accident.*

Maybe I don't have to choose. Not between Glen and Felix, not between my current job and the one in Rotterdam. Maybe there's a job in Newfoundland. A different career entirely. Another man. A completely different life.

A knock on the door. Mona's brought coffees and croissants from downstairs. A plate of eggs.

"Good morning," I say, clearing a spot where she can eat at the desk. It seems Joan's made enough protest signs for all of us. I replace the cap on a red marker. Mona shuffles over, sets down her plate, and then hauls from her handbag a full-size bottle of ketchup.

"You want some?" she asks, thwacking the glass bottle.

I shake my head, take a croissant.

"I wanted to talk to you without your dad around. He went to the pool. It's about your mother's ring. The one that went missing."

"I have it."

Mona drops her fork. "*You* have it?" She leans back in the chair, closing her eyes in relief. "Oh, thank God." She sputters her coffee. "Where'd you find it?"

"In your pantry."

Her eyes grow. "In the pantry," she repeats. "Of course. In the little Tupperware. I knew I'd seen it some place weird." She pauses. "And you took it?"

"I thought *you* took it."

"Well, I did, for a while. Your dad kept losing it. He'd take it out of the satchel, slide it on and off his pinkie. Leave it on the counter. A week after the wedding, I found it in his suit when I took it into the drycleaner. He thought he'd lost it at the church! I told him to put it somewhere secure. He wanted to give it you, here, but then he lost it again and I had to find a replacement." She dabs her face with a napkin and then begins rifling through her purse. "I bought this," she says, palming the imposter ring. "I know it's not an exact replica, but your dad's been just sick about it. I'm so relieved you have the real one."

"He wanted to give me her ring?"

Her voices drops to a whisper. "All those years, he'd thought he'd given it to your mom. The matching earrings, yes, but not the ring."

Typical of my father. To assume he'd given it to her. How perfectly inattentive. How predictable. "Émile," I say, remembering his portrait, the soft shape of his hand on the portfolio, his wistful smile.

"Yes!" Mona shovels back the remainder of her eggs and then moves onto a croissant. On the TV, an excavator creeps across the narrow causeway connecting Oak Island to the mainland. A team of decrepit men with crushed dreams and hardhats watch and wait.

My voice cracks. "I don't think my dad really knew my mom."

"It's possible," Mona agrees. "I mean . . . I've read the emails, but he loved her, Claudia. I see it in his eyes when Stompin' Tom comes on the radio or when I pull the snap peas from the garden, or polish with Pledge. But Émile loved her too." Mona sets her plate aside and pats my knee as if to indicate the conversation is over.

"It's kinda sad."

"Or romantic," she counters. "That's the sober joy of marriage. Of life in general, really. It's not the choices you make that cause life to be rich and tedious. It's the ones you *didn't* make. It's all the possibilities and options you rejected. Every decision you ever made *for* something was also a decision *against* something. Or someone."

"Then how do you reverse that? How do you make better choices so you don't end up dead on an airplane, or alone like Émile?"

"Or alone like you," Mona says, tapping my shoulder. "All you can do is accept your own finitude."

Finitude. Not a word I expect to hear from Mona. Not now, coming out of her orange lips. Not when she's dressed in a Minnie Mouse sweatshirt and leopard print leggings with a Jenga stack of bangles on her wrist. I want her to talk *Wheel of Fortune,* sales on boxed wine and Beach Boys reunion shows. I don't want her talking about my *finitude.*

"We're all on borrowed time, Claudia. When you reach my age you realize there'll never be enough of it. The reality is, there never was."

I wonder if this is the point in the sermon where she tells me I should start getting up at four to be more productive, have my groceries delivered, or switch to audiobooks so I can learn about time management while also commuting to work or climbing the Stairmaster.

"So?" I ask, unable to hide the exasperation in my voice. I'm a single mom. Of course I know about time and there never being enough. Why does she think I still have a rooster border in my kitchen or the donation box I filled last year still in my hallway? The fuck does this have to do with my mom staying married to my dad?

"So, use your time wisely."

"That sounds reckless," I reply.

She shakes her head. "Reckless is living like you're entitled to tomorrow. Reckless is thinking you'd someday get to Paris, and getting runover by a banana boat instead. We all know we're going to die, and yet we act like immortals. Finitude," she repeats. "That's the key." Mona stands, leaves her egg plate behind, and heads for the door. "Now what in the hell does one wear to a protest?"

My head is reeling. "Something comfortable?" I suggest. "I imagine we'll be on our feet for a long time."

"And sneakers in case we have to run from the police."

I stare at her.

"I'm just saying. We should prepare for anything."

She backs out the door. I glare at her stained plate, the sad men of Oak Island. I open the hotel room safe, pluck Mom's ring from the corner, slip it on and message Felix: *meet me somewhere?* He begins messaging back immediately and I focus on the ellipsis, waiting, waiting. Nothing.

Instead, a message from Glen. *I'm coming to the protest.*

I want him at the protest. I want him there as Joan's father, whether to give her money or to reason with her, or to convince her when it's time to leave or where to stand, or when to resist. I text him a thumbs up. Someone's at the door. Mona, back to retrieve her plate, or her bottle of ketchup, which is sitting atop one of Joan's posters.

"I'm coming," I holler, screwing the lid back on the ketchup. I open the door.

Felix.

thirty-nine

"HI" IS ALL I CAN MUSTER. I'm barefoot, still in pajamas and clutching the ketchup bottle with an alcoholic's grip, and yet I feel I might levitate, my heart is a helium balloon.

Felix wears jogging pants and an overcoat. His hair is wild, and the collar of his pink T-shirt is ratty and stretched. There are beads of rain on his shoulder. "I had to see you," he says, stepping into the room. He holds my face, kisses my cheeks, my neck, my mouth, but it's the hug that does me in. The quiet desperation of it, the longing. The kind you see at airports and liberation parades.

He whispers, "Come with me."

I set the ketchup on the bathroom sink and tell him I'll meet him in the lobby. The kids could be back any minute and they don't need to see Felix lingering at the door. He heads for the stairs.

I change, brush my teeth, leave a note for Wes and Joan saying I'm going for a run, which is what I'm dressed for. I pass by the pool on my way down to the lobby. Everyone is there and a ripple of nostalgia passes through me. Swimming pools are sanctuaries. I've sought their alchemy from the time Wes and Joan were big enough for bathing suits, and plump enough not to turn hypothermic. We've swum to celebrate: birthdays, hat tricks, Saturday nights. We've swum to forget. You can blame anything on chlorine, especially tears.

The lobby is crowded with check-outs. Felix sits in a club chair, flipping through a magazine, but stands when he sees me coming. "Do you care where we go?" he asks, taking my hand. I don't. I will go anywhere with him right now. Walcrotch, Jupiter, jail.

We step into the drizzle and Felix hails a cab to the neighbourhood of Montparnasse. We stop in front of a cemetery on a quiet, tree-lined residential street. He pays the toll in cash. "I bet Glen's never taken you to a cemetery before." He winks, and I remember just weeks ago standing with Glen in front of Mom's headstone after Dad's wedding. The exchange had been awkward, my first inkling that Glen was interested in . . . however you want to call it. A re-coupling? A salvage operation? But we'd been to other cemeteries before we had kids, mulling over the graves of Titanic and Halifax Explosion victims. We were young then, naïve about our own mortality, our *finitude*. Those tombstones could have been marking the unlived or benign: an ox shoe, a wizard's wand, a bus pass. I never thought about death there or about the dead, their unrequited dreams or missed milestones. I thought about life. My own.

"I've always wanted to come here," Felix says. He charges through the gate and down a pathway, periodically stopping to read the inscription on a mausoleum, or to run his hand along the mossy exterior of a tilted headstone. "So many artists and philosophers." He gazes up at the sky, where a single band of sunlight pulses through a fissure in the clouds. "My favourite graves to visit."

He rushes through rows of plots, zig-zagging from stone to stone — Egyptian, Renaissance, Gothic, Art Nouveau — pausing to catch his bearings, catch his breath. Who is he looking for? I pass a centenarian's grave, then a terrorist attack victim's. In the distance, a caretaker rakes a grassy mound at the edge of the cemetery.

Finally, Felix stops. *Jean Paul Sartre* and *Simone de Beauvoir*. Together. Their headstone is festooned with lipstick prints, Metro tickets and wilted flowers. Private messages are rock-pinned to the grave's base. I don't read them but note that at least one is written in Arabic, another in Dutch. Felix crouches, runs his fingers over the grave's sandstone surface.

"It's the philosophers who truly rest in peace," he says, "because they lived in turmoil. I find that comforting."

I find it depressing. Philosophers are assholes. They make it their life's work to ruin everyone else's life by constantly searching for meaning, questioning the status quo, telling the truth. They live in turmoil because through it all, they learn there is no meaning. The rest of us already know that. It's why we shop at Winners, pretend to like chickpeas, and share Facebook posts of blind and jittery baby animals or elephants playing soccer. Why we take pictures of our salads or our biceps, or our sad, desperate faces, and hashtag them with apologies. I'm pretty sure it was Sartre who said, "I exist, that is all, and I find it nauseating."

Felix pulls a small, fortune cookie–sized slip of paper from his pocket. I can't make out what he's written, but I help him find a stone to anchor it to the grave and then I wander over to a bench. When Felix has finished his pilgrimage, he joins me.

"What's wrong with you?" I ask. The question doesn't come out how I want. It sounds vague and almost accusatory, as if the wrong I'm assigning is this cemetery visit, not whatever illness has him leaving notes for dead philosophers.

"I have a heart condition," he replies.

So do I.

"And it's terminal?" Haven't they solved all heart conditions now? Aren't there stents and pacemakers and pigs for that? Has Elon Musk not figured this out?

"I have less than a year."

Less than a year? A surge of panic. It's such a cruel estimate. Less than a year can mean three hundred and sixty days or three, another birthday or another Tuesday. It can be months; it can be minutes.

"And there's no cure? No experimental treatment?" Joe Rogan probably has one. Or Diane on Twitter. Maybe the cure is buried on Oak Island. Maybe if he just ate more broccoli or shared a meme about body positivity, he'd feel better.

"We've tried." I picture his "we". His team of doctors, surgeons, specialists, counsellors. His eyes are glassy. "You know, I've made peace with my diagnosis. Every time I travel, I come to places like this. Places where people suffered much more violent deaths. Beheadings, tramplings, falls from buildings. At least I *know* I'm going to die. I can prepare for it."

I think of my mom. Of all that was unsaid or undone because she didn't know when she boarded that plane home from Cuba, that she would never touch down. She would never again pick up her grandchild, phone a friend, make love, spread butter on a muffin, feel the rain. But maybe it's easier that way. I can't imagine preparing for my own death. I'd overthink the invitations and the theme as if it were a child's party.

"And now I don't want to die."

I touch his knee. A sparrow flutters in the foliage. "I'm going to the protest tonight."

"A big one," Felix replies. "We've been talking about it all week."

"You're going?"

"Of course."

We sit in silence. I resist the temptation to fill the space with empty words. I listen instead to his breathing and study his chest, imagine his faulty heart, what it looks like. A gelatinous anemic jellyfish or an overripe avocado? Grenade? Or sandcastle? I imagine going down on him. I imagine shooting him up with morphine. I imagine marrying him. I imagine visiting his grave, leaving him a message anchored beneath a stone. Less than a year. Do I have room in my heart for more grief?

He rests his head on my shoulder like an old friend, and for a moment I believe this is how it'll end, in nauseating melancholy, in nothing, but then he works his way from my shoulder up my neck, to my ear lobe. I feel the tip of his tongue, his hot breath, his mortality in my ear, his finitude on my cheek, and it's so overwhelmingly desirable that I gasp.

He seizes the moment, jolting up from the bench, grabbing my hand. We race to the exit. We make out in the back seat of the taxi like teenagers, hands fumbling, bodies shivering. I apologize to the cab driver, a simple *désolé*. For my sexuality, my age, my humanity. We pull up to a hotel, grander than mine, not as grand as Glen's.

Glen. Fuck.

We take the stairs, it's only three flights. Is he struggling? Am I going to kill him? It takes several passes of his key-card to get inside his room. His tidy, small room, with polished shoes lining the wall, a desk covered in papers, and an oxygen tank. A pharmacy is on the bedside table. A tube sock, white and furled and feeble, sits idle on the red carpet and somehow it makes me want to cry. I will remember this sock forever.

He climbs onto the bed, pulls me on top of him. I can barely stand the intimacy, the spark, the want in his eyes, his grip on my hips, unyielding. I kiss him, memorize his tongue. He is all over me, pressing, cupping, mouthing. I reach into his pants and pull on him. He is hard and beautiful. I come just from holding him. So does he, recklessly, on my collarbone, my shirt cuff, my cheek. I can feel the tears well, a cocktail of shame and relief, hope and despair. I close my eyes, note the softness of his arm against mine, his end on my upper lip. After a few minutes, I sense him get up. He returns with a warm wash cloth and I wipe him away.

I fix my shirt, sit up, feel the hardness of the bed's headboard against my confused spine. He puts on glasses I've never seen him wear and recites climate statistics like poetry. He will go to the protest with fellow oceanographers. He will clap and chant and cheer. I will look for him.

He goes to the mini fridge and prepares an ad hoc picnic. Pastries, pistachios, Jujubes, pastel M&Ms. Sparkling water. I ask what he knows about Rotterdam. He asks what it's like to be a mom, and it catches me off guard — this interest in the familial — and I tell him stories. About Wes and Célestine, how to get rid of head lice, the horror of loving and, at times, barely being able to stand my children. I explain indoor shoes, soccer evaluations, parent-teacher interviews, movie nights and loneliness.

' "We're leaving tomorrow afternoon," I say, choosing a fat orange Jujube from a paper plate. "In fact, I should really go soon and pack. We're doing one last family dinner before the protest. When are you flying home?"

"I'm not flying back to Nova Scotia," he says. He reaches for one of the pill bottles on the bedside table, swallows two tablets and then reaches for another bottle.

"Where are you going?"

"Switzerland."

"Switzerland," I reply, trying with my tongue to pluck away the bits of Jujube cemented to my back molars. "Another conference? Vacation? Ski trip?"

He shakes his head, opens his mouth, and then closes it as he watches me figure it out. The answer sits in the scattered pill bottles and in his trembling hands. It's still on my cheek and on my shirt and probably on the note he left on Jean Paul Sartre's headstone. The end.

forty

JOAN LOOKS STUNNING. She wears the bougie store dress I got stuck in, lip gloss, mascara. She's styled her hair in serious braids, the way she does for a playoff game or final exam. The bartender has reluctantly agreed to stash Joan's protest signs behind the bar. He's old and has frown lines deep as gutters, but seems taken by her enthusiasm.

I sit between Glen and Dad. Dad is dressed in head-to-toe black, Glen, sharp and comfortable: old concert T-shirt, blazer, expensive jeans, Lacoste sneakers. He's not here for the climate, or for Joan. He's here for me, and I can't look him in the eye because I'm still wearing the shirt from this morning with Felix on the cuff. I dried it with a hairdryer and covered it with a cardigan.

A thin-faced conquistador plunks crusty loaves of bread at either end of the table. Mona's the first to break off a piece and slather it with butter and a sprinkling of sea salt. Emma complains that the bread is spicy, so Dan orders her a fancy mocktail chockful of cherries, orange wedges and umbrellas.

"How come you're wearing a tux?" I ask, only now noticing my brother's burgundy velvet jacket, crumpled shirt and his black bowtie, stiff as drywall.

"The boys took me shopping," Dan says.

"Isn't it great?" Liam slurps his beer. He's also dressed up, a baby oligarch about to take on the Vegas strip. Wes too, dressed for prom. Célestine will be protesting with her family. Wes plans to join them. Only Mona has taken my advice to dress comfortably. She wears a black Costco leisure suit, flamingo earrings, Sketchers, and massive sunglasses. She's ordered two bottles of wine for the table, a Chenin Blanc and a Côte Rôtie. I start with the red.

The appetizers arrive: canapés, escargots Bourguignonne, Bouchées à la Reine, blood sausage paired with apples, salade Lyonnaise, mussels. Dad clears his throat. He wraps his hand around the bowl of his wine glass, nearly dragging his elbow in pate, and lifts it from the table for a toast. I feel a trickle of guilt. I was supposed to do the final tribute. This trip was mostly my idea, derived from my own need to get some closure and simultaneously to honour Mom's unrequited Paris dreams. But I've prepared nothing. No speech, no notes. I think only of myself and Felix's death wish and Glen's persistence and the mini love grenades that detonate every time a memory is triggered: rumpled sheets, confessions, a shared laugh, a bare flank. I twist her ring on my finger in frenetic apology.

Dad attempts to stand, but his legs catch under the table. The dining chairs are heavy and don't slide in and out easily. As he falls back into his seat, a little crumple of wrapper tumbles from his pocket and lands on the floor. I pick it up.

"Why don't you just say what you're going to say from here," I suggest, resting my hand on his back while trying not to be patronizing. "We can all hear you." It's true because we've been seated in a corner, almost a separate room. Either it's Mona's plastic earrings or the fact that Emma has brought a three-foot stuffie with her to dinner. Or maybe they know I have half a handcuff and Felix's sock in my purse. I remind myself to deal with these items in the morning before we go through airport security.

"I'd like to propose a toast —" Dad interrupts himself to sip from his water glass. I play with the little ball of garbage on my lap, tugging at its edges, waiting for him to get on with it. It's not often I get off on a salad, but the one in front me looks divine and I'm starving.

"To Mother Earth," my father says, eyes misty.

Wait, what? I look at Dan. He shrugs, clinks his glass to Joan's, and repeats the phrase. "To Mother Earth." I clink glasses with the giant stuffie and throw back my entire glass of wine in one greedy gulp, a goddamned pelican. Does he mean Mother Earth as in the *planet*? Or is this a posthumous nickname he's given Mom because she liked gardening?

Dad raises his drink, as if he might dump it over his head. I pour another glass of wine, to the rim, emptying the bottle. Glen watches my father with abject fascination the way one might revere a gorilla with a kazoo in its hands. "Oh, Mother Earth," he says, more of a lament than a statement. "We've done horrible things to you." Is he swaying? "We've hurt you, abused you, cut your forests, poisoned your rivers, raped you."

"Assaulted you," I interject, burying my face and gesturing toward Emma. But it doesn't help because Dad's eyes are still closed. "We get it," I continue. "We've done terrible things to the earth, but let's move on with it so we can make it to the next course and get to the protest."

"I just feel so responsible," Dad continues.

Mona nods in agreement, smuggles a half-loaf of bread into her handbag.

"We're all responsible," Glen says, resting a hand on my thigh. "It will take hard work to fix."

"I think that's brave, Grandpa," Joan says. "To admit your responsibility. After all, it is your generation's fault."

"Joan —"

"No," Dad interrupts. "She's right. We made most of the mess and even when we started to hear the warning signs, we ignored them." A tear trickles down his face.

"Yeah," Dan says, oblivious. "Didn't your company dump a ton of toxic waste into a lake?"

"No." Dad shakes his head.

Joan blows out a sigh of relief. I do the same.

"It was a river."

For fuck's sakes.

The waiter appears annoyed that he's been stuck with our table, but perhaps also hopeful we'll leave a fat Canadian tip. "How ees every-sing so far?"

I can't answer. I haven't touched my salad, and my father's having a breakdown. Emma uses the stuffie as the table spokesperson. "Three out of five stars," she replies. The server ignores her.

"Can I go meet Célestine now?" Wes asks.

"You haven't eaten," I reply.

"I had some bread."

"You ordered a steak. Who's going to eat that if you leave now? No. You can meet her afterwards, when one of us can get you there safe."

Wes looks to Glen, Glen glances at me. "No," he agrees. "After."

Wes mumbles something about "not being a baby."

I stab my lettuce. "This protest is a serious thing," I say. "So let's get out there and participate. Grandma never got to see the climate change movement. She wasn't around to hear Greta Thunberg speak, or to see the first Tesla. She never even got to use a reusable shopping bag. I agree with Joan. Grandma cared about the environment. She never wasted food, we walked whenever we could, and she recycled everything from wrapping paper to yogurt containers, so let's just enjoy our last night in Paris, as a family, go to the protest, and then get some sleep. Tomorrow's going to be a long day." I dab dressing from my chin, knocking the paper garbage ball from my lap with my napkin. I bend to retrieve it, placing my face dangerously close to Glen's lap. I reset my napkin, unravel the wrapper. I smell the watermelon before I read the label. It's a friggin' cannabis gummy. Dad's high. I look across at Mona, who is sawing through the crust of her French onion soup with a steak knife.

Glen leans into my ear. "As a family," he whispers.

forty-one

WE'VE MISSED THE BEGINNING of the climate march from Paris's opera district and take the Metro straight to the end destination, la Place de la République. The subway car is crowded with protestors, weary Saturday shift workers, and tourists. One protestor is dressed as the Grim Reaper and Emma watches him closely as if unsure if she should flee for her life or ask to borrow his cardboard scythe. I imagine for a moment that he is real and here for Felix.

Dad naps on the train, head on his chest like a newborn and Mona fixes her hair beside him with a plastic pick. The rest of us test the group chat and hammer out the details of a family plan in the event we get separated. Glen is tasked with making sure Wes is safely delivered to Célestine and her family, where he'll get an hour with them before he's to return to us. Dan is assigned Emma, Dad and Mona. I get Joan and Liam, who's become his cousin's right-hand man in protest.

When we stumble up from the underground, a crowd is singing "La Marseillaise" in a cacophony of voices: gravelly men, maestros, boys, baritone ladies. The sun's beginning to recede and hundreds cradle candles. The statue of Marianne, the "personification of Paris" at the centre of the square, is cast in hazy blue light. French flags compete with signs and banners varying in sophistication, from laser-printed placards to hand-painted bedsheets. A man in a New England Patriots jersey licks a soft-serve and observes with curiosity as if unsure what's being protested. Glen and Wes negotiate their way through the masses toward the Célestine meeting point. I watch until they're blurs.

In every direction, I search for Felix, but there have to be twenty thousand people here. The mood is somewhere between hope and despair. Some protestors weep and I can't tell if their tears are real or performance. Others shout angrily at anyone who will listen. Parents hold signs that claim "ce n'est pas trop tard." A lone vagrant bangs a hand drum and begs for money.

An organizer with a red megaphone shouts a proclamation, rousing the crowd. Her French is muffled and I don't understand what she's saying. People respond with applause. Dad and Mona have found a tree to lean on. Mona checks her safety-vest-orange lipstick in the tiny seashell-shaped compact and I'm struck again by Mona's . . . Mona-ness. My father's wife. I try to imagine Dad giving my mom an ultimatum. Where and how did he say *it's me or Émile?* In "winning" did he not calculate that he was also losing? A marriage of conformity. I observe the couples around me. Couples that look alike. Couples that look like they had a fight last night and were up until two in the morning hating themselves and each other. Couples who look like they still make love on a sun-streaked bed in the middle of the afternoon.

All marriage involves loss.

"This is wild," Dan says, careful not to lean too close to my ear so that Emma doesn't tip from where she's balancing on his shoulders. "I've never been to a protest before. Can you hold this?" He hands me Emma's stuffie, which I reluctantly accept and pin under my armpit.

Of course Dan's never been to a protest. He started attending the Pride parade when Hannah first came out as gay, and continued when he came out as trans, but those had been in celebration of and not in protest against. The crowd suddenly roars and Dan joins them, fist pumped and whistle sharp.

I temporarily lose Joan and Liam, igniting a spark of panic. How far could they have gone? On tiptoes, I search. They resurface above the crowd. I can't tell what they're standing on — a statue? A bench? — whatever it is must be stable because their upper bodies move with confidence and conviction. The youth are here in droves.

I join my dad by the tree. "Those gummies," I shout over the noise. "You didn't buy them here."

"Smuggled them in," he replies, a mischievous smile on his face. "With my diabetic candy."

"You could've been arrested. They have tracking dogs."

He shrugs and then whistles in response to some sort of climate prompt.

"Well, I hope you don't have any left because you can't take them back."

"They help my knees."

Glen texts: *where are u?*

I describe the tree, the stilt walker teetering beside it, the bald woman with the three German Shepherds on blue leashes. In a few minutes Glen's by my side. He pulls a flask from inside his jacket, downs a hearty a swig and passes it to me.

"What is it?" I ask, sniffing the opening.

"French whiskey."

I take a shot and hand it back. It burns and soothes. Like a marriage. A troupe plays homemade instruments. Back and forth with the flask until I feel warm, a tea light in my chest. I read the signs: *sauvons la terre! La terre est en danger!* Macabre artwork. *There is no Planet B.*

No plan B either. Glen was my plan. A man in a wheelchair is attempting to pass. I don't see him right away, my vision skewed by a mock funeral procession also moving in this direction. Glen grabs my wrist and tugs me to the side. I appreciate his grip. I drop Emma's stuffie and one of the pallbearers steps on it. Fuck. Now it has a footprint on its neck. I don't even know what "it" is. Probably a video game character. I brush the dirt from its green fur. The wheelchair jitters by and Glen hands me the flask. I have no plans.

A news crew moves through the crowd. I try to hide the stuffie behind my back. The last thing I need is to make the front page of the French paper clutching a large plush creature of indiscernible breed.

"We should move closer to Joan," I suggest.

Glen nods and we push our way forward. Protestors cling to lampposts. We pass an elderly couple in black tie, arms linked and chests proud, steps: synchronized. We get close enough to see that Joan and Liam are standing on a bench. A news crew films them. Joan doesn't even seem aware. Her arms stretched overhead holding one of her signs, her mouth wide open, shouting, a right Joan of Arc. Liam, on the other hand, is filming himself being filmed. I can't see Dan. I send a text to the group chat: *everyone ok?*

Mona sends a photo of Dad posing with a Grim Reaper, a different one from the train. This one is seven feet tall and masked, hopefully not here for Dad. The crowd surges as police in riot gear advances through. They move with authority, a precaution. A good thing.

I go to respond to the group text, but notice something odd in the background of Mona's picture. Figures dressed in black, in fatigues. I want to show Glen, but as I'm motioning for him to look, a text arrives from Felix: *I want to taste you.* My face flares and I shove the phone in my back pocket.

"What?" Glen asks, expectantly.

"Nothing."

He presses something into my palm, a small silk sack. I whittle my finger through the cinched opening and dump the contents into my hand. It's a heart. Not the smooth polished hearts you'd find in a gem store or washed up on the beach or punctuating a text, but a tiny anatomical one with valves and ventricles and veins. It's intricate, mixed metal and miniature glass. Fine art.

"I bought it after seeing the Wall of I Love Yous," Glen says. "At this little shop on the Champs."

The splashes represent fragments of a broken heart. Gathered together, they form a full heart.

I stare at the piece, observe the detail of each miniscule glass vein, the silver aorta, the gold vena cava, every fragment fused or soldered together. Fixed. I look up at Glen, his expression hopeful, alert. I believe him. The reconstructive possibility of an *us,* because Georgia's right: I'm still in love with him. A fact, perhaps cruel, perhaps foolish, probably regrettable, but a fact nonetheless.

I think of the books Joan used to collect. *5000 Awesome Facts (About Everything!).* My father would read them to her at bedtime after they'd both had a snack and she'd recite what she could remember the next morning at breakfast: *an avalanche can travel 80 miles an hour, the first candy canes were made without stripes. The heart can continue beating even when it's disconnected from the body.*

I can't stop loving Glen and yet when I study the little mechanical heart, I imagine not that it's mine, or his, but Felix's: fixed and whole and healed. I feel him suddenly, Felix. The weight of his chest on my rib cage, his frantic mouth and gentle gaze. I search for him in the crowd.

"Auntie Claudia!" A shriek behind me. "Why is Bobo on the ground?"

Shit. I tuck the heart back in its delicate sack, and pick up the giant stuffie.

"He's dirty!" Emma shouts, batting debris from its fur.

I ignore her, take a pull from Glen's flask and perform a headcount. Joan and Liam are still standing on the bench not ten feet from us. Joan shouts climate phrases, alternating between French and English. Liam continues to film, holding his phone in the air and slowly turning three hundred and sixty degrees. Dan's gotten himself a drink, an Italian soda, and he slurps it obnoxiously.

"Where are Dad and Mona?" I ask, noting they're no longer hanging off the tree behind us.

Dan shakes his head. "I wasn't looking. You were in charge of them."

How far could they have gone, high and practically immobile?

Another crowd surge, out of nowhere. Dan's Italian soda lands on my foot. I kick it away. By the time I find my balance, Glen is gone. "Find Wes," I holler, hoping he can hear me, but there's too much noise. Chatter, bongos, electronic music, tear gas. I swim through the crowd toward the bench, toward Joan, but the protestors have been replaced by riot police.

"Yellow vests," someone says, though the only vests I make out are bullet-proof, or in the case of the well-dressed man face-down on the pavement, fur.

"Joan!" I shout.

I can't see her, but I'm certain the hand jutting up from the crowd and filming the chaos ahead belongs to Liam.

"Meeting spot!" I yell, circling, elbowing people out of my way. Where is the meeting spot? The buildings surrounding the square all look the same. *Just look for the golden arches*, we'd collectively told the kids, like the predictable, disappointing tourists we are.

Breaking glass. I cover my ears and duck as a bottle sails over my head. People run. I'm caught in a horde, one that moves like a landslide in a single preordained direction. I submit out of fear that any protest will get me trampled. I pretend I'm in a mosh pit in 1992, safe, alive, but instead of moving away from the square, the horde moves toward the statue, the centrepiece, the stage. My feet barely touch the ground.

Someone sets off a flare, and in the ensuing panic, the horde disperses. A police officer grabs my arm and shoves me in a direction he presumes, I hope, to be safe. At the end of the square something is burning, a trash can or an Uber. It's hard to tell if it's an act of terrorism or performance art. Sirens howl, families flee and under a red and white awning, Wes and Célestine kiss like end times.

I make my way toward them, past a sobbing woman shielding a baby stroller, a dog devouring a relinquished kebab.

"Wes!" I call. "Wes!"

A fire truck blocks my passage to the café where he and Célestine are making out. I haul my phone from my pocket with trembling hands: *where is everyone??* I text.

Dan is the first to reply. *McDonald's.*

Who's there?

Me, Emma, Liam.

No Glen, no Dad, no Mona. No Joan.

My legs start to give. I grab a light post for stability, wait for the fire truck to pass so I can cross toward the golden arches, but a scuffle erupts to my left. Too close. I bolt across the thinning square, past hooligans and citizens, reporters and cops and that's when I see them. Dad and Joan hurling bricks through a shop window.

forty-two

A CLIMATE PROTEST and there's garbage everywhere. Discarded placards, plastic cups, a single dreadlock. Police carry away a protester who resembles my mother: demure and cooperative and practically dressed. She's stretched between two cops like a hammock, a tennis shoe print on her cheek. I watch her exit. The sway of her body, the way her tailbone grazes the cobbles sweeping away cigarette butts and parched leaves. I imagine my mother being carried this way off the plane, up the narrow aisle, past the saddened passengers and shoddy lavatories, the cockpit with its mysteries, switches and wrap-around windshield.

I close in on the row of storefronts, where piles of glass litter the sidewalk and wiry rioters climb through open windows like soldiers, athletes. I stare with curiosity as they return seconds later with armfuls of alarm clocks, cigarettes, cell phones and heaps of clothing.

I search for Joan and Dad in the chaos but it's Mona I find first, vaulting out of a store window with a stack of berets under her arm.

"What the hell are you doing?" I ask, yanking her into an alleyway.

"Protesting," she says with wide-eyed hysteria. She smiles and then frowns, the weight of the moment becoming brazenly clear. Her expression acknowledges that she's crossed a line, that it was thin as glass and too easy. This is what happens when you live in the moment. She brushes her hand over the berets stacked in the crook of her arm, pinching the stalk of a grey one, as if contemplating its return to the store. Instead, she hurriedly stuffs the entire lot inside her giant klepto handbag.

"Where's my dad? Where's Joan?"

"They were right behind me," she says. We peek around the corner into the shop. Empty. Shelves and displays are tipped. An ugly bowler hat balances on the edge of the counter. I pause to check my phone in case Joan and Dad have made it to McDonald's.

A text from Dan: *have you seen Bobo?*

What the actual fuck, Dan.

Felix: *are you safe?* Above it, his last message lingers like the scent of a party: *I want to taste you.* My face flares all over again. *I'm safe,* I reply. *You okay?*

Glen: *Your dad and Joan have been arrested.*

Arrested? Can children be arrested in France?

Where are you? I reply.

Glen says, *Head toward the burning police car.*

That's comforting. What then? Douse myself in gasoline? I grab Mona from the alley, stubbing my toe on a brick, and tug her towards the burning cop car. It's been flipped. Mona and I cover our noses with berets. The fumes are nauseating, acrid. Fisher-Price sirens wail. Just beyond the car, on a film-set-worthy strip of sidewalk, are Dad and Joan. They sit, side by side like cell mates, legs splayed, hands tied behind their backs. Blood drips down my father's face from a spot on his head, turning his hair into cotton candy. Joan sits tall and defiant. One of her sleeves is missing. Her braids are frizz. Glen is arguing with the police.

"Qui êtes-vous?" a cop asks. He's short and robotic with Mediterranean skin, his accent heavy and neck thick as a cheese wheel.

"I'm her mother," I reply.

He asks Mona the same question.

She points to my father. "His wife."

I stare at my father's pink hair and knurled spine. The man who is my father, but also a stranger with his own black box of thoughts and longings, secrets and regrets. Who knows if he really likes shredded wheat and curling and tree tinsel and free healthcare or what he really thinks about fatherhood or Paris. Who is a man when he's not a father?

I try to imagine what Mom would think of the zip-ties on her granddaughter's wrists, the gash on Dad's forehead, the trash-strewn streets, and the lone police horse with the magnificent hooves and polite eyes, the air both promising and rancid as a revolution. There's nothing to imagine. This moment *is*, because she isn't.

Glen whispers, "They're being charged with vandalism and malicious destruction of property."

"They can't be. We leave tomorrow." I want to go home. The urge is acute and physical as fever. I want the chatty crows in the yard and the cleats in the hallway. The carpet stains and giant glasses of abandoned juice. Mom's yellowed funeral bulletin. I miss my horrible ensuite with the oak vanity and peeling laminate and double sinks: mine, Glen's. I can picture him there: shirtless and shaving, his feet bare, body covered in bike scars and stories.

Mona leans in. "Have you tried bribing the police? I heard they're very bribable here."

"I don't have any cash," I reply. Maybe they'll accept a dozen Eiffel Tower figurines, or a sheath of berets or bread. Where's Bobo?

"I tried that already," Glen spits. "They wanted a thousand euro!"

"A thousand? For fuck's sakes." I rifle through my purse, uncover a few stray bills, half the handcuff, the parfait spoon, Felix's sock. Felix. I check my phone.

Safe, he's replied. *Back at the hotel. Can I see you again? One last time.*

Last supper, last call, last place, last post. Last. How potent and permanent. How devastating. I don't know whether to beg him to stay, or help him pack, stop him from dying or assist him. I'm not sure if I'm capable of either.

I type back: *I'll try!* and feel immediately shitty about my response. My last night in Paris, his last night. And I can only *try*.

Mona limps toward the officers. "Let me talk to them," she calls over her shoulder.

Glen sighs, rubs his face. "We need a lawyer." Stress has always looked good on him.

"A lawyer?" I reply. "I was thinking an ATM. They want a thousand euros, I'll get 'em a thousand euros."

"A thousand euros *each*."

"Each? That's criminal. They just got caught up with the wrong crowd."

"The wrong crowd? Claudia, this isn't some afterschool special. Joan started it. She threw the first brick."

"And the cops can prove that?"

"They have video."

My heart plummets. "That's it though? They just have her throwing a brick?"

"It comes at the two-minute mark. Right after your father's failed attempt to throw a café chair through the front door of a pharmacy."

Maybe he needed Voltaren.

I watch Mona dabbing at my father's head wound with a napkin. "You're right. We need a lawyer."

"And where are we going to find a lawyer on a Saturday night?" Glen asks.

I reach into my pocket. My fingers find the silk bag. The heart is in pieces. Beneath them, the damp scrap of legal paper. I pull out my phone and dial with a shaky hand: Émile Fontaine.

On the fourth ring, he answers. "Bonjour?"

The deepness of his voice startles me. He sounds six foot five. I picture a woodsman, a prison or point guard, not the gentle, refined legal professional in his law firm portrait. Not the man who loved my quiet, well-behaved mom.

"Bonjour?" he repeats with heightened curiosity. Music drifts in the background.

It's late. I clear my throat. "Bonjour," I squeak. "It's Claudia. Janice's daughter."

He drops the phone; I hear it clatter on a hardwood floor, the shock in his breath. He mutters something upon its retrieval.

"Claudia?" he replies. "Êtes-vous à Paris?"

"Oui, avec toute ma famille."

Silence follows. A magnetic, crackling silence. It's the sound of wonder. It's a lot like the sound of love.

"We're in trouble," I say. "My daughter and father have been arrested at the climate protest."

"Pour quelle raison?"

"Vandalism and destruction of property." I fill in the details: bricks, broken windows, blood, video evidence, the drugs in Dad's pocket, the bribe.

His instructions are firm: pay up. I ask a few more questions until he urges me to get on with the exchange, "avant qu'il ne soit trop tard." Before it's too late. The words sit on my chest. "Too late" is a CLOSED sign, a dial tone, the back of someone leaving. It's a Swiss clinic, a stroke, a pool drain, a coffin on your palm like a drink tray. It's Cathy's parked car waiting solemnly in your driveway for Wes to get his license. I can barely stand. Across the square, I spy the Grim Reaper from the train, scythe on his shoulder, black robe blowing in the wind. He's looking for someone.

"Okay," I reply. It's as much of a response as it is an attempt to psyche myself up about breaking the law in a foreign country. I exhale. "What about after? I think my dad needs to see a doctor."

"Bring heem here," Émile says. "Best to avoid anyting on record. I'm not a doctor, but I can get heem cleaned up. I'll send you my address." A long pause and then, "Bonne chance, Claudia." The last part comes out as a thin whisper, as if it had been squeezed from the back of his throat.

I stay on the phone for a second and listen to Émile's soft fossilized sobs.

forty-three

"**WHAT KIND OF LAWYER** suggests we actually pay off the cops?" Dan argues. "Isn't the whole point of a lawyer to use the law?"

"The kind of lawyer who knows that if we don't, we're not going home tomorrow," I reply.

"We're staying?" Wes asks. He squeezes Célestine's hand. The air around them hums like a Louisiana swamp, alive and busy. Hopeful.

"Dad has cannabis gummies in his pocket," I whisper to Dan. "If the police find them, we're screwed."

Emma is bent over a sandwich board mourning Bobo's loss. She looks like she's pulled an all-nighter. She threatens to call her mom.

"I don't even think I have a thousand euro," Dan says.

I tell Wes and Liam to watch over Emma as Dan and I cross the street toward an ATM. People sip wine at a café seemingly oblivious to the protest carnage only a square away. It's almost inspiring and yet exactly why the climate is in ruins. It's easier to ignore, let others sort it out. Laissez-faire.

Dan jams his card through the ATM slot and follows the prompts. He can only withdraw two hundred euro.

"What do you mean you can only get two hundred?" I push him out of the way. A line forms behind us. I can't remember my pin. Why can't I remember my pin? I can remember my childhood phone number, my student ID, the code to a lock

I owned ten years ago, the number of crackers in a sleeve of saltines, the entire lyrics of Snow's "Informer." Not my pin. After a third failed attempt, my card is licky boom-boom down.

"What are we going to do?" Dan whisper-spits, his face red as a cockscomb. "How can you forget your pin?"

"How do you have only two hundred dollars?"

"Allison-Jean's taking all my money," he replies. "She wants to redo the kitchen."

I look at my brother and feel sorry for him. How quickly a life can change. How suddenly a person can lose.

We cross the street back to where the kids are gathered on a lonely strip of sidewalk. Liam is doing his best to comfort Emma by telling her Bobo's been reassigned to a new little girl, as if Bobo's a body guard or a guardian angel and not a ten-pound sack of synthetic fibres constructed by an overworked nine-year-old in Bangladesh. Wes and Célestine are holding each other as if they're the last couple on earth.

I stare at Dan. "What are we going to do?"

"Isn't that Bobo?" Wes says.

We all look to where Wes is pointing. A man with a leather jacket old as the Bee Gees walks toward the Metro with Bobo head-locked under his arm.

"Bobo!" Emma shrieks.

I shove my brother. "Go," I urge. "Get Bobo." We need a win.

Where can I get two thousand euro? I check the time on my phone. I've been gone thirteen minutes. How long before the cops give up on the "arrangement" and throw Dad and Joan in jail?

"Auntie Claudia?" Liam says. "You okay?"

I smile at my nephew, the neglected middle child, eighteen and lost as a library book.

"I need money," I say.

He brightens. "How much?"

"Two thousand euro."

"I got you."

He's *got* me? When I was eighteen, I still had a piggy bank. Liam pulls out his phone and then nods back toward the ATM. I motion for him to go without me. I don't trust Wes and Célestine not to elope.

Liam returns with two thousand crisp euros.

"How?" I ask.

"Crypto," he says with the nonchalance of an x Games snowboarder.

Crypto, I repeat inside my head. All this time spent contemplating love and brooding over the meaning of life and I could've been accumulating my fortune in bitcoin and NFTs. Maybe I should convert it all to the digital space. Virtual money, virtual reality, virtual love. Who needs flesh when you can have pixels? Why touch a face when you can touch a screen? Digital hearts can be upgraded. Digital hearts can be fixed.

Back in the square, fire crews have doused the flaming cars and garbage bins. Cops direct stragglers and onlookers to exits. A gentleman with shiny shoes and a fat cigar smokes outside a bodega, his posture loose as if this is any night in Paris. Champagne and blood. Party hats and steel-toed boots. Hope and despair. Mona's in the distance conversing with the police, upholding the myth that an "investigation" is taking place.

The night wears like a wet mitten, the air brisk, the minutes cold. I shiver, pull my sleeves over my hands, press my arm against the sharp brick of cash in my pocket. I should be back at the hotel packing and checking in for my flight. I've neglected my work email for two days, ignored the LinkedIn message from the recruiter. Tomorrow, I tell myself. Tomorrow I'll be on a plane and everything will go back to normal and what happened in Paris will stay in Paris and who goes to Switzerland, will stay in Switzerland.

I text Émile: *I just give them the money?*

Oui.

How do I know they're not going to go back on their word?

Trust me, he says.

I pick up my pace, dodging remnants of protest. A rainbow scarf, a lost backpack, a child's soother. Mona sees me coming and waves. Another fifty feet and this will all be over. I glance up at the earnest moon and take comfort in its surety, fumbling for the bills in my pocket and head toward what resembles a TV set. The cops who skipped leg day, the angsty teen, the bad grandpa, the second wife, the ex.

"You have the beeznus?"

It's not the Mediterranean cop who asks, but the leathery one with the Crocodile Dundee skin, tin soldier pants, eyes like glazed buns.

"He means the money," Glen says.

"The bribe," I correct.

"Claudia," Dad interrupts. "Just pay them already. I need my pills."

"Can you at least take their handcuffs off?" I flash the wad of euro in front of Mediterranean Cop. "Before I hand over the *beeznus?*"

The cop eyes me with a mix of scorn and . . . admiration? He takes a step forward, chest inflated, hands on his hips like a seventies-era detective sniffing out a scam. His body odour is sex.

"Your wife ees very bold," he says at last. To Glen.

"I'm not his wife," I say. "I'm her mother. His daughter. Can you just uncuff them so we can get on with it?"

"You two aren't married?" He shifts his muddy gaze back and forth between Glen and me. "But you are a beautiful couple. And you are in Paris. What are you in Paris for if not for each other? If not for love?"

I want to believe he's kidding. That he couldn't possibly care about the nature of me and Glen's relationship while actively extorting us, but there's an undeniable curiosity in his face, a cliché so on point I nearly laugh.

"We're in Paris to remember my mother," I say.

He motions to a brick resting next to Joan's ankle.

"Your mother was an activist? Une criminelle? Une femme radicale?"

"I don't know," I whisper. "I never knew her."

forty-four

GLEN TAKES THE MONEY and pays Med Cop, while Crocodile Dundee releases Dad and Joan. Mona eats a loaf of bread.

"Now what?" Dad says.

I check my phone, click on Émile's address. A five-minute walk.

"We need to deal with that." I gesture to my father's head wound, his blood the cheerful red of grenadine or geraniums.

"I'll call an Uber," Glen says.

"We can walk."

"Back to the hotel?" Mona asks, brushing crust flakes from her chest.

Joan tugs on my sleeve the way she did as a toddler. I stumble from the force, from the memory of her doughy hand, fingernails like pincers, her expression somewhere between madness and God. Joan of Arc.

"I'm sorry," she says, tears so crystalline I can nearly see my reflection. She sniffs. "I got kinda carried away."

"Did you start it? Is what they said true?"

She opens her mouth to speak but says nothing, a silent admission, and then wipes her tears with what remains of her sleeve. Glen sidles up beside me, where I need him, where I want him. I feel a shift in my body the way I do when I step through my front door. It's the promise and comfort of home.

"What you did was wrong," Glen says, checking Joan's bare arm for scrapes and bruises. "You could've been hurt and God knows what kind of punishment you might've faced if your mom wasn't able to get you out of this mess."

I don't tell them it was actually Liam and his bitcoin empire that paid for her release.

"It's good to believe in something," I say. "And it's good to fight for what you believe. We need that. The world needs that. I mean, look around."

A pigeon hobbles across the pavement, one leg a faded stump, feathers a child's craft, pecking at a climate sign smeared with blood.

"But you can't go around breaking the law."

"Am I in trouble?" she sobs.

"Yes," Glen says. "But your mother and I will need to discuss what that means."

Mona wraps a scarf around Joan's shoulders. I have no idea if it's one of hers, or one she stole during her Paris crime spree, but despite the scarf's gaudy pattern and dizzy fringe it's exactly what Joan needs.

I forward Émile's address to the group text, clear a mangled barricade and head south across the square. Dan and company beat us there. Bobo's been recovered. It dangles from Emma's hand, a poor dance partner.

"What is this?" Dan asks, staring up at the beige building. It's beautiful in its simplicity. Only the balconies are complicated, severe and tight as mesh.

"This is the house of Émile Fontaine."

"He a fashion designer?" Wes asks. A hickey the size of a Liechtenstein pulses from his neck.

"He was grandma's boyfriend," I explain.

"Before she met me," Dad chimes with misplaced bravado.

"Grandmas have boyfriends?" Emma asks, her nose scrunched in disgust. She fondles Bobo's giant plastic eyes.

"Yes," I reply. "Grandmas can have boyfriends."

"So why are we visiting our grandma's boyfriend?"

"Because he's the one that got Joan and Grandpa out of trouble. We're going to thank him. Plus, he's offered to help clean up Grandpa's head so we don't have to go to the hospital and hand over any more *beeznus*."

My family stands obediently around me like mercenaries promised a cot and paycheck and a second chance. I push the buzzer to Émile's apartment and we all look up as if he might appear in a window, as if he'd always been expecting us.

forty-five

THE FIFTH FLOOR. If there's an elevator, no one sees it. We ascend the black staircase in single file. After sitting for too long hunched on the sidewalk, Dad can barely bend his knees. It's uncomfortable watching him cling to the banister, hearing him grunt with each flight. Célestine is still with us, silent, dragging Wes behind her. Tomorrow she'll hijack our plane and kidnap him.

Three missed calls and a text from Allison-Jean. *Cindy and I have reiki tomorrow, Harrison will pick Emma up from the airport.* I nudge Emma up the final flight of stairs. Allison-Jean and Dan will do their best to make their divorce amicable. They'll attend parent–teacher interviews and spring concerts. They'll co-host birthday parties and share pictures when one of them can't be there to watch Emma's piano recital or Harrison's graduation ceremony or Liam's first trip to space. But for now, the divorce is fresh and terrifying and raw as an exit wound. This is why Emma clings to Bobo. Bobo represents *before*.

Mona keels over on the top stair to catch her breath. A door at the end of the hall opens and Émile steps out, finely dressed. He looks just like his photo, perhaps a little smaller, a tad older.

"Soyez la bienvenus," Émile says, extending an arm. Dad and Dan shake his hand. I give him a hug. His presence is warm and benign, unthreatening as a sloth. He gestures us into a sitting room with built-in shelves and palatial drapes, velvety couches and stiff militaristic chairs. An ancient rug covers the floor. Laid out on the coffee table is a medical tray: angled scissors, bandages, rubbing alcohol, gauze, an unmarked jar of ointment. I can't help but notice the stack of books beside it: an atlas of untamed places, another on textiles, and a thin irregular-sized book on lighthouses — did Mom give it to him?

I take Joan to the bathroom, fill the sink with warm water. She washes the makeup and dirt from her face, unravels her braids. I pluck a tiny shard of glass from a crease in her dress.

"You okay?" I ask as she scrubs her hands. The pipes bray and we both look up like the ceiling might cave in. In the mirror, Joan's lip quivers.

"I'm sorry I ruined our last night in Paris," she sniffs.

"You made it more complicated and expensive, but you didn't ruin it."

She frowns. "I got arrested and Grandpa has a hole in his head."

"Those things are true, but somehow I think Grandma would approve." I pull a burr from her hair. "I feel like we were meant to end up here, tonight, all of us together. Perhaps not for the reasons we did, but life rarely unfolds how you think it's going to. We can dream and plan and practice and work hard — and those are good things to do — but it doesn't mean life will work out the way we hope." I dab at a scratch on her neck with my finger. "Disappointment comes from expecting life to be different than it is. Peace comes from recognizing that."

"You're rarely peaceful," she says.

"Rarely?" I ask.

She shrugs. "I don't know. You just always seem stressed."

"Probably because it took me nearly forty years to figure that out."

Joan smooths her hair with her mangled gel-tip Paris-themed nails. "I'm still going to play professional soccer," she says.

"Yeah," I nod. "You probably will."

She examines her reflection one last time before drying her hands and nudging open the door. "You should have seen Grandpa, though. This guy in like, coveralls and a ski mask blew up a store and Grandpa dove through the window headfirst. It was crazy."

I stay in the dim-lit bathroom tracing the floral wallpaper and contemplating whether Dad's behaviour is a new stage of older adulthood: the terrible seventies, the first signs of dementia, or the first signs of Gerald. For all I know, it could've been an attempt to end his long, boring, mostly well-behaved life. A radical end to a predictable existence. Why grieve, when you can hoard? Why die of pneumonia when you can bleed out in a tourist shop in the name of Mother Earth?

I hear the electric razor before I see it: Dan shaving Dad's head. Bloody tufts of hair fall to the floor. Mona sweeps them up with her hands. Émile's given her a garbage bag to collect the mess. Everyone else is eating. Cheese, bread, strawberries. Emma sits cross-legged on the couch fishing through a bowl of wrapped chocolates, leaving Bobo facedown under the coffee table.

"Have you enjoyed your time in Paris?" Émile asks. He seems pleased and not perturbed by having a house full of guests, as if revelling in the experience of a large family with the blessed knowledge they'll be gone tomorrow taking their regrets and grievances with them, their dysfunction, their DNA.

Have we enjoyed our time in Paris? I don't know if I would call implosion enjoyable.

"My dad made me look at a bunch of dead bodies," Emma blurts.

"The catacombs," Dan corrects.

"Ah yes." Émile smiles, crosses his legs like a storyteller and leans back in his chair.

"Versailles was cool," Liam offers, gagging down a piece of cheese. He's probably already bought Versailles and made plans to turn it into a nightclub.

The conversation continues. I only hear fragments: Notre-Dame, Disney, rats, soup, bitcoin, bikes. I imagine another life where my mom, who wouldn't be my mom, is sitting in the pale gold bergère chair across from Émile in a sweater she purchased in Scotland. They've just come from the American University of Paris where a handsome oceanographer with a heart problem gave a lecture about marine ecosystems and loneliness. They're having a glass of champagne in honour of their anniversary. Fifty-two years? Fifty-four? They don't know. They stopped counting after twenty-five, the years since a glorious blur. Quiet nights reading, warm afternoons tending the balcony herb garden, harvesting the basil and thyme, winters in Norway for the aurora borealis and fish for breakfast, summers in Malta. A charitable organization registered in the Philippines. It wasn't perfect. Two miscarriages, homesickness, an almost affair, skin cancer, arthritis, botched investments, disagreements over the cutlery drawer. But, love.

"Is that a yes?" Dad asks.

"Huh?" I stare up at my bald father, his head patched as an old pair of jeans, Mona hovering behind him, a squat Vegas bellhop.

"Émile's offered to show us the roof."

Right. The roof. I rise from my chair and follow the procession through the kitchen, down a narrow hall to a windy staircase. The stars are pink. I wait at the bottom, watch Mona give Dad a helpful shove. Célestine and Wes have temporarily detached and the boys walk up in tandem, glued to something on Liam's phone. Emma makes it a third of the way up, then comes barrelling back. Bobo wants to see Paris. Bobo wants to see the stars.

"You coming?" Glen asks. He leans against the railing, weary and distinguished, a five o'clock shadow. Somewhere in Émile's apartment a bygone clock announces midnight.

"Dan up there?"

"He went to the bathroom."

"I'll be up in a sec."

Glen nods. "I'll wait," he says, turning. "I'll wait for you."

Glen, waiting. *For how long?* I head down the hall toward the bathroom, knock softly on the door.

"Who is it?" Dan calls.

"It's me."

The door opens a crack. I slip inside. Dan's sitting on the closed toilet, head in his hands.

"You okay?"

"I can't believe we're going home tomorrow."

"Thanks to Liam," I reply. "I think he's rich. You should keep an eye him. As much as Emma and Harrison. I mean, probably more. Emma's young, but tough. And Harrison, he's thriving. The worst is behind him. Liam needs guidance. He needs his dad. Maybe you and he can go into business together, flip houses, buy a country."

"Things aren't going to change," Dan says. "I'm gonna go home and Cindy will still have her shit in my closet and her stupid charcoal toothpaste on my side of the sink. They already replaced my Nespresso with a tea caddy."

I hand him a tissue.

"I guess I just thought she'd change her mind and we could go back to the way it was."

"You won't always feel that way. Georgia can help you find a chic little condo downtown. You can finally buy that ugly BMW you've always wanted. Order pizza, without it having to be marked on the calendar. You just need a fresh start."

"Yeah," he says, hands on his lap as if poised to get up and go for it.

"I've got an idea. Wait here." I go back to the sitting room and get the razor. Bits of Dad are still mangled in the blade. I tap it on the edge of the sink, plug it in and hold it up. "Yeah?"

Dan doesn't object. I shave my brother's head. Above, the bathroom light flickers. The razor emits a pleasing hum. It sounds like a fresh start, even if it's symbolic, especially if it is. When I'm done, Dan leans forward on the toilet, studies himself in the mirror.

"Looks good," I say.

He wipes his face on his jacket, adjusts his bowtie, stands. "What are you gonna do about Wes?" he asks.

"What can I do? He's going to have to learn like everyone else."

"That love is awful?"

"I was going to say hard."

"And?"

"And so we love." And hurt. "Go," I say. "Go see Paris from the roof. Take a picture, make a wish. Check that Wes and Célestine haven't jumped."

I clean up the hair and then stop in the kitchen for a glass of water. I find a teacup in a cupboard, hope that it's for everyday use. The rim might be real gold. The tap chugs to life. I don't wait for the water to cool. Off the kitchen is a study with deep red walls and high ceilings. More books. I look to see that no one's searching for me and then tiptoe toward the study. It's both grand and simple, masculine and quaint. Manuals, law texts, stone sculptures, a tiny glass horse blond as a beach, Sable Island. On the wall, a portrait of my mother, the one I never knew: green, hopeful, childless. The teacup drops from my hand.

forty-six

"**EET IS FROM A PEECTURE.**" Émile's materialized behind me, an apartment-sized broom and dustpan tucked under his arm. "My favourite peecture of her. One of my old partner's wives was an artiste. I had her paint eet."

"I've never seen it before," I say frantically trying to pick up the broken teacup.

Émile steadies my shaking hands, assumes the clean-up. "Eet was taken on a Saturday in June, the day before I went back to France." He dumps the porcelain in a waste basket beside his desk.

"Sorry," I say.

He waves a dismissive hand. We both gaze at the painting. Joan looks so much like her.

"You want to see zee original?" He slides open a thin drawer and removes the photograph from a yellowed, but otherwise immaculate envelope. The photo is black and white with a crease in the corner most likely caused by Émile's thumb. On the back, my mother's signature cursive, sleek and Victorian: *I will always love you. Janice.* Below her name, a heart. One I recognize from birthday cards and lunchbox notes, Christmas tags and the margins of cookbooks. The last on a postcard she'd sent the kids from Cuba that cruelly arrived a week after her death. I traced that heart a thousand times.

"You never married," I say. "Why?"

"I told her I would wait."

"But you knew she was married and she had us and a job and . . . she lived in another country."

He shrugs. "Hope."

"Or despair? I mean, was it worth it? Waiting all those years and ultimately ending up alone?"

"I have zee memories."

"But they gotta be like sixty or whatever years old! She's been gone ten years and I'm starting to forget things. Mannerisms, expressions, the sound of her voice. The other day Joan asked if she had the same colour eyes as Grandma and I actually had to look it up on Facebook because I couldn't remember."

"Blue."

"It just seems crazy to me that you waited for nothing."

"J'étais fou amoureux."

There's a tiny brass shovel on a trophy mount, centered on his desk. I can't read the engraving. Émile notices me eyeing it.

"Charity work," he explains.

I think of Oak Island. All the years those men sacrificed in pursuit of treasure. The earth they've disturbed, the nests they've tipped, the trees they razed and all the things they may have missed: grad ceremonies, game nights, goodbyes. Last times.

"People make hope out to be so noble," I say. "But it's not. It's deceiving."

Émile smiles, touches my shoulder. "You're just like her."

I am? How? Was my mother exasperated? Negative? "Rarely peaceful," as Joan observed?

"Contemplative," he explains. "Always thinking. Comme un philosophe."

I feel the wretched, stinging, healing, high of tears. This is how I'll remember her now. In the uncertainty. In the questions I can't answer, the things I can't explain. I twist Mom's ring from my finger. "Would you like this, Émile?" I hold it up to the bleachy light. An appreciative nod and the ring disappears inside a tight mottled fist. For a moment, a needle of regret. I want it back. I want her back, but I see in Émile's weary expression, his desperate fist, the ring is exactly where it belongs. Home.

"What's going on?" Dad appears in the doorway. I'm still startled by his shorn head. How it makes him look both tough and vulnerable. A war vet. A love vet. And then he sees her portrait.

"Is that Mom?" Dan pushes Dad out of the way and gazes up at the painting.

"Grandma was hot," Joan says.

They're all here.

"You should check out the roof," Wes says with a hint of pleading, clutching Célestine's hand. "Dad's still up there."

"I'll go up in a minute."

Emma ponders the portrait, stroking the lichen tufts of hair on Bobo's head. "Dad said she was old."

"When she died," Dan corrects.

"People grow up and they change," Liam adds, placing a brotherly hand on Emma's shoulder.

"Like Harrison," Emma says.

"Harrison, Grandpa, Mom . . ." His voice trails off and his phone pings.

I use the interruption to propose a toast.

"We don't have glasses," Joan says.

"I can feex zat." Émile races out of the study and returns with a tray of crystal champagne flutes and a bottle of Moët & Chandon. "I've been saving zees for une occasion spéciale."

Hopefully not for sixty years. He pours the champagne, distributes the glasses. Emma gets Perrier.

"To Janice," he says, holding up a glass.

I raise my glass. She would have liked to come to the party.

forty-seven

THERE'S A SMALL WINDOW at the top of the stairs, the kind you'd find on a ship. All I see is blackness. I picture the ocean. Felix in his yellow rain jacket leaning over the side of a boat, lowering an underwater camera into the darkness. Or maybe, lowering his arm, so he can feel the sea's secrets lap across his hand one last time. I imagine his IV-pricked hand, his hospital bed angled and adjusted to scientific perfection, the white room, the tidy blankets, his fingertips activating the valve to begin the end, the sound of the ocean tumbling from an invisible speaker easing him to sleep. Low tide.

How could his case for medical assistance in dying have been refused in Canada? How can an oceanographer die in landlocked Switzerland? How can he die alone?

The door swings open.

"You okay?" Glen takes my hand. "Come see."

He leads me to the edge of the roof. The city of lights. Golden, magnificent, somber. Music in the distance. Empty streets, shuttered blinds, a bicycle locked to a tree.

"When I was in China, I punctured a tire. Of course, there was only one bike shop in the area and they didn't have the right size tube. A cyclist I'd met in the Tibetan highlands suggested I order a new one from TaoBao, which is like the Chinese Amazon, but I was freaking out because the site said it would take three to five business days and my visa was expiring in three."

A cloud, all popcorn edges and white face paint, drifts by.

"So, what did you do?"

"When it didn't arrive on the third day, I had to make a decision. Go to the embassy and apply for an extension on my visa, ditch my bike for some cheap replacement, or fix the tire."

"You're terrible at fixing things."

"*Was* terrible," he says. "But I needed to try. Even if it wasn't perfect."

"Aren't you supposed to carry a spare? Or a patch?"

"No spare, and I'd given my last patch to Vivienne. That's how we met."

I think of Vivienne now, somewhere out there with her Moulin Rouge voice and dusty bike. She was the one who knew Wes and Célestine would end up at the Wall of I Love Yous that night at the Eiffel Tower. Would she have also predicted that Glen and I would end up here, on Émile's rooftop surrounded by plants and constellations?

"How'd you do it?"

"Sandpaper and glue. That got me within three kilometres of the border. After that I had to fill the hole with grass and I had to ride so slow that I could barely keep from tipping over, from crashing. By the time I crossed into Laos, the tire was completely flat." He laughs at the memory. "But it felt so good to have fixed something. It felt so good to have tried."

"I broke the heart," I say, running my fingers over the silk pouch. "It got crushed in my pocket during the protest."

"It can be fixed," Glen says.

"Felix's going to Switzerland to die. Alone. Like Émile's probably going to die with no one beside him to tell him he mattered."

"You love him." Glen says. "Felix."

"I don't know what to call it. It all feels kind of the same right now: grief, joy, sorrow, love. It all aches."

Glen nods. We gaze at the street below. It's going to rain.

A couple exits a building and briskly crosses the street, as if they know a downpour is imminent. I wonder if they're married, divorced, illicit, or new.

"You have to go," Glen says. "To Switzerland. I'll get the kids home. I'll deal with school and soccer. You just . . . go. I've always done what I needed to do and I know it probably prevented you from being able to do the same. And I'm sorry. I wish it hadn't taken me ten years and sixteen thousand kilometres to see that, but it did and it changed me. I hope it can change you too."

He doesn't know I've already changed. Because of Felix. Like the lid of a jar someone loosens so you can open it.

"I have to go with him."

Glen holds my face and kisses it. It's the kiss you give when you know someone's coming back. He heads for the stairs. "I'll see you when you get home."

The first drops of rain ping like dimes off the eaves and the couple takes cover under a print shop awning. Émile's plants buckle and crimp in the wind and a maple seed blows over the tip of my shoe. A memory of my mom splitting one of the seeds and sticking it on her nose, another on mine. I smile, shielding my phone from the rain, and text Felix: *I'm coming with you.*

He replies with prayer hands. I dig through my purse to find Mom's pewter prayer hands resting at the bottom in the everyday dust. Felix and I exchange logistics and I call Mallory to ask her to change my flight. The rain picks up and turns the city into a gauzy golden glow. I raise my face to the clouds. A crack of thunder and then the sky peels away.

I run for the stairs, wring out my clothes, and shake my wet hair. I quietly close the rooftop door behind me and listen. Down below, they are singing her funeral song: "Under the Boardwalk." Émile was playing it earlier, when I'd called from the square. I head down the pink stairs to the landing. He is belting the chorus like he himself is under a boardwalk and it becomes clear as a headstone: this was not just mom's funeral song; it was their love song.

I walk down the hall to where the party's erupted: in the kitchen. Dan sings off-key, Mona claps, Dad conducts. The teens sip champagne. Emma tosses Bobo up and down until it hits the ceiling. Happy tears run down Émile's cheeks. Everybody wears stolen berets in kaleidoscope colours.

I hug my wet clothes to my chest and try not to focus on tomorrow, on Felix, on goodbyes, on all the grief I've signed up for. Instead, I picture the gravestone with the lipstick prints, ticket stubs, and secret notes. The only thing Sartre got right: life begins on the other side of despair.

ACKNOWLEDGEMENTS

A giant cockscomb of gratitude to the one-and-only Kelsey Attard of Freehand Books: tireless advocate, champion and editor extraordinaire. I owe you a lifetime of acknowledgments for always being in my corner. Huge shout out to my agent, Stacey Kondla, for placing my work with heart and hustle and to Natalie Olsen for designing the cover to *Coq*. You always get it "right" and then some. Mad love to my writing peeps, my adored first readers: paulo da costa and Judith Pond, who push my writing in all directions and into new and otherworldly places, from the catacombs of Paris to the moon. Bradley Somer, the best Brad, brilliant writer, generous friend, confidant, mentor, poutine aficionado. Leanne Shirtliffe, my fiercely loyal friend, poet, changemaker, soul whisperer. And the profound Elizabeth Withey, who I deeply admire and simply love to be around. I still think of our grizzly bear encounter. I still think of your response.

Highest fives to Naomi Lewis for naming Bebe the rat and David Frevola for naming Petit Vert.

Heartfelt thanks to my readers and friends. Those who have purchased, read, and shared all of my work, all of my books. Those simple acts of affirmation have kept me going. At times they've kept me alive.

My family: Big Frat. God, I love you. Through the endless grind, the joy and the sorrow, the wtfs and hallelujahs. My kids, Pippa, Hugo and Odessa. Each of you enlighten me through your reckless pursuit of being. I love learning from you, I love loving you. Alfie, your quiet presence is a balm. Mom, Dad, Amy, and Mandy: my pillars, my DNA, my heart, my soul. Reta, for all the affection, all the support. And to all the members of my writing community, my soccer teammates, and friends, I'm so grateful you're in my life. And a final hats off to the 5:00 am crew at the Signal Hill Centre Tim Horton's for fuelling this book.

For where your treasure is, there your heart will be also. Matthew 6:21

ALI BRYAN is an award-winning novelist and creative nonfiction writer who explores the what-ifs, the wtfs and the wait-a-minutes of every day. Born and raised in Halifax, Nova Scotia, she now lives in the foothills of the Canadian Rockies on Treaty 7 Territory, where she has a wrestling room in her garage and regularly gets choked out by her family. *Coq* is her fourth novel. For more, visit www.alibryan.com or @alikbryan on IG.